I0728791

Letters
to the
Editor

PAUL MICHAEL GARRISON

Owl Hollow Press

Owl Hollow Press, LLC, Springville, UT 84663

Library of Congress Cataloging-in-Publication Data
Letters to the Editor / P.M. Garrison. — First edition.

Scripture quotations taken from the New American Standard Bible® (NASB), Copyright © 1960, 1962, 1963, 1968, 1971, 1972, 1973, 1975, 1977, 1995 by The Lockman Foundation used with permission. www.Lockman.org, except for Rom. 14:23 taken from the King James Version. Public domain.

Quotation from "God's Grandeur" by Gerard Manley Hopkins. Public domain.

Summary:
As Detective Kate Baxter works to find the culprit in a series of death threats against a high-profile magazine editor, it's her turn to drag everyone's dirty secrets into the light—but not before at least one body hits the floor.

ISBN 978-1-945654-33-6 (paperback)
ISBN 978-1-945654-34-3 (e-book)
LCCN: 2019954542

For Naomi and Melissa,
Good readers, good friends

Chapter One

I *'m coming for you.*

It would be the last letter. He had decided at the plan's inception what it would say: *I'm coming for you.* Simple, direct, with an air of imminence. By now he had the timing down; the sixth letter would arrive tomorrow. This one would follow fast after, closer than the others had, but the timing would be according to plan. Everything was according to plan.

Only the snipping of the scissors and the muted passage of occasional traffic disturbed the stillness of the night. He worked meticulously by the yellow light of a single desk lamp, cutting out the letters from a magazine. He unscrewed the cap of the rubber cement, releasing its acrid vapor. Painstakingly, he pasted each slick little rectangle onto the white construction paper, positioning each piece, not in a straight line, but in a ragged one to replicate the look of the letters he'd seen in thriller movies and on television. One had to take artistic satisfaction where one could find it.

In the beginning, he hadn't been sure whether the latex gloves were necessary; he had felt silly purchasing them, but he refused to ignore any possible precaution. He always worked with several sheets of paper under the letter so that nothing from the desk would come into contact with his work. They hadn't gone to the police yet, but he knew they would and he'd come too far to risk identification now.

A plastic bag to his left contained the butchered magazines from previous nights' work. He placed everything but the letter and envelope into that bag and stowed it in the lower left-hand drawer. He locked the drawer and pocketed the key. He would need to get rid of all that soon. He had a plan for that as well, but the time wasn't right. Not yet.

A soft thud fell overhead. He froze, his heart beating wildly. Silently he rose and strode to the doorway, listening. When he heard nothing more, he returned to the desk, folded the paper, put it in the envelope, and sealed it. The name and address were already printed on the outside.

Nathanael Carver
199 Adams Road
Fulton Springs, IL 60188

He would mail it tomorrow. And in less than a week, it would all be over.

Chapter Two

"**N**ate?"

Nathanael Carver turned abruptly from where he sat at his desk to see his wife, Amelie, standing in the study doorway.

"What?"

"Lunch is ready. I've been calling for you. What are you doing in here?" She moved toward the desk.

"Nothing really." He shoved the paper he'd been studying underneath a stack of manila folders. By now, she was standing at his shoulder.

"It's another letter, isn't it?" It was more statement than question. Nathanael sighed and slumped back in his chair. Amelie leaned forward and gently pulled the paper from under the folders. The glossy, clipped letters pasted to the page threatened, *It won't be much longer now.*

She released the page and placed a hand on Nathanael's shoulder. "Will you go to the police now?" Her voice was slightly husky.

He sighed again. "Yeah, let's go."

THE SOUND of gunfire filled the room as Kate Baxter squeezed off another round. She paused for a moment to inspect the target at the end of the shooting gallery. The bullet holes ranged from two to four inches away from the center, all to the right.

"Well, at least if you aim for his sternum," shouted Sergeant Polanski, who had been shooting in the next stall, "you should get him in the heart."

Kate glanced over her shoulder at him and then looked back at the target. She squared her shoulders, raised her gun, narrowed her eyes, and fired one more shot. It hit dead center. She pulled off her ear and eye protection and looked at the sergeant.

"I'll hit him wherever I aim for. I just have to focus a little harder."

Polanski laughed. "I believe it."

Kate felt her phone vibrate. She prayed it wasn't her parents. Their conversation that morning was what had driven her down to the range. Today, Saturday, was supposed to be her day off, and normally she would have preferred to stay away from the station, but the need to vent had been greater. She suspected a correlation was developing between the time she spent on the phone with her parents and the time she logged at the shooting gallery and was a little concerned at which way that ratio was tipping. She checked her phone; it was the station.

"Looks like I'm needed upstairs."

Polanski smiled. "Duty calls."

If they had paged her on her day off, it was probably something or someone important. As she walked up the stairs, she tried to make herself look as presentable as possible. She pulled back her hair and fixed her ponytail, which had come loose when she yanked off her headgear. She was almost to the lobby entrance when she decided to tuck her T-shirt in.

"Need any help with that, Baxter?" offered a passing patrolman named Nash. Kate turned around to face him as he arched an eyebrow in what he must have thought was a sexy leer. He waggled his fingers at her. "I'm pretty good with my hands."

"Drop dead, Nash."

Nash gave a token snort of laughter. "I think you're hot too," he said as he sauntered down the hall.

Kate silently berated herself for not stepping into the restroom to fix her shirt.

In the lobby, an attractive middle-aged couple stood at the high front desk. They looked as if they'd stepped out of an advertisement for Viagra or Aleve.

The man had full, black hair veined and specked with silver. His face was clean-shaven and, though lined, still handsome with a strong jaw and a Roman nose. Small silver-framed spectacles did nothing to hide the dark, brooding eyes. Although a little thick around the middle, he appeared to be in fairly good shape. He wore khakis, a button-up, and a suede blazer. In his left hand he held a manila folder. His other arm was wrapped protectively around the narrow waist of the woman.

The wife, at least that was Kate's assumption for the moment, was a stunner. Her shoulder-length hair was a light, brilliant blonde, a color that would easily camouflage encroaching white or silver, not that it appeared she had any. Understated makeup complemented the natural beauty of her pink complexion and symmetrical features: warm brown eyes, thin nose, and small mouth. The drape of her pink cashmere sweater and tan pants showed off a figure many younger women would envy. She clutched a leather bag at her side with a hand that sported two diamond-encrusted rings.

"Good afternoon," said Kate.

"Detective Baxter," said Parkman, the officer behind the desk, by way of introduction. "This is Nathanael Carver and his wife. They'd like to file a report." Kate shot Parkman a look; they'd paged her for this? He just smiled back.

She shook hands with Mrs. Carver and then Mr. Carver, whose hand was quite moist.

"If you'll follow me, we'll go to my desk," said Kate. Turning away, she unobtrusively wiped her hand on her jeans. Kate led the couple into the back of the station, through the maze of messy desks, past officers and petty criminals. An occasional phone rang, keyboards clattered, and a woman with a bruised cheek and split lip sobbed convulsively while Sanchez cajoled her into requesting a restraining order. *I should not be here,* Kate thought. *Potter should be here; he's on duty today, not me. I should be cleaning out the refrigerator. I should be cleaning the bathroom. I should not be here.* She pulled two chairs with cracked green leather seats over to her desk and looked at the Carvers. She resented them already. She inhaled and smiled.

"Have a seat. You'll have to forgive my dress." The three of them sat. "I was down in the shooting gallery and wasn't expecting to be called in." Kate pulled out a pencil and legal pad to make record of their interview.

Mr. Carver simply nodded and placed a protective hand on his wife's arm.

"What's the trouble?" Kate asked, trying to make her voice sound reasonably concerned.

The husband handed her the folder. "For some time, I've been getting these in the mail."

Inside it, Kate found a creased page of white construction paper with letters clipped from a magazine. They spelled out the message, *You need to die, Carver.* Using a letter opener, she flipped it over; the next one read, *Death comes to everyone, Natty.* The third said, *Carving you up will be a pleasure,* and the last, *It won't be much longer now.* Underneath the last letter was a white business envelope with Nathanael Carver's name and address printed on it. A patriotic stamp marked the corner next to a partial postal mark, of which she could just make out the word *Olivet*, a small city that bled into Fulton Springs.

"When did these start coming?" Kate asked.

Mr. Carver swallowed before answering. "About a year ago, I think. I didn't take it seriously at first. Amelie," he gestured to his wife, "has been trying to get me to come speak with you guys for the last couple of months, but I didn't think there was any real danger. Not until this last letter."

"So these four letters have been spread out over a year?"

"No. At first I threw them away. These are only the most recent ones. The first few came over the course of several months, but recently, they've been coming one every month," he explained.

"How—" Kate broke off at the sight of the unassuming brown-haired man walking toward them—Potter Davis, her partner. "Will you excuse me for just a minute?" She met Potter at what she hoped was out of the Carvers' earshot.

"Aren't you on duty today?" she said under her breath. Potter was tall enough that she had to tilt her head back to look him in the eyes.

"Yeah," he answered in similar fashion. "Aren't you off today?"

"I'm supposed to be; they paged me—to take a report for those people. They didn't page you?"

"I was in the can. I guess they couldn't wait five seconds."

Kate wrinkled her face. "I hate someone right now. I'm not sure who. But someone is responsible for this, and I am hating them."

"D'you want me to take over?" Potter asked.

"No, but come take notes because as soon as we're done, I'm gone and this is in your lap."

Back at the desk, Kate introduced the Carvers to Potter and explained he would be filing the official report for them as well as helping with any investigation that was necessary. Taking his cue from Kate, Potter tore her notes out of the notepad and sat down at his desk, just across from Kate's, and began typing as Kate continued the interview. This way, by the time the interview was done, the report would be too.

"I was going to ask you, how many letters total?"

"I'm—I'm not sure. Maybe seven, eight, something like that," said Mr. Carver.

Mrs. Carver spoke for the first time. "The first one I found was face-up in the kitchen trash."

"I didn't want to worry her since I thought it was nothing," Mr. Carver explained to Kate.

"Why did you think it was nothing?" Kate asked. "Do you get letters like this all the time?"

"Not exactly. I've never gotten death threats before, but I have gotten hate mail. I figured this was the same thing, just a little more juvenile and extreme." Kate raised her eyebrows and waited for him to continue. "I'm one of the chief editors over at Roving House Publishers. People don't always like what they read in our publications, especially when it's about them."

Kate interrupted. "You do news, current events stuff, right?"

"Yes, our tag line is 'Anything But Fiction.' We've got two magazines, *International* and *Truth Will Out*, and we just opened a book division about a year and a half ago."

Kate was familiar with the two periodicals; *International* was a news magazine dedicated to what was happening outside the United States, and *Truth Will Out*, a general news rag with a muckraking slant, prided itself on its investigative reporting and exposés. She could see how Carver would have made some enemies there.

"And what exactly do you do at Roving House as a chief editor?" Kate asked.

"I was in charge of *Truth Will Out* until they opened the book division and I switched over to that. It was partially for a change of pace and a promotion of sorts."

"Can you think of anyone, Mr. Carver, who would be upset with you enough to send these letters? Someone with a grudge from when you worked on the magazine, somebody who might be jealous of your promotion, somebody from your past, an ex-wife?" Kate asked.

Mr. Carver laughed. "No ex-wives. Amelie's been the only woman in my life." He reached out and clasped her hand, and Kate wondered if Mrs. Carver liked sweaty palms. "I can think of a few people but not someone who would seriously do this. I mean, even one of our new book authors has sent the house some pretty irate mail. Celebrity writers can be extremely temperamental and not always the most stable folk."

"I'll buy that," Kate said. "Could you make a list for us?" Before Kate finished the question, Potter held out a pad of paper and a pen to Mr. Carver. "Anybody you can reasonably think of," she continued. "And why they might have it in for you. Perhaps someone from another publishing house? There are at least five major publishing ventures in town. Is your new book venture cutting into anyone else's business?"

"Not much," he answered. "We're focusing on current events books, true-life stories, mostly pieces with a quick turnaround. We've got some memoirs and biographies with a more literary vein lined up, but most of the houses in town deal in fiction."

Kate knew he was overstating the case but ignored it and turned to his wife. "What about you, Mrs. Carver? Can you think of anyone who would want to kill your husband or at least make him think his life was in danger?"

"No," she answered. "Nate's a likable man. Most of the people who were angry with him at the magazine weren't really mad at him; they were mad at the stories that got printed, and they had to blame someone."

As soon as the woman started speaking in her fluffy, innocuous tone, Kate realized she would have nothing interesting to say. Kate turned her attention back to the letters. As she flipped back and forth between them, she noticed a distinctive red *r* that occurred in each letter. There were no other letters matching the color and size, but the *r*'s repetition seemed like a calling card.

"All the letters seem to contain this red *r*. Does it look familiar, mean anything to either of you?"

Mr. Caver barely glanced up from the list he was making. "Looks like a pretty standard typeface."

His wife studied the letter. "It does look familiar, but I couldn't say why."

"Do either of you remember what the earlier letters said? The ones you threw away."

"The first one I found said, *You deserve to die, but I'll wait for now*," answered Mrs. Carver.

Mr. Carver stopped writing momentarily. "They've all been pretty general like that," he said. "I can't say for certain what all of them have said."

"So there hasn't been any hint at what the person's upset about?" Kate asked. "No I-know-what-you-did-last-summer allusion? Nothing that would connect to either your personal or professional life?"

The wife looked at her husband as he shook his head.

"Hmm. What about this?" Kate pointed with the letter opener. "One of the letters refers to you as Natty. Do you ever go by that?"

"No," he answered emphatically. "No one's called me that since elementary school, unless it was to mock me, which is what I figured he was trying to do." He handed the finished list to Kate.

She scanned it and shot Nathanael Carver a wry look. "I thought you said you couldn't think of anyone who'd seriously do this."

The editor gave a tight-lipped smile. "Wishful thinking, no doubt."

"Any of these people live in Olivet?"

Amelie Carver looked up quickly and then away.

Mr. Carver shrugged. "I don't know. I'm sure some of them might. Most of the people on that list aren't people we interact with socially, as one would expect, since they're people who likely hate me. It's hard to say who actually lives where unless you have their address. Olivet's practically part of Fulton Springs nowadays. You can't tell where one stops and the other begins."

While Mr. Carver gave commentary on Fulton Springs' urban expansion, Kate glanced over at Potter to see if he had caught the wife's reaction. He had. He leaned forward in his chair and gently asked, "Did you want to say something, Mrs. Carver?"

She looked back at him a little dazed and dropped the strap of her purse, which she had been weaving about her fingers. "What? Oh, no. I'm sorry; this is just—it's all getting to me."

Kate stood. "We'll get these letters put into evidence and tested by the crime lab. Has anyone touched them, to your knowledge, besides the two of you?" They both answered no as they joined her standing. She handed Mr. Carver one of her cards, and Potter did the same. "If you think of anything that might help or if you have any concerns, you give one of us a call," she said. "Especially if you get any more letters. We'll start looking into this and be in touch in a few days, Tuesday by the latest."

The couple thanked them both. Potter printed out copies of the report, which the Carvers signed. He then went to file the report while Kate walked the couple back to the lobby. Before they separated she said, "Mr. Carver, I'm sure it won't do much good to tell you not to worry, but it's highly likely that somebody's just trying to scare you."

He nodded. "That's what I've been trying to tell Amelie all along."

"And while I think that's probably true," Kate continued, "I do want you to be safe. Do you have an alarm system on your house?"

Mrs. Carver shot her husband a dark look as he answered that they did not.

"If you'd like, I can put you in contact with some reputable companies. For now at least, you want to be sure to keep your doors and windows locked. Do you own a gun or anything you could use to defend yourself?"

"I have a handgun."

"You might want to keep it handy. Just in case."

"Oh, trust me, I will."

Chapter Three

That night Kate found herself, by no accident, in Olivet. She had no intention, however, of doing any investigative work. She was stretched out on her friend Heidi's couch, her feet propped on the rough edge of the coffee table. Heidi, all of five-two with curly auburn hair, handed her a glass of iced tea.

"Sounds like a crummy day," Heidi said as she settled her compact figure back in the center of the papasan chair, which sat snugly between the entertainment center and the front door of the cramped living room. She picked up her grade book and continued recording test scores.

"Yeah. Thanks for listening," Kate said.

"That's what I'm here for. To mold the young minds of the future and to listen to whiny policewomen."

"Yeah, some friend you are."

"Whatever. Oh, look. Jason Awlinson must have actually studied; he got a B–. That's me right there, making a difference."

"Are the guys coming over?" Kate asked.

"Danny's on his way. He said they're short-handed at the hospital right now, so he had to work late. I told him I'd make him dinner. Spence isn't coming. He's working on some lead for a big story, but he refuses to say what it's about."

They spent a few moments in companionable silence, the tick of the timer in the kitchen the only sound in the tiny house. Kate sipped her tea and thought about neither her parents nor her job, having purged her soul of both issues. Finally, the quiet was broken when a two-handed rhythmic knock drummed against the door. Heidi reached over and turned the knob, and in came

Danny, fresh from work, still in his white gym shoes and light blue scrubs.

"Hey," he exclaimed. "It's the sin'ster spinsters!"

Kate threw a pillow at his head while Heidi reached down and grabbed some hair through his scrubs and pulled.

"Ow! And you wonder why you're still single?"

"Well, we don't wonder why you are," Kate said. "Aren't you cold? Summer's over." Despite the evening chill, Danny wore only his lightweight scrubs. She noticed a large dark smear on his right side and leaned forward to look at it. "What is on the side of your shirt?"

Danny looked down as he made his way to the beige armchair on the other side of the room. "It's probably just blood."

Kate leaned back. "That I can deal with. I thought maybe it was puke."

"I can't," said Heidi, rising from her seat. "You are not sitting on my furniture in bloody clothes. I'll get you a T-shirt." She exited quickly to her bedroom.

"It's already dry; it's not coming off," Danny called after her.

"I don't care. It's disgusting," she called back.

"You really think one of your shirts is going to fit me?" he asked as she handed him a folded white T-shirt. He stripped off his scrub top and handed it to Heidi, who held it by two fingers.

"I'll go put this in the wash for you," she said.

"Thanks." He pulled the T-shirt over his short-cropped dark hair and onto his lanky frame. The well-worn cotton tee hugged his form like spandex, its hem hovering above the waistline of his pants. Green letters on the front spelled out *Go Big Green* in an arch across his accentuated chest. Kate whistled loudly. "Hey, look at this," he said. "Suddenly, I'm built." He struck an exaggerated fashion pose.

"Hardly," Kate tried to say, but her laughter obscured her reply.

Heidi came in and looked Danny over as he lounged vampishly in the armchair. "It's definitely you," she said.

"So what's going on?" Danny asked.

"Not much," replied Kate. "We're about as boring as we could be for a Saturday night."

"That's not true," Heidi objected. "Kate has a new case. Some guy's getting death threats, but don't ask because she won't tell you any of the interesting stuff. Between her and Spence, everyone's getting hush-hush about their jobs."

"I can tell you stories from the hospital," Danny said. "I just can't give you patients' names."

"It's hardly a case," Kate said. "It's probably someone just trying to scare him. You know how many murders there were in Fulton Springs last year? Twelve, six of them were gang related, three were bar fights, two were domestic, and one was a mugging. None of them terribly mysterious." She paused, reflecting on the interview. "But there is something going on with the wife. I don't know if it's connected to the threats though."

"Cool," said Danny. "Nancy Drew is on the case." He got up and stood in the kitchen doorway. "Where's my dinner?"

"It's in the oven. It'll be done in a couple minutes," Heidi answered.

Kate read the words printed in green block letters on the back of Danny's shirt, *Olivet High Track & Field*. She turned to Heidi and asked, "How many post office branches do you have in Olivet?"

Heidi didn't look up from her grade book. "One, why?"

"Just thinking."

THAT NIGHT when Kate got home, she found Louis, once again, sleeping on top of the landline that she kept for security (to her friends' amusement). For some reason, he had taken to napping there. Perhaps it was his way of ensuring she paid attention to him. She picked the cat up and buried her face in his long striped hair. She listened to him purr, his body vibrating like a friendly incoming text. She set him on the floor.

"Go find Joan," she said. He wrapped himself around her leg, apparently uninterested in seeking out feline companionship. The phone's message indicator blinked at her; it was from Spence.

"Why aren't you home? You said you were off today. Do you have Tuesday night free? I'm going to this big social function for work, some elegant publishing house bash, and I need some arm candy. Seriously, though, I'd like you to come and maybe use your investigative prowess a bit. Plus, if you make me take Heidi, I will never forgive you—and also if you tell her I said that, I will never forgive you. Give me a call tomorrow after church and let me know."

Kate laughed. She'd made plans to meet Heidi after church for lunch; she'd call Spence after that to tell him she didn't have to work Tuesday night. Slipping into the Fulton Springs' publishing circle couldn't be a bad idea right now. Besides, she had a little red dress in the closet going to absolute waste.

Chapter Four

Sunday afternoon was beautiful, with a brilliant blue sky and a fervent sun that defied the chill of autumn. Amelie stood at the window, toying with the top button of her sweater. The warmth of the sun's rays was starting to become unbearable. She undid the button and moved back into the shadows of the unlit living room, where Nate sat in the recliner, his feet up, one hand massaging his forehead. It seemed as if the trip to the police station yesterday had done more to agitate than calm him.

She went up behind him and slipped her arms around his neck. "Is your headache any better?"

"Yes, it's almost gone."

"Do you want to go for a walk? It's pretty outside."

"I don't think so. I have a lot on my mind. I just need to think some things through."

"All right," she said. She had known he would say no; in fact, she had been counting on it. "I'm going out in the backyard. I've been inside all day. I could use some fresh air."

As she moved away, he caught her hand and turned in his chair to look her in the eyes. "I love you. You know that, right?"

"Of course," she answered. "I love you too."

"I'm sorry about all this. I know it hasn't been easy for you."

"It's not your fault, Nate."

"I know I haven't always been there for you as much as I should, but I'd do anything for you." He gave her hand a squeeze.

"I know." She squeezed back. "I'll be back in soon."

Amelie closed the back door and locked it. That way if Nate changed his mind and followed her out, she would hear the door. She walked across the lawn, which had barely begun to brown, to the slatted fence that marked the property line between their house and the one behind it. She looked back at the house before removing her cell phone from the pocket of her khakis. The desire to make the call had been gnawing at her ever since the interview at the police station. She dialed the number from memory; it rang only twice before the party on the other end answered.

"It's Amelie." Her voice shook. "You promised—you promised me you didn't have anything to do with the letters."

MASON STOOD at his bedroom window, hardly able to believe his good fortune. He was looking down into the neighboring yard. Since the weather had turned cooler, she did not come into the backyard as often. During the spring and summer, she had been out there constantly, planting flowers around the house, lounging in the hammock in the shade, throwing garden parties and barbecues, and sunbathing. Once, last summer, when he had come home for lunch and found her sunbathing, he had called in sick for the afternoon so that he could stay and watch her. He knew she was older, perhaps even twice his age. But it didn't matter, not with her looks.

He pulled the cord to release the slate gray Venetian blind. He had chosen this particular color because it blended into the perpetual dimness of his room, making it less noticeable when the blinds were partially open. Placing two fingers between the slats, he created a gap at eye level and pulled the other cord. The blinds tilted, making it harder to see inside. It would be safer watching her from between the slats. A few times she had looked up and caught him watching with the blinds up; he had just nodded and waved as if it had been happenstance. She had smiled and waved back, and he had been forced to withdraw. The window on the other side of his bed didn't have as good a view, but it sufficed on those occasions. Too many incidents, though, would draw unwanted attention.

From his second-story view, he could see her pacing back and forth, talking on her cell phone, but she had come too near the fence for him to see her face, just the top of her head. Without taking his eyes off her, Mason reached over and picked up the binoculars off the corner of his crowded nightstand. He raised them to his eyes and focused them. She moved away from the fence, still on the phone, but now she faced away from him. He willed her to turn around so that he could see her face. She was wearing the baby blue sweater again. The one with a row of pearl buttons down the front. He guessed it was one of her favorites. His too. She had her hair up; she didn't do that often. A striped silk scarf, blue and cream and white, was knotted around her smooth neck. Mason swallowed; it had been a long time.

She finally turned around. So beautiful. Mason exhaled; he hadn't realized that he'd been holding his breath. But she looked upset, her brows knitted together, an anxious hand rubbing the base of her neck, pushing back the unbuttoned neckline. A tear escaped and glided down her satin cheek. She wiped it away. It saddened him to see her like this, but in truth, it was what he needed. He set down the binoculars and picked up his digital camera; he kept both near the window at all times. It took only a moment to adjust the lens. He began shooting.

Chapter Five

"So, what do we know?" Kate asked as she passed Potter's desk Monday morning.

"I know that you're late."

She sat on the edge of her desk, facing him. "I had to stop at the gas station." Something in the way he was looking at her unnerved Kate. "What?"

He dropped his eyes and shrugged, unflappable as always. Kate shook her head. Even though they worked well together, she didn't profess to understand her partner. They clicked intellectually, sometimes to the point that it freaked her out, but personally, she found Potter...socially distant. She could respect that; she just couldn't understand it.

Potter brought up his notes on the computer. "I've done background checks on the Carvers and have been working my way through his list. There's about a dozen people."

"So what'd you find on the Carvers?"

"Nothing that doesn't match up with what we already know. Nathanael Carver, 50. Bachelor's in journalism from Ball State, graduated top of his class. Worked at some newspaper in Muncie, Indiana, before he moved back to his hometown of Fulton Springs, where he got a job writing for *Truth Will Out*. He quickly transferred to the editorial staff and rose through the ranks.

"She's a career socialite of a moderate sort, dabbles in charity work and uncontroversial causes. She's a member of one of Fulton Springs' founding families. She was a Weston before she got married, so between his job and her family, that puts them pretty near the top of the Fulton Springs social scene. She didn't go to college but lived in Europe for a while after she finished prep school. They met up when he moved back here. No kids. They've got money, but they're not really loaded...unless you compare their income to what you and I make."

"But money could be a motive," Kate said.

Potter made a face indicating that he doubted it.

"Did you see those rings she was wearing?" Kate asked.

"Yeah." He shrugged. "I still doubt it, though. Anyway, they've never been in trouble with the law. A few speeding tickets for him, and a couple parking violations for her." He leaned back in his chair and put his hands behind his head. "Guess how old she is."

Kate took a stab. "Thirty-seven."

"Fifty-two," he said flatly.

"You're kidding me."

"A full two years older than him."

"Nobody looks that good at fifty-two."

"Unless you count Sophia Loren, Tina Turner, Ann-Margaret. Should I go on?"

"No, really, that's okay." Kate held up her hand. "I'll take your word for it. Anything else on her?"

Potter looked her in the eyes before answering, and she could feel it, the *click*. "You mean other than the fact that she's guilty as proverbial sin? That she's hiding something from us and her husband? That she's got some connection to something or someone in Olivet?"

"Yeah, besides that."

"No." He paused. "Whatever she's hiding may not be related to the case."

"Or it could be."

"Then why convince her husband to go to the police?"

"Throw off suspicion."

"Maybe."

At that moment, a loud gurgling noise rose above the general office clatter. Kate looked at Potter in amazement. "Was that your stomach?"

"I came in early."

Kate grabbed her coat. "Come on," she said. "I didn't eat either. Bring your laptop, and we can finish this over breakfast."

"Do you think someone's really gunning for him?" Kate asked Potter. She pointed the Crown Vic toward a nearby McDonald's.

"Hard to say. It's gone on too long to simply be a practical joke. It could be someone who's just trying to mess with his head. You know, tear him up. And that kind of thing can escalate. Turns into addiction and requires a bigger thrill."

They ate in the car. Munching on breakfast sandwiches and hash browns, they discussed what little evidence they had and the list Carver had compiled. The letters had borne only two sets of prints, Nathanael's and Amelie's. There was nothing extraordinary about their materials that would make them easy to trace, except of course the pasted-on letters. Potter handed Kate full-sized color photos the lab had taken of the letters.

"I haven't looked at them much," Potter admitted, taking back a few of the photos for inspection. "I spent most of my time on the phone. It's not nearly as glamorous as on TV, huh?"

Kate laughed. Potter had completed his detective training just over a year ago, right before he had transferred from Carol Stream.

"Well, this red *r* in each letter tells us he's using the same source each time," Kate said. "Whether he's using more than one or not, who knows? The letters were from coated paper, probably cut from magazines."

"So the *r* is probably from the title or from a recurring column. Something with a heading that always looks the same."

"We track the *r* down, we narrow our search."

"Really?"

"It couldn't hurt."

"You're going to check all the magazines in the world?"

"No, I was going to have you do it. Did you get anywhere with the Olivet Post Office?"

"Have you ever known the post office to be helpful? We're going to have to pull some serious rank to get anywhere with them."

They set the letters aside, and Potter pulled out the list Carver had given them. He had categorized the entries. The largest group contained those whose careers or images were ruined under Carver's editorship at *Truth Will Out*. While not an exhaustive list, it included four politicians, three celebrities, and a university president. The other three on the list were newer enemies: a current author, a rejected author, and a rival publisher.

According to Potter's research, two of the politicians had died of natural causes, one of heart disease and one of cancer. One of the celebrities, a Hollywood actor, had died from a drug overdose while serving a prison term. No one they had left behind seemed to hold a grudge against either Carver or the magazine. This was not the case with the other deceased celebrity. Stacia Chodorova, a former figure skater and Chicago socialite, had drunk herself to death after *Truth Will Out* had published an article cataloging the unreputable and illegal activities she had been implicated in.

"She had an older brother," Potter said, "who at the time of her death held the magazine responsible. Guess where he lives."

"Olivet."

"Bingo." Potter mentioned that only two of the other suspects had direct connections to Olivet. The rejected author and the other celebrity, a former radio host, lived there. "But it's possible that whoever's sending these letters might not live in Olivet. If I were sending death threats, I'd be willing to drive out of my way to get a misleading postmark."

"Or they could be sending the letters to an accomplice in Olivet to mail. The writer could live anywhere; all we can say is that we know the letters are coming through Olivet. Actually, all we can say is that the *last* letter came through Olivet. Not a very strong lead, huh?"

"Stronger than your red *r*, I imagine."

They decided to head back to the station to draw up a further plan of attack. As they rolled to a stop in the parking lot, Potter asked, without looking at her, "So, when did you start smoking again?"

Kate instinctively gripped the steering wheel a little tighter but kept her voice nonchalant. "What do you mean?"

Potter turned to face her. "I could smell the smoke on you when you walked by me in the office. The smell was slightly stronger inside your car, and I'm guessing that rectangular shape in your inside pocket"—he gestured to it—"isn't a tin of Altoids." He picked up the container of mints in the console and rattled it. "I am a detective, after all."

Kate felt a guilty flush rising in her neck and tried to fight it back. Sunday afternoon, there had been another row on the telephone with her mother, one that had rendered her incapable of paying attention to the evening sermon. It had also delayed her getting to sleep, and that morning, nothing had sounded as good as a smoke.

"This morning, actually," she answered levelly.

"Look, Kate, I don't really care if you smoke or not. It's none of my business. But if you don't want people—"

"You're right. It's not your business." She opened the car door. "Come on; we've got work to do."

Chapter Six

An endless chase, round and round. The alligator and the man. Impossible to tell, really, who was chasing whom. Likely, they were chasing each other. One would think that eventually, eventually, one would have to win out, but Grant Innerst had studied the scene set in silver time and again and knew that there was no end. Amazing how the ring could still draw him into contemplation after all these years, but that was one reason he liked it so much.

The medium-width band currently rested on his right hand above the middle knuckle of his middle finger. He rotated the ring slowly, letting its scene unfold. The ring was composed entirely of a stick-figure man running from, or after, a similarly wrought alligator. Or it could be a crocodile; it was impossible to tell. *A crafty crocodile weeping in the sacred Nile*, Grant let the words roll around in his mind. He thought of it mostly as an alligator though. The open jaws nipped at the man's feet, and the man's arms extended past the tail, perhaps in an attempt to grasp it. Thus the infinite loop was complete, a symbol of survival, of living dangerously.

A short horn blast from the SUV behind him pointed out that the light had changed. Grant pushed the ring down snugly against the knuckle, closed his fingers around the top of the steering wheel, and turned.

The sky was overcast, a disappointment after yesterday's sunshine. It was still warmer than usual, but the threat of rain hung heavy in the air. It would have been the perfect day to stay at home, curled up on the couch with a good book or a good woman. Grant smiled. Well, he would've had to leave the house to find either of those things, at any rate. Perhaps he still could.

He eyed his cell phone in the passenger seat, where it lay on top of his briefcase, plugged into the car charger. No, there was work to be done; he wasn't as dispensable at the office as he used to be. It wasn't so much that Grant believed in self-denial as that he believed in seizing the alligator by the tail. You didn't do that by staying home on a gloomy Monday.

He surfed through radio stations until he found one playing a song with a driving beat, something to dispel the gray before it could settle inside him. He beat out the rhythm on the steering wheel, the ring making a thud with each hit.

Grant followed the traffic to downtown Fulton Springs and parked in the usual garage. After turning off the car, he turned the knob to extinguish the headlights and then moved the ring from his middle finger to his ring finger, where it fit. He grabbed his phone and briefcase and jaywalked across the street to Roving House.

About two hours later, a notify message that said *Coffee* popped up on Grant's screen and announced a recurring appointment. Grant tossed aside the red pen he'd been using to hatchet his way through an article by the staff's newest writer, whose training was going too slowly, and grabbed his mug. He took the back stairs two at a time and walked into the tomblike ambience of the book division.

The large space was divided into cubicles that housed multiple desks and their corresponding editors, proofreaders, and layout personnel. The quiet wasn't always this pervasive, just usually. As he walked down the center aisle, he glimpsed proofreaders and editors hunched over their proofs, some of them plugged into their smart phones or computers, an occasional hushed consultation between coworkers. Some of the staff had resented being moved from their respective magazines, but a few expressed relief at the slower pace. Grant found it stifling. He liked the hubbub downstairs.

Grant poked his head into the open doorway of the office at the back of the room. Nate Carver sat at his desk, like his many workers, hunched over a set of papers. Grant shook his head. Nate still dressed the part of an exec even though he was largely holed away from the public eye. The sleeves of his white shirt were rolled up a few notches, to keep the cuffs clean, no doubt. In adherence to a dress code expired many years ago, he wore a tie, and a pin-striped charcoal suit coat hung on the back of his chair. Grant couldn't remember the last time he had worn a tie. Before heading to work that morning, he had thrown himself into a pair of red corduroys and an overpriced black sweater.

Nate still hadn't noticed him. He waited a moment more before saying, "Coffee." Nate started so violently that Grant jumped himself.

"My word, Innerst. Don't sneak up on me like that."

"I wasn't sneaking, and I think you scared me more than I did you. It's time for coffee. Are you ready?"

"Yeah." Nate stood up and winced as he straightened out his arms. "My elbows are killing me." They walked down a short hallway to the book division's small break room.

"You need to stop leaning on them." Grant flicked the lights on.

"Easier said than done. I tried editing on the computer, but that kills my eyes."

"What's the death of a few thousand more trees?"

"Spare me. Anyway, as soon as I finish with this book, I'll be doing mostly acquisitions. I plan to outsource most of the editing. Except for the occasional big shot, of course."

They lapsed into silence. Nate walked over to the window as Grant poured for them both.

"Looks like it's going to come down," Nate said after a few moments.

"Tell me about it," Grant replied.

"So, I'm assuming you were on the invite list for the Chapman bash. You going?" Nate walked away from the window and joined Grant, leaning back against the edge of the counter. He took a long gulp, the wisps of steam fogging his glasses.

"I don't know. I was waiting to see how some personal matters panned out first."

"Business before pleasure, Grant. You're the editor of a prominent magazine now. You need to make connections, your own connections."

"Can't rest on your laurels, huh?"

Nate laughed. "No."

"Well, you shouldn't have left such big shoes to fill." Seeing Nate was about to protest the flattery, he rushed on. "You're right, I think. I should be there. It's dangerous letting personal matters interfere with business."

"So what was this personal matter, if I may ask?"

Grant tried to suppress his grin but couldn't. "Just trying to score a date."

"A date? You were going to skip this for a date?"

"A hot date. And if you were young and single, you would remember how important such things are to people of my age demographic."

"Oh, brother." Nate took a swallow of his coffee. "Why don't you just bring her?"

"A publishing reception isn't exactly my idea of showing a girl a good time. Are you dragging Amelie to this thing?"

"Yes. It took some persuading. Usually she's up for any occasion to put on the glitz, but she's got that stupid book club on Tuesday nights. She's some kind of officer now, so she thinks they can't meet without her. She said she'd get them to reschedule."

Grant swirled the remaining coffee in his cup and stared into the foamy pit of the dark whirlpool. "You're lucky to have her."

There was a moment before Nate replied, "I know." Another moment passed before he asked, "Do you still have our spare key?"

"Yeah, why?"

"Things have been kind of stressful lately for us. I was thinking of taking Amelie away somewhere. Maybe for a week or two. I think it would be good for us. If I did, could you take care of the plants and mail?"

"Sure."

"I'd ask the Thompsons, but they've already left for Florida, and I don't know that there's anyone else in the neighborhood I'd trust with it."

"It's no problem," Grant said. "When are you thinking about going?"

"I don't know. It would have to be after I wrap up the Boudreau book."

"How's that going?"

"Awful. I'm beginning to think Chapman played us a dirty trick when he let us steal Boudreau from him. He's temperamental, his writing isn't even that great, he challenges me on every change, and I told you how a couple of weeks ago—" Nate stopped, frozen in mid-gesture.

"What's wrong?"

Nate turned to look at him. "I think I may have made a very bad mistake."

Chapter Seven

Kate listened as Benny explained what Potter had already told her about the letters, that the paper and envelope were common enough to not be traceable. He added that the clipped characters had been affixed using rubber cement; that the aging of the materials was consistent with the timeframe Carver had given them, at least as far as Benny could tell; that the envelope was self-adhesive and, thus, there was no DNA from saliva; and that he had found two additional sets of prints on the envelope, both belonging to Olivet Post Office employees. Kate listened as Benny recited all this, but she was thinking about Potter and what he had said earlier about her smoking. Neither of them had said much on the drive over to the crime lab.

"Which brings me to my question—are you listening to me?"

Kate looked at Benny's round face. With his smooth cheeks and curly mop of black hair, Benny could almost have been cherubic, if it weren't for the large-framed glasses and the chronically annoyed expression.

"Yes," Kate answered. "Fingerprints belonging to Olivet Post Office employees."

"Okay, well, look like it then." He looked at Potter. "Which brings me to my question—why are you here? I could've told you all this over the phone; in fact, I already gave you most of this information."

Potter scratched behind his ear. "Kate wanted to look at the letters again."

"The photographs weren't good enough?"

Kate thought about kicking him in the throat but instead made her best attempt at a smile. "Please, Benny?"

He gave an exaggerated sigh. "Oh, fine. Put on some gloves." He escorted them back to an examining table on which the letters were spread out.

"Why are you in such a bad mood, Benny?" Kate asked as she began to survey the letters.

"I'm always in a bad mood. It's who I am."

"That's not true," she said, doubting the veracity of her objection. "Have you tried removing any of the letters to see what's on the back? We're interested in finding out what magazines the writer used. Might tell us something more about him or her."

"Just this one." Benny walked over and, using a pair of tweezers, picked up the initial character from the second letter, a heavy black sans serif *D* on a white background. He flipped it over for them to see. Underneath the crusty smear of adhesive residue, the little rectangle was black except for a bit of blue in the lower left corner.

"Not much help, huh?" Benny said as he placed the character back in place. "Before I go ripping all these off, let's try something." He walked to a light table and lay the letter down on it. He flipped the switch on the side of the table, illuminating its surface. He waved Kate and Potter over. "Bring the others over here. Your friend used cheap construction paper. You can see through it no problem, and you can see the other side of the magazine print as well."

"It's difficult to make some of them out," Kate commented.

"Yeah, there's a little competition for your eye, and anything from the cover is going to be thicker. But in the long run, I think it'll beat tearing all of them off. If there are some you can't make out, we can remove those." Benny peered more closely at the first paper. "I don't think you're going to find much."

After ten minutes, Kate was about ready to concur. Most of the little rectangles yielded only solid colors or snippets of patterns or undecipherable photographs. A few were backed by other large letters, and occasionally a square would bear a few partial and cryptic words.

"I think I may have something," Potter said from the other end of the table. He was looking at the most recent letter. He pointed to a large white *e* set against a background gradient of dark blues. "The dark background makes it difficult to make all of it out, but I'm pretty sure that says, 'August,' and it looks like that's a 2."

Kate looked more closely. "All capitals and bold. It's probably not regular copy."

"Looks like we've got a date then," Potter said.

Kate's first inclination was to laugh, but since she had no idea whether Potter was consciously making a joke or not, she swallowed the impulse. She turned to Benny.

"Let's take this one off."

"Demanding, aren't we?" he muttered as he went about gently removing the square.

"Please, Benny," she amended.

"See, that really wasn't so difficult, was it? Here you go. You're right; looks like it's the cover date." The little phrase had barely made it onto the square; in fact, part of the *A* in *August* was clipped off. But whatever magazine the scrap was from, the little white letters clearly spelled out that it was the August issue of that year. The background was a deep plum, and above the words were a couple thick, red swishes.

"Well, it's someplace to start," said Potter.

Kate picked up the little square and set it down next to the word *longer*. The background perfectly matched the color behind the red italic *r* that ended the word.

"Yes," she said. "It certainly is."

Potter gave a little snort that might have been a chuckle. "That'll make the magazine search a little easier, won't it?"

"We should start with the Roving House publications."

"Makes sense to me," said Potter.

Benny peeled back his glove to check the face of his watch. "I don't mean to be rude, but do you guys need anything else?

Andreeson's going to be in soon, and real people make him nervous. I want him in a good mood today."

"Why's that?" asked Kate.

"Not that it's any of your business, but I want Friday off."

On their way out, Potter turned and caught the door before it swung shut.

"Thanks again, Benjamin," he called. "Have a good time on Friday. Tell her I said hello."

A slow smile pushed Benny's cheeks to greater heights. "I'll do that," he said and turned away as Potter let the door close.

"Benny's got a date?"

"It would seem so." They headed toward the parking lot.

"Do you always call him Benjamin?" Kate asked.

"Most of the time anyway."

"Why? Everybody else calls him Benny."

Potter looked at her. "Because it's what he likes to be called," he said.

"You guys are obviously tighter than I realized."

"He introduced himself as Benjamin when I first came. Most people introduce themselves how they want to be called. It's pretty simple." Potter yanked open the driver's side door and climbed inside the unmarked Crown Vic.

Kate made a mental note to check Potter's theory out, although for the life of her, she couldn't think of Benny as anything but Benny. She got in the passenger side. Potter already had the key in the ignition.

"I want to ask you something…about what you said this morning."

Potter didn't turn the key. "Yeah, I figured."

"If you don't care whether I smoke or not, why did you bring it up?"

Potter leaned back in his seat and pursed his lips. He started slowly, "It doesn't matter to me whether you smoke or not. What matters, I think, is whether *you* want to or not. I don't think you should smoke if you don't want to smoke. And if you're hiding it, that tells me you don't want people to know and probably that you don't really want to. Otherwise, why would you have quit in the first place?"

Kate wasn't sure how to reply, so for a moment, she said nothing. He was right, at least in one sense. She really didn't want to smoke, but then again, it felt so good, comforting really. So maybe she *did* want to. She'd quit because she knew it was bad for her physically. And of course, any form of tobacco use was frowned upon by the conservative little church she went to, so she had made sure the people there never knew. She hated to think there might actually be a spiritual dimension to it because that only compounded her guilt. It was only three weeks ago that she'd quit. Somehow, she doubted that three weeks constituted a fair run.

Finally, she answered, "I'll have to think about that."

"Yeah." Potter started the car and headed for the station.

Chapter Eight

Mason swore in disgust and leaned back in his swivel chair. He should shoot Ricky for giving him this project. Mason was designing a new layout for the scads of little advertisements that appeared in the backs of magazines. Totally boring and a total waste of his talent. He reached down into his knapsack and pulled out a small sketchbook. He opened it to the drawing he had done yesterday of Amelie crying. He had exaggerated the openness of her mouth, the wideness of her eyes. Tears flowed down both cheeks. Sad yet sensual. He flipped back near the front of the book to a full body sketch he had made in the summer. He wondered if this was indeed what she looked like underneath her clothes.

"Hey—" Mason flipped the notebook shut. The girl who sat next to him, Kelli or Karri or something like that, was leaning over her desk at him. "Whatcha got there?"

Her voice was thick. She was gawky. Little rounded glasses perched on her beak nose, and her over-dyed hair was pinned up into a nest on the back of her head.

"Nothing," he said and put his hand back on his mouse.

"Is it for your next book? The first two were awesome."

Mason looked back at her. Maybe she was worth noting. She was probably just a few years younger than he was, definitely legal. Her body wasn't bad, nothing like Amelie's, but...

"Yeah."

"Cool. Can I see it?"

"No." She looked disappointed, so he added, "I don't show my stuff until it's done."

"That's cool." She turned back to her computer but after a moment tried again to ignite a conversation. "You ever been to Etched in Skin?"

"Yeah." Mason reached back and fingered the Japanese characters tattooed on the back of his neck. "That's where I got this."

"Cool." She traced one of her thin eyebrows with two fingers, their stubby nails painted blue. "Well, I'm going after work to get a new piercing." She already had a row of rings in each ear and a stud in her nose. Mason wondered where this new piercing would go. "You wanna come? After, we could go for a drink or whatever." Her chest rose and fell more rapidly than before.

"Sure." He flicked the knob of his tongue ring between his teeth; she smiled. If she turned out to be totally lame, he could always just pretend she was Amelie. Mason was good with pretend.

Chapter Nine

"**D**id you hear my phone ring?" Kate asked Potter. They were driving to Olivet to follow up on the leads they had there. He answered that he hadn't. Kate punched through the menu to view the details of two missed calls. "This thing's a piece of junk. I told Polanski I can barely get reception at my house." The station-issue phone was a constant source of frustration.

Both missed calls were from the same number. Although she didn't recognize the number, Kate dialed the person back. After two rings, a high, slightly breathy voice answered.

"Roving House Books. This is Cynthia."

Kate made an educated guess at the caller's identity. "May I speak with Nathanael Carver, please?"

"And who may I say is calling?" the voice asked sharply, taking Kate back a bit.

"Kate Baxter."

As Kate waited for Carver to pick up, she covered the receiver and told Potter, "I'm talking to Minnie Mouse, and I think she's hostile." Potter didn't seem terribly interested. Kate sighed; he was so little fun. Danny would've been amused. She thought it would be fun to have Danny for a partner, but the thought of him with a gun made her shudder.

Carver picked up. "Detective Baxter? I've been trying to reach you."

"Yes, Mr. Carver. I'm sorry I missed your calls. Is everything okay?"

"Yes—well, I hope so. Have you spoken with Eirik Boudreau? He's on the list I gave you."

"We're actually following up on the list right now. But no, we haven't spoken with Mr. Boudreau yet." Kate looked at Potter with arched eyebrows to make sure she was correct on this. He shook his head.

"Good! I'm going to ask that you not."

"Not speak with him?"

"Yes."

"So, you now have reason to think he couldn't be involved with the threats?" Kate asked.

There was a brief silence on the other end of the line before Carver replied, "No, but it's a rather delicate situation."

"Why don't I come by later this afternoon, and we can talk about this in person? I'd kind of like to take a look around Roving House."

Once again Carver didn't answer immediately. When he did, he said, "No one here knows about the letters, and I'd like to keep it that way, as much as possible."

Kate assured him of her ability to employ discretion, and with a fair amount of reticence still in his voice, Carver consented.

A few moments later, Kate and Potter stood at the door of Pyotr Chodorov, brother of the deceased Stacia Chodorova. Kate had reviewed Potter's notes on the way over. The siblings had come to the States six years ago from Russia as Stacia's figure-skating career was rising to its peak. Besides being her legal guardian, Pyotr had been her coach at the time. He later took a backseat as Stacia's popularity and fame grew. Her career ended abruptly when an injury from a car crash left her unable to skate competitively. By that time, Pyotr was little more than a spectator in his sister's life.

Stacia's status turned to celebrity-martyr as she supported herself through interviews and appearance fees. She'd already received the advance on a book deal when a *Truth Will Out* article showed Stacia to be far from a suffering saint. Most shocking was the allegation that through her new social ties to organized crime, Stacia had taken out a hit on the other driver involved in the collision that had ended her career. The hit man, who was arrested for conspiracy to commit murder, had implicated Stacia at first but later refused to testify against her. Stacia never saw jail time but died a year later from alcohol poisoning.

The little brick house was a modest one, not anything like the estate the Chodorovs had first inhabited when they'd moved to the Chicago area. Kate rang the doorbell. The thirty-something man who answered looked nothing like the pictures Kate had seen of the sandy-haired skating princess. His black hair was spiked, and a hawk nose and large chin dominated his face. He wore black-framed glasses, a turtleneck sweater, and jeans.

"Hello?" His one-word greeting was enough to distinguish the heavy accent.

"Mr. Chodorov?" Kate asked.

"Yes, I am him."

Kate and Potter displayed their badges as she explained they were with the Fulton Springs Police Department. "We'd like to ask you a few questions."

Pyotr briefly scanned the street. "Yes, come in please."

He showed them to a sparsely furnished living room. The mantel over the fireplace held a few family photos but was largely a shrine to Stacia, displaying publicity photos, framed articles, trophies, and medals.

They had barely sat down when Pyotr asked, "May I ask what your visit is for?" the words rushing out a little too loudly. He shifted in his chair. "Last time police come to my house was to talk to my sister, Stacia, about trouble she is in. I am not part of such things." His right hand hovered around his mouth and chin, occasionally flailing out open-fingered and emphatic at Kate and Potter.

"We want to ask you some questions about Nathanael Carver," Kate answered. "Are you familiar with him?"

Pyotr's mouth tightened. "Yes, I know him."

"We understand that at the time of your sister's death, you held him somewhat responsible—"

"*Somewhat?* He is more than somewhat! He let his filthy magazine print awful things of Stacia. She was—" he struggled for a moment "—devastated, you say, ruined. Yes, I hold him responsible, more than somewhat." Pyotr sat back in his chair, his jaw set firm.

"It's evident you still feel that way, Mr. Chodorov," Kate said. "You do realize that Nathanael Carver did not write any of the material about your sister?"

"He printed it. Is same thing to me."

"Have you had any contact with Mr. Carver since your sister's death?" Kate asked.

"Just right after. I tell newspapers what I think of him and his magazine and Stan Cohen, man who wrote article. I write him letter, I think. That's all. Why do you ask me this?"

Kate looked Pyotr in the eyes. He wasn't masking his anxiety at their presence nor his distaste for Carver. She decided to lay the situation out plain. "Someone's been threatening Mr. Carver. You've been very vocal about blaming him for Stacia's death." She stopped there, letting him draw the conclusion.

Pyotr absorbed the information quietly, his eyebrows rising ever so slightly. "This is nothing to do with me. Now, you will excuse me. I have better things to think on than Mr. Carver and his problems. I am due to give lessons soon." He stood and showed them out.

Back in the car, Kate said, "I think we can cross him off the list."

"Because?"

"His English. Look at the letters." She pulled out the copies and read through the messages. "They're all grammatically correct. For goodness' sake, they're even punctuated. Chodorov still doesn't have a strong grasp on his articles or prepositions, not to mention verb tense. A nonnative speaker's errors are usually more pronounced in writing than in speech. We should be able to tell if Chodorov had written these. He didn't."

"He's obviously still pretty torn up over Stacia's death," Potter commented. "It's too bad how it all happened."

"Well, I'm sure it's hard for him, but I find it kind of hard to pity someone who drinks herself to death," said Kate.

Potter looked at her. "She lost her career near its peak. I can imagine how she might be a bit unstable after that."

"Potter, the woman put out a hit on a soccer mom. She was

a lot more Tonya Harding than Nancy Kerrigan. I'd save my sympathy for someone else." She pulled out Potter's notes on the next Olivet suspect. "Let's move on to the next one."

Chapter Ten

Amelie watched as Talitha took an extended drag on the cigarette she held in a red rhinestone-studded holder. "Well, girlfriend," Talitha finally said. "You said you wanted to chat, but apparently what you want to do is dish."

"I'm serious," said Amelie. She took another sip of her daiquiri. The two women sat at a sidewalk table at Marcadé's, an upscale restaurant in downtown Fulton Springs. The morning's gloom had not fulfilled its promise of a downpour, offering a mere smattering of drops around luncheon before dissipating, and now the bright afternoon sun echoed the previous day's warmth. She'd had to convince Talitha that this would be their last chance this year to enjoy an outside table.

"Of course, I keep secrets from my husband." Talitha brought her margarita to her bronze-painted lips for a sip. "Do you honestly think Rupert knows my tennis instructor is a twenty-four-year-old college boy with the body of a god? Or that I never liked his mama or her cooking? Or that I have my own credit card that doesn't have his name on it? Of course, he doesn't, and there's no reason he needs to."

"So you think it's all right…to have secrets from your husband?"

"Honey, *everybody* has secrets. You don't think Nathanael has some? It's the quiet ones you have to watch. Still waters, and all that."

Amelie had never thought of Nathanael as having secrets, probably because she'd always been preoccupied with her own. She traced around the rim of her glass with a manicured finger.

"The real question," Talitha continued, "is what kind of se-cret are we talking about?" Amelie couldn't discern Talitha's

expression behind the mirrored sunglasses. "Because there are secrets that don't do anybody good to know, like Rupert
knowing about my tennis instructor. There would definitely be no good in that—for anyone. But then there are secrets that if you keep them, they will swallow you up whole."

Amelie smiled. "What if it's a little of both?"

Talitha gently threw her head back with a faint snort. "Then, girl, I'd say your life must be a lot more interesting than I thought."

Amelie wanted to ask about that tennis coach but didn't. "Have you ever had a secret that you wanted to tell, but there just wasn't the right person? Or maybe you wanted to tell Rupert but couldn't?"

"You know I'm pretty much a cards-on-the-table type of girl. If I've got something to say, it's going to be said." With her free hand Talitha patted her towering mound of thick, glossy curls to ensure none had come loose. "If you have something you want to tell Nathanael, then tell him."

"I've tried. It's just…"

"It's obvious the man still loves you." Talitha put her cigarette down. "I don't think there's much you could tell him that would change that."

Amelie sighed. How many times had she started to bring up the subject to Nate, only to stop short or quickly change the
topic? And what was the point anyway after all these years? Having secrets had been fun at first. She relished keeping them, not necessarily from Nate, but from everyone. Having something private, just her own. But the tricky thing about secrets was that they compounded, and just as Talitha had pointed out, sometimes they could eat you alive. When they gripped you with their long, sharp teeth, there was no getting loose, and what Amelie knew was even worse was that sometimes, you didn't even want loose.

Chapter Eleven

"If those walls could talk," Kate said. She and Potter were parked outside a large white plantation-style house. While the small grounds surrounding it were overgrown and the fountain in the center of the circular drive had run dry, the house seemed in good condition still. It belonged to Sonya Rashad.

"Yeah, tell me about it." Potter winced.

They sat there for a moment, looking at the house, which would probably never outlast its notoriety.

"Given the suspect's history," Kate said, "I think you might have better luck handling this one alone. I can wait here."

Potter cocked his head at her. "I was thinking it might be better if *you* took this one, given the suspect's history."

"She'll react better to a man. She'll get a lot more hostile, a lot more quickly, with me."

Potter grimaced as he opened the door and got out. Kate smiled and watched as he crunched along the crushed stone walk, littered with fallen leaves, to the large veranda marked with white pillars. He rang the doorbell and waited.

Sonya Rashad had come to the Chicago area, still in her prime, from New York City. A former high-end call girl, she no longer seemed particularly interested in plying her trade. Rather, she was interested in teaching it. Building off the traveling business executives and politicians already in her little black book, Sonya had quickly assembled an ample clientele for her band of protégés. Olivet's proximity to Chicago, as well as several smaller cities such as Fulton Springs, made it an advantageous base of operation.

As her business blossomed, she became harder to prosecute due to the political standing of a good number of her local clients. But as with all business ventures founded on such dubious ethics, Sonya's did not last. It toppled at the instigation of a disgruntled senator whose husband had been less than circumspect. Names were named, careers were ruined, divorce settlements were filed, and Sonya Rashad had her brief share of national headlines, a successor to the legacy of Heidi Fleiss.

The legal brouhaha had ceased only the beginning of that year. And about that time, according to Potter's notes, Sonya's publicist approached Roving House with a book proposal. It moved forward initially, but when it failed to go through, Sonya took it personally and poorly. After several indecorous phone calls to Nathanael Carver's office and a public scene or two, she was threatened with a restraining order before she finally desisted. It hadn't taken long to locate a more willing publisher, but Sonya did seem the type to nurse a godfather of a grudge.

The large oak door finally opened, and a thin brunette in a black pantsuit stepped out. With the windows rolled up, Kate couldn't hear anything of what was being said, but she watched closely to see what impression she could gather from Rashad's body language. She had taken Potter's hand readily enough, but when he showed his badge, she took a step back and crossed her arms. Then the arms uncrossed, and a wraithlike finger vibrated in front of Potter's face. The actions were accompanied by an increase in the decibel of conversation, for the female party at any rate. If not the words, Kate could hear the tone.

Potter raised his hands open palmed in a defensive, placating gesture. Sonya's hands shot up over her head, fingers splayed. The made-up mouth distorted as the volume increased further, and while it was muffled, Kate could make out a good deal of the tirade, which was composed almost entirely of expletives. The woman swore with dexterity, combining terms in creative ways.

Kate opened the door, and while she stayed at the car, she unfastened her gun holster, just in case. Potter himself had deftly placed one hand near his gun while he tried to interject into the madam's monologue. When he failed to break through, he turned and walked steadily, but not quickly, back toward the car, his hand still near his gun. Kate admired his cool; she would've been on the verge of either decking or cuffing the stupid chick. After a few blistering comments on Potter's manhood and paternity, Rashad retreated into the house with a resounding slam of the front door.

"She's got quite a mouth on her, huh?" Kate said.

"Yeah, that's an understatement."

"So what are you thinking?"

"We can probably mark her off. There wasn't any profanity in the letters, and if she'd written them, there would be. It's pretty much her mode of communication."

"She's pretty volatile though," Kate countered. She didn't really consider Sonya a viable suspect but enjoyed playing devil's advocate.

"Yeah." Potter slid into his seat, and Kate followed suit. "If she were still ticked at Carver, she'd have tried something already. We can keep an eye on her, but she's not the type to wait around."

"Who is? That's the question. You know, you probably could've brought her in on disorderly conduct."

Potter looked out his window at some neighbors who lingered on their porch. He shrugged. "What's the point? She's not the type who would learn from it."

Kate looked at the dashboard clock. The afternoon was almost gone. "I need to drop by Roving House to talk to Carver before they close. I don't think there's time to see this last guy." She consulted the list. "Will McGlynn."

Potter was looking at his phone. "It's just as well. They want me back at the station. I haven't got much background on him yet anyway. He's the radio guy."

"We can get him tomorrow. Can you drop me off at Roving House on the way back to the station?"

"How'll you get back?"

"I'm a big girl. I can take care of myself."

"I have no doubt about that."

Chapter Twelve

Joyce Wickenseimer stood in the doorway of Mr. Innerst's office, holding a sheaf of proofs he'd asked her to get. He was talking on the phone, and she didn't want to interrupt. It unnerved her, working for someone so young. She'd seen his employment papers and knew he was younger than both her sons. It lurked in the back of her mind that he would eventually replace her with someone younger. She'd never felt that way with Mr. Carver. Even though he was still younger than she, the distance was not so much, and she knew that he appreciated her years of experience. But young people today…

She ventured a timid knock on the open door. He didn't hear.

"Oh, I think it's worth waiting for," he said into the receiver cradled between his shoulder and jaw. He continued rummaging through a desk drawer. "Well, he did seem agitated…No, it didn't have anything to do with that. Something to do with the book he's working on."

Joyce wondered if she should just walk in and lay the papers on the corner of the desk. She took a tentative step in.

"Later this week then." He turned slightly and saw Joyce standing just past the threshold. His face darkened. "Just a minute," he said into the phone. He covered the receiver. "What?"

"I—just—here are your papers." She thrust them out. As soon as he had them in hand, she retreated to her desk.

As she left, she heard him tell the person on the line, "No, it was nobody. Don't worry about it." She heard the door closing.

He had called her nobody. Joyce could feel the residual heat still flushing her cheeks as she sat at her desk. She was so nervous around him that she always seemed to do the wrong thing. Mr. Carver had been much more formal, yet she had always felt at ease with him. A little less than half an hour had passed when she turned to find Mr. Innerst perched on the edge of her desk.

"Oh, Mr. Innerst, I'm sorry. I didn't hear you," she stammered. "What can I help you with?"

"Well, first, I want to apologize." He gently took her hand, clasping it between both of his. "I didn't mean to speak to you so sharply in my office a bit ago. You startled me, but that's no excuse and I'm sorry." She began to protest, but he continued. "And second, I want to say how much I appreciate all you do around here for me. It doesn't go unnoticed."

"Well, thank you, Mr. Innerst, but I'm just doing my job."

"And you do it very well." He beamed a smile at her as he let go of her hand. "And I've told you before," he admonished, "call me Grant. You did before I became senior editor, and I'm still the same person."

"Okay, Grant." She felt the heat rise into her cheeks again.

"I'd tell you to take the rest of the afternoon off, but somehow I don't think you would."

She sat up proudly. "You're right. I wouldn't."

He laughed. "Well, keep in mind you have the option. Thanks, Joyce." He rose and walked back toward his office.

"You're welcome," she called back, her eyes shining behind her bifocals. Maybe she needn't worry so much about losing her position after all. And my, wasn't he a good-looking boy.

Chapter Thirteen

Kate was surprised to find no receptionist in the small Roving House lobby, but signs clearly indicated what departments were located on what floors. On the third floor, she walked out of the elevator into the book division, trying to look as little like a cop as possible. She was wearing her gun but was positive no one would see it under the trench coat, but then she thought the trench might be enough to give her away. Danny always teased that it made her look like Columbo, but the threat of rain had been imminent for days.

Not seeing a clear sign of where to proceed, she plunged into a maze of cubicles. She got only a few steps before she was halted by a soft, high voice.

"May I help you?" The voice sounded as though it wanted to do anything but help.

Kate recognized the distinct contradiction of vocal quality and inflection—the receptionist she'd spoken with earlier. Kate pivoted to her left to see the receptionist's station, cleverly hidden behind a half-wall. The stalwart, iron-haired matron behind the desk hefted her bulk out of her rolling chair with impossible grace. Kate blinked and checked the nameplate, *Cynthia Nixon.*

"I believe I spoke with you on the phone. I'm Kate Baxter. I'm here to see Nathanael Carver."

Cynthia's mouth puckered as she lowered herself back into her chair, like a dragon retreating into its lair. She told Kate to wait please. After a quick conference on the telephone, she coolly informed Kate that Mr. Carver would be with her in a moment.

Kate took that moment to survey the art pieces hanging on the walls, which turned out to be book covers pressed between glass plates. Two held just the front cover, one, the entire dust jacket. There were only three; there wasn't wall space for much more than that. Kate reasoned they must be the newest releases from Roving House until she realized they were probably the only releases since the book division's inception was so recent. Three books? That made it small potatoes indeed in the publishing world. The likelihood had to be pretty slim that a rival publisher would be upset enough about competition to send death threats.

"Kate!"

She turned to see Carver walking toward her. It was not lost on her that for the first time he had called her by her first name. A deft show of familiarity to conceal her reason for being there. She had to smile.

"Let me show you back to my office." As they walked, Kate asked Carver about the book division's recent birth and current status, saving the question she'd been mulling until the door to his office was closed.

"Wouldn't it be pretty unlikely that you're treading on a rival publisher's turf?"

"Yes, I mentioned that at the station."

"But you also listed Linley Chapman on your suspect list. Is that a private grudge?"

"No," he answered. "That's connected to Eirik Boudreau."

"Who is also on your list. The guy you were concerned that we'd already contacted."

"Yes." Carver wet his lips. "I'd like to see Roving House become a bigger competitor in the book market. The titles we have out now are doing well, but we need a bestseller to persuade the powers-that-be to invest more capital in our division. We're hoping Boudreau will give us that bestseller."

"Because?"

"Because his last book was. It was also his first book, and it was published by Linley Chapman."

"I can see how there might be some ill will there."

"The reason I was concerned about your speaking with

Eirik Boudreau is the same reason he broke with Chapman. He's temperamental. Sometimes I think he's borderline volatile."

"Which is why he made it on the list."

"Exactly. But we can't afford to lose him. Not at this point."

"How could you afford to get him in the first place?" Kate asked.

"He had a falling out with Chapman, and I convinced our owners he would be a good investment. They put up the money for an acceptable advance, and when Boudreau tore up his contract, we were there waiting."

"Was that the exact order in which the events took place?"

"What do you mean?" Carver countered.

"I was wondering whether you just happened to be in the right place at the right time or if maybe you'd been whispering in Mr. Boudreau's ear before he tore that contract up. Because otherwise, I'd have thought he'd head straight to a big house like Simon & Schuster."

Carver gave a small smile. "You're very perceptive."

"It helps with the job." Kate took Carver's ensuing silence as a degree of confession and pressed forward with the conversation. "So losing Boudreau would not only risk the advancement of your division but also put a financial strain on the company."

"Yes. We'd have to ask for at least part of the advance back, and I imagine things would get pretty ugly."

"How much are we talking?"

"I'm not at liberty to say, but it was in the six-figure range," Carver said.

Kate whistled. "We'll check him out as quietly as possible," she said. "But I'm not willing to ignore him completely. It wouldn't be smart or safe. We'll be indirect for now." Carver nodded slowly, and she judged that he was satisfied for the present. "Before I head out," she continued, "I'd like to take a look around. Mind giving me a tour?"

"Not at all." Carver showed her quietly through his department, explaining the division of labor. As they finished their tour of the floor, he said, "Most of our human resources, all of them really, have been siphoned off the two magazines. Some people have come up here permanently, but most are just drafted to work on a specific project or part of a project. In that case, they usually don't move up here, and they split their time between our project and their magazine work. Some tasks, like proofreading, we outsource."

"I thought you said those girls back there were proof-readers," Kate said, referring to some college-aged girls in a nearby cubicle.

"Interns. They're here for class credit. Most of it we out-source. Eventually, and I hope soon, we'll get to the point that we can afford our own permanent staff."

"How many books are you working on now?" Kate asked as she watched a balding, middle-aged man work on a Mac, positioning diagrams in a text file.

"We've got a dozen for this next year, not counting the Boudreau book." Carver motioned to the man. "This is Bob, our only full-time compositor up here." Bob turned around and smiled. "When he can't take a project, we give it to someone in the composition department downstairs."

"Composition?" she asked.

"They put the page together, the text with the art and photos," Carver explained.

Bob turned around. "The department downstairs is actually called Page Layout."

Carver threw his hands up. "They keep changing the names on me. I guess I'm just old school."

"I can respect that," said Kate as they walked toward the el-evator. "Doesn't each magazine have its own page layout department?"

"Actually, no. Right now there's only one department for both magazines in design and layout. There are certain staff that are assigned to one publication or the other, but a lot of the 'underlings' in both departments take their assignments from a collective queue. It keeps things moving for both magazines."

Passing the ever-watchful Cynthia, they went down to the second floor, which housed the writing and editorial staffs for both magazines. On the way, Carver explained that Roving House kept the writing and editing staffs of both publications equally far from the designers and compositors on purpose. "It's a peace-keeping measure," he said. "Everyone wants the best resources and the most ready access to them."

Before they entered what seemed to Kate an identical copy of the cubicle maze on the preceding floor, she quietly asked Carver if anyone else had been up for his promotion.

"It's hard to say. I know I was the first one they offered it to, but they didn't mention who they were considering if I didn't take it."

"Have you picked up on any professional jealousy?" Kate asked.

"Not really."

"What about the editor in charge of *International*?"

"That would be Mya Duritz. I suppose she could have been up for consideration."

"Then let's go meet her."

Kate could understand why Carver hadn't listed Duritz on his list of suspects. His reflective attitude in considering her indicated that there had probably never been any forthright animosity between them like the others he had listed, but that didn't mean she was without motive. People killed for things less trivial than a promotion.

Mya Duritz was a stout woman of medium height. She wore her bleached hair in a mannish cut, and her ill-fitting gray pantsuit, heavy features, and minimal makeup did little to accent her femininity. She exuded a sense of business. After Carver's vague introduction, they were interrupted by the magazine's staff three times, and in each situation, Mya issued a brisk, authoritative answer in her husky voice. From the way she glanced frequently at her computer screen and occasionally rifled through papers on her desk, it was apparent that she viewed Carver and Kate as an interruption, but her replies never went beyond borderline brusque.

Kate was venturing into her sixth minute of small talk, not one of her strong points, when Carver's cell rang.

"I need to answer this," he told Kate.

"Oh, I'll be fine here," she said. Out of the corner of her eye, she saw Duritz grit her teeth as the woman took the opportunity to dash off an email. Carver stepped out of the office. Kate immediately took a seat. She crossed her legs and leaned forward conspiratorially. "Since he's gone, can I ask you a little question?"

Duritz eyed her warily. Kate had judged from the interaction between the two that there was no strong friendship between Carver and Duritz, and this was the only card she could think of to play at the moment.

Duritz picked up a pack of cigarettes and tapped them on her desk. "What?"

"Do you really think he can handle this book thing? I kind of have my doubts."

The look on Duritz's face was priceless. "Aren't you his friend?"

Kate scrunched her face. "Not so much."

Duritz gave a chuff of laughter and leaned back in her chair. "Then who are you?"

"Let's just say I've been asked to look into things, see how they're going." Kate feigned a semi-nervous glance at the door and then looked back at Duritz. "So?"

"He's doing pretty well so far," she said.

Kate heard it in her voice. "But?"

"He's put all his eggs in one basket," Duritz replied after a moment. "Boudreau's." Kate nodded that she understood. "And he's got the owners to put so much money up that if something falls through, which with Boudreau is likely, it could hurt the entire house, not just his division. And—" She broke off, eyeing the cigarettes that she still had in her hand. Kate recognized the look.

"And it's not like someone else—" Kate made an open gesture toward the woman. "—couldn't be doing just as well, maybe smarter?"

Duritz smiled humorlessly. "You said it, not me."

Kate stood as Carver opened the door. "That sounds interesting," she said to Duritz. "I'll look forward to reading the issue." She gave the other woman a veiled wink.

"Good," Duritz replied.

Kate turned to Carver. "I think I've bugged Mya long enough. You'd better get me out of her hair."

They left the magazine editor's office to continue their tour of the floor.

"Did you learn anything?" Carver asked.

"Oh, yeah," Kate replied as she texted Potter to dig up what he could on Mya Duritz.

THE ONLY light in Grant's office was the yellow glow of the small desk lamp. Blinds covered the glass panes that looked out on the rest of the floor. No one in the company was blessed enough to have outside windows, unless you counted the part-time receptionist who sat mornings in the downstairs lobby. But Grant enjoyed the dim cavelike ambience, especially while writing.

Since it was nearly quitting time and he had nothing pressing on his desk or in his inbox, Grant had picked up his pen. The phrase that had come to him on the morning commute had lodged in his brain, and he believed it would serve as the kernel from which his next poem would grow. He was quickly making a name for himself as an up-and-comer in literary journals, and he had a stable of unpublished poems that he intended for a new collection. To those around him, he disclosed little if anything about his literary ventures. In fact, there was a great deal that Grant did not disclose to much of anyone.

He stared at the phrase he'd written on the small pad of blue paper, *A crafty crocodile weeping in the sacred Nile.* Underneath was very little poem, just questions brought to mind by the phrase. Why was the crocodile weeping? If he was crafty, were his tears true? Why emphasize the river's sacredness? The crocodile was in the water, not on the shore. How was that important? As Grant read over his notes, the idea of the poem, its truth, surfaced. He smiled to himself as he wrote on the bottom of the page, *It's a trap.*

He stood and stretched, glanced at the clock on the wall, which told him he may as well leave for the day. He'd take the poem home and perhaps get a semblance of a rough draft before bed. He shut down the computer and peeked through the blinds to survey the state of the office.

Now that was interesting. Nate was standing in the middle of the office with a woman Grant had never seen before. She was much younger than Nate and pretty, at least from this distance. The khakis and trench coat didn't belie much style, and her dishwater-blonde hair was pulled back unceremoniously in a ponytail, but the more he looked at her, the more Grant was sure she had potential. Who was she, and what was she doing with Nate? Or rather, what was he doing with her?

"BEFORE WE go downstairs, I want you to meet someone," Carver told Kate. He knocked twice on a door and opened it unbidden. The office was completely dark. "I guess he must have slipped out already." He shut the door and looked at his watch. "I guess it is about that time. Grant was my associate editor at *Truth*, and he took over when I moved on."

"So you know him pretty well?"

"Oh, yes." People were migrating toward the elevator, so Carver motioned Kate toward the back stairwell exit. "He's more than a colleague. Young enough to be a son, but more like a good friend."

"I see," Kate said. "So he's not a probable suspect?"

Carver laughed. "I wouldn't think so."

"He wasn't interested in the position you got, at all?"

Carver paused, his left foot still on the last step. "You know, I don't know. We never really talked about it like that. I remember his congratulating me and such…we had a party and he came, of course. But he never really said much about whether he would've liked the job himself. We talk shop a lot, and he seems pretty…neutral about my division."

Kate gave a "hmm" as they started through the page layout, or composition, department. More cubicled desks, these with flat screen Macs that displayed full-page spreads or sections magnified so closely that only a handful of partial lines showed. The compositors were making last-minute changes, saving files, and shutting down their computers. The department comprised mostly women in their thirties and forties, all dressed in casual business attire with one or two in dresses.

Thus it was a bit of culture shock when they passed into the bohemia of the design department, which showed no sign of closing shop for the evening. The cubicle walls there were shorter, and nearly every shelf and wall was plastered with artwork ranging from color printouts of Picasso to hand-drawn cartoons. Kate noticed a few older artists among the rows of art tables and Macs, but by far, Roving House was mining the younger crowd. Nearly two-thirds of the department seemed to be paying homage to the sixties and seventies, clad in patterns and styles commonly marketed as "vintage." Most of the rest were decked out in jeans and T-shirts, with either a distinctively hipster or punk overtone. Hair ranged from shaved to free-flowing waist length, and not all the colors were of God's creation. Body art seemed popular as well. Kate looked down at the Asian figures tattooed on the neck of the guy seated in front of her. She wondered what they stood for and if the guy himself even knew.

As they walked back toward the lobby, they passed a hallway. The glinting of light off rectangular objects mounted on the wall caught Kate's attention, and she stopped.

"What's down this way?"

"Oh, nothing exciting," Carver answered. "Just some conference rooms, accounting, HR, things like that."

Kate entered the hall anyway. On one side the wall bore glass-plated covers from *International* and the other side, *Truth Will Out*, much like the book covers she had seen mounted in Carver's division. Carver explained that they put up the most recent issue of each, moving the rest down the line, until they were retired.

"If we ever end up with a bad cover, we make an exception and retire it early," he joked. "But, of course, that rarely happens."

Kate was barely listening. She was peering at the most recent issue of *Truth Will Out*, letting pieces fall into place. What had arrested her attention was the full-cover photo of a little Shirley Temple of a girl leaning against the backdrop of a woman. One could tell from the girl's stalwart face that she was fighting back tears, and her hand clutched a rose to her little chest. The headline proclaimed a wrongful death suit brought against a Virginia corporation.

The picture was pathetic in a piteous sense, but Kate's attention drifted to the magazine title, set in red italic. She was specifically interested in the *r* in *Truth*, as she had seen quite a bit of it lately. She next took note of the color of the woman's coat, a deep purple, on which the August date stood out sharply in white letters. Other letters from other headlines rose out toward her: a *w*, an *h*, and a *t*. They had been part of the message, too.

She moved down to the next issue, intently studying it. She thought she recognized some letters there as well and wished she had kept the photocopies of the threats instead of giving them back to Potter. She turned to Carver, who was studying her.

"Do you keep back issues of these?"

"I'm sure there are some around somewhere."

"See if you can get me the last five issues. I think I'm on to something."

Chapter Fourteen

Kate had hoped to catch a ride with her friend Spence, but when she arrived at the *Fulton Springs Tribune*, a block from Roving House, she found he wasn't in.

"You don't know where he is?" she asked Marty Schultz, a reporter whose desk was close to Spence's.

"No. Boy Wonder's been out most of the day." Marty removed his bifocals and rubbed at his right eye, then ran his hand over his prominent forehead into his thick mane of silver hair. "On the verge of another big story, no doubt."

"Wow," said Kate. "Professional jealousy seems rampant today."

"Look, I've been on this paper since your friend was in training pants. I had to wait my turn before the paper'd give me a crack at a big story, and now they've pulled me off hard news to write this family-friendly feature crap."

"I imagine you're so good at it too."

Marty made a face. "I'm not saying he isn't a good writer. You just have to put your time in. That's what I'm saying."

Kate knew exactly what he was saying. She'd risen to her position too quickly for the comfort of some of her older coworkers. She'd even heard the dirty phrase *affirmative action* tossed around. She hoped it wasn't true and worked hard to disprove it. Those people were slow to come around, but once they saw her work, they usually did.

"Yeah, I know what you're saying." She backed away from his desk. "You're jealous."

"You know what's wrong with your generation? You don't have to work for anything. You get it all handed to you on a platter."

Kate laughed involuntarily. "As much as I'd love to continue this discussion, if Spence isn't around, I need to find another ride. Unless, Marty, you'd like to hand me one on a platter."

So much for that idea, she thought, standing on the sidewalk outside the *Tribune*. She should have called Spence instead of trying to surprise him at his desk. She pulled out her cell and rang Danny at the hospital.

"When do you get off?" she asked.

"'Bout a half hour. Why?"

"I'm downtown. Can you give me a ride back to the station when you're done? If you play your cards right, dinner may be involved."

"Ooo—wait a minute—someplace cheap or someplace nice?"

Kate sighed. "How about that Greek place you like?"

Danny laughed. "Philo's? Where the chef always comes out to flirt with you?"

"Yeah, don't make me reconsider my offer."

"I'm there. Things have been pretty slow today; I'll see if I can knock off early."

He picked her up twenty minutes later. As they settled into a booth at Philo's Kitchen, Danny said, "I love eating out with you."

"Why's that?"

"Free appetizers." As if on cue, the waiter laid down a large plate of *dolmas*.

"On the house," he said, smiling at Kate. He winked and left.

"See," said Danny. "Why don't medical personnel get free stuff? We serve the community as much as cops, and you can obviously tell that I'm medical personnel." He gestured to his scrubs, blood free this time. "Other than looking like Columbo—" She kicked him under the table. "Ow! You don't necessarily look like a cop."

"The presence of nurses at a business does not deter criminal activity. The presence of police does."

"But you're off duty, and we've already established you're not in uniform, like me." He pointed at himself with both hands.

"Give it up and just eat your grape-leaf thingies."

They spent the meal in companionable conversation. Just as Danny had said, the chef, a very large, authentic Greek, did come out to the table and pay his respects to Kate, which she returned as coolly as politeness allowed. Danny alternated between laughing into his sleeve and scarfing down the complimentary baklava brought just prior to the chef's arrival by the waiter who kept giving Kate the eye over his boss's shoulder.

"Maybe you should consider dating Greek men," Danny suggested. He pulled his Geo Metro up outside the police station. "They're very into you. It's like you're the American Aphrodite."

"Funny." Kate opened the door but didn't get out. "You said you talked to Spence on Sunday?"

"Yeah, he was at evening service. Why?"

"Is he okay?"

Danny looked at her blankly, his mouth hanging open slightly. "Yeah. Why?"

Kate shrugged. "I just haven't seen him in a couple weeks. That's kind of rare, you know. I've just had a few messages from him, but I can never actually get him on the phone."

Danny shrugged back at her. "He's busy. He said he's working three or four regular stories, plus some extra stuff. He said he was gonna see you tomorrow."

"Yeah, but I don't even know when or where because we've only gone back and forth on voicemail, and he answers maybe every third text. Seems like he's overdoing it at work."

Danny snorted. "Like you're one to talk about that. He's a big boy; he can take care of himself. He's almost as old as you."

"Watch it—I've got a gun. Don't forget we're running tomorrow morning."

He groaned as Kate got out of the car.

"Hey, it's not my fault you've been off three weeks. You're gonna get fat."

Danny scowled at her and sucked in his cheeks and nonexistent stomach, making himself look emaciated. He released and said, "You just bring it on, Jackie Joyner-Kersee, and we'll see who has trouble keeping up." She shut the door, and he threw his car, named the Purple Mosquito, into reverse and peeled out.

It was a quarter till nine when Kate walked in her front door. She removed Louis from his nesting place up against the phone and found several messages waiting for her.

The first was from Spence, saying he'd pick her up for the reception after work at the station. Kate made a general sound of disgust and flopped down on the couch. That meant she would have to take everything—dress, heels, makeup—to work. And worse, she would have to change at the station. She started preparing herself mentally for the catcalls before Spence's message even ran out.

Another message was from Terri at the YMCA, asking if Kate could teach her kickboxing class that weekend. Kate rolled her eyes. Another thing to do, but the extra cash would be nice. If Marty was right about having everything handed to her, why did she have to budget so diligently to make her mortgage payments?

The next message was from the vet, reminding her of an appointment she had scheduled for Louis and Joan. Come to think of it, she hadn't seen Joan in a while. Perhaps there was some mystical link between Joan and Spence; they were only around at the same time. Kate went to the kitchen to check Joan's food dish. It was empty, but Louis could very well be taking care of that.

The last message elicited a heavier sense of dread than the first had. "Kate, this is your father. Your mother's been trying to get hold of you. She thinks you won't answer because it's her. You know she didn't mean that you wouldn't ever get married. She does have a point though—"

Yeah, thought Kate. No decent guy wants to marry a cop.

"—you could be making it easier. Anyway, I want you to call her and talk things out. Love you."

Kate clunked the back of her head against the doorframe, took a deep breath, and then called. It didn't take long for the conversation with her mother to wind back to Kate's career not being suitable for a lady, especially a Christian lady, and to her parents' worry about her being in such a dangerous position.

"Mom, that's one reason I took the detective position." Kind of. "So you guys wouldn't have to worry so much about me being on the street."

"You still go out for investigations to all sorts of bad parts of town, don't you? And crime scenes?"

"Yes, but I spend most of my time at a desk. Doing research, phone calls, you know, the real life-threatening type of stuff."

"You're still around all those criminals!" Her mother's voice shrilled slightly. "And those other policemen. Robbie's told us what kind of men they are."

Kate added her brother to the list of people she wanted to throttle. "Mom, I can handle myself! We've been through all this before. It's just the same thing over and over." She threw one hand in the air in a plea for divine aid. "You don't think God can protect me on the police force as much as anywhere else?"

"Don't be sacrilegious; of course I do. But He wouldn't have to, if you had a safer job!"

They were pretty much yelling at this point, so Kate stopped, breathed for a moment, and then said, "Mom, I've got some work to do, so I'm going to go before I say something we'll both regret."

"You're not going back—"

"Goodbye, Mother," Kate said firmly and hung up.

She sat down on the arm of a chair and pressed the heels of her hands against her eyes. She very badly wanted to shoot something. It was too late to go to the shooting range, and shooting anything else would likely end her up in trouble with the neighbors.

She fished a cigarette out of the pack in her coat pocket. Thirty. She was thirty, and she still let them drive her nuts. She lit up. She wasn't a kid; at times, she didn't even feel young anymore. She took a long drag. Why couldn't they just let it go? She'd been on the force for what—six, seven years? And if they couldn't let it go, why couldn't she make herself not care that they wouldn't. She exhaled a stream of comfort into the dimly lit living room air. The irony that her mother was driving her to smoke was not lost on Kate. She took another drag and thought about how her mother would unspool if she knew. Louis rubbed up against her leg. She picked him up and rubbed her cheek against his soft fur. Finally, she stood up.

"C'mon, buddy. We've got work to do."

Chapter Fifteen

It was still dark as Mason drove by Amelie's house. The clock on the dash read a quarter till six. He slowed the car to a roll and extinguished the headlights so as not to attract attention. He'd gone out of his way to drive by the front; he didn't see it often. She lived on the last street of the neighborhood, facing a row of massive pines and spruces.

Mason turned the little gold Volvo around at the street's dead end. Nothing else stirred in the scant illumination of the sparse light poles and the nearly sunken moon. He could see the house better now that it was on his left. He stopped directly across and wondered what it would be like…just to walk up to the front door. To go inside, to see her sleeping there.

The thrumming of the motor lulled his senses as he sat there. The hunter green door appeared black in the dimness, its spray of dried flowers like a skeletal hand reaching down to the knocker. Mason put the car in park and got out. The crisp air invigorated his lungs and tingled against his skin, his jacket and jeans too thin to keep it out. He walked to the end of the sidewalk, leaving his car idling behind. A dog barked, startling him. He jerked his head to the left but didn't see anything. Then he heard it again, the yap of a small dog. His eyes darted to the windows of her house, still darkened.

Mason got back in the car. He didn't have time for this now. He'd only come home to wash his face and change his shirt. He needed to get his hours in early this week because he had to pick up his housemate, Trav, at the airport Friday afternoon.

Kassie—as her name had turned out to be—had surprised him when she asked him up to her apartment. The shots of vodka she'd downed at the bar must have dulled the tenderness of her fresh piercing. Still, he hadn't intended on spending the night, but she had started whining at him to stay when he began dressing to leave. He'd given in to shut her up. He disliked the cloudiness of her voice, nothing like the soft clarity of Amelie's. Occasionally, not too often, he would call the Carver house just to hear her. Kassie was asleep when he left, but he'd left her a note. He'd even drawn a little abstract sketch of her sleeping on it, making her appear prettier than she was. She would like that. Girls liked that kind of thing.

His right brow throbbed, but it was a good pain. He resisted the urge to finger his own new piercing. Kassie had marveled at how he hadn't even flinched as it went through. Afterward, she had insisted he hold her hand as the piercer had done her naval. It had been fascinating to watch, heightened by the simultaneous squeeze of pressure on his hand.

He parked the car in the drive, but instead of going inside, he circled around to the back of the house. A voice in his head reminded him that he should be getting ready for work, but a stronger impulse led him to scale the wooden fence.

He was riding a successive string of thrills: the shots of tequila at the bar, his own piercing, then Kassie's, going back to her apartment—and now, with a soft thud, landing in the neighboring backyard.

He'd figured out long ago which windows were the bedroom. She usually had the curtains drawn back during the daytime; she liked the light. And sometimes at night, with the lights on, there were shadows. That excited and bothered him at the same time, bothered him because the man's shadow was someone other than him. He tried not to think about the husband much, but it was hard not to.

Mason looked for a few moments at the darkened panes, hugged by darker shutters. His quickened breath cast small puffs into the early morning air. He stole up to the back door, slowly reached out his hand, and grasped the knob. The cold unyielding metal felt good under the fire inside his skin. He turned the knob.

It moved but barely, chinking softly. He swallowed. The battering in his chest slowed slightly, but the burning did not subside. He closed his eyes and pressed himself against the door, feeling somehow closer to her by doing so, letting the coolness of it seep into him, the sharp cold of the glass pane against his bare cheek.

He didn't know how much time passed, but something made him open his eyes. And there, out of the corner of his eye, he could see a snatch of light, part of dim misshapen rectangles projected into the yard. A muffled voice came from above.

He pushed away from the door. The bedroom lights were on. He reversed quickly across the yard, eyes locked on the windows to ensure no one looked out. He could see only one dark form moving about. When he felt the fence at his back, he scrambled back over into the safety of his own yard.

After catching his breath, he hurried into the house. The clock in the hallway told him that now he'd probably have to work late or through lunch. In comparison to what was happening, that seemed unimportant. He shucked his jacket onto the living room couch and peeled out of his Metallica T-shirt and wifebeater on his way up the stairs, careful not to catch either on the stud in his eyebrow. He tossed both shirts on the floor near his closet and went straight to the window.

Grabbing his binoculars, he made a gap in the blinds and peered through. She stood near the window; he could tell it was her from the silhouette. Another much fuzzier, dark form became more distinct as it neared her. The husband. Mason watched as the taller silhouette came up against the smaller, enfolding it, the head bending down to take or give a kiss.

In that moment, Mason Lenkov envied Nathanael Carver more than he could say."

Chapter Sixteen

As Amelie descended the stairs, she could hear a constant whir and steady thud coming from the den, off to the right of the foyer. They were familiar sounds. At the foot of the stairs, she peaked into the den as Nate reduced the speed of the treadmill to a walk. She continued down the hall to the kitchen, where she put on coffee for him and tea for her. She was stirring sugar into her tea when Nate entered.

His face and neck were flushed and glistening, his hair as wet as if he'd just showered. Large beads of sweat stood out on his forehead, and rivulets ran into his dampened gray athletic shirt. After he finished downing a large glass of water, she handed him his coffee. He leaned forward to kiss her for the second time that morning, just lightly on the lips. He exuded a pungent musk.

"Careful," she said, pulling back when he lingered over her. "You'll get me all sweaty."

He took a sip of coffee and gave her a wry smile. "There was a time when you didn't mind."

She gave a small laugh. "I was younger then." She returned his wry look. "And so were you."

"Touché." He started toward the kitchen table and winced. He steadied himself with a hand on the counter and flexed his right knee several times. "I think you may've jinxed me."

"Knee giving you trouble again?"

"Both of them actually."

Amelie walked to the drawer where they kept odds and ends, including much of their over-the-counter medicines. She took out a small bottle of ibuprofen and set it near his hand.

"Maybe you should see Dr. Keller. Tell him your arthritis is acting up again."

"Maybe." He popped a couple tablets into his mouth and washed them down with a swig of coffee. "The price of living, I suppose."

Amelie had drifted over to the back door, where she was looking at her reflection in the glass pane. "Time is our enemy." She noticed large smudges on the glass. She'd have to speak with the cleaning woman about being more thorough.

"HOW DO you do that?"

"Do what?" Grant asked.

"Hit the ball to exactly where I am so that I have to cripple myself to return it." His friend Kipp stood behind him on the racquetball court.

"I aim." Grant served the ball so that it returned over the line low and to the opposite side of the court from where Kipp had been. He heard a grunt and the sound of impact as Kipp's sturdy frame slammed against the wall in a failed attempt to return the ball.

"You're a punk, you know that?"

Grant smiled and moved to the box on the other side of the court. He served again, a hard hit that bounced straight back to Kipp, who darted to the right just enough to backhand it. The round lasted for several hits, challenging enough for both men to leave traces of their gym shoes on the floor, but in the end, the point—and game—went to Grant.

"One more?" asked Kipp.

Grant checked his sports watch. "I need to clean up and head to work. But you're getting better, really."

"Thanks. Maybe next time I'll even win a game." They both chuckled as they made their way to the locker room. "Maybe we should switch to something I'm better at, like football."

Grant rolled his eyes at Kipp. "Yeah, one-on-one football. That would work."

After the shower's hot water had stripped away the oil and sweat, Grant wrestled against the temptation to stay under the therapeutic spray. The health club's showers had terrific pressure, and the steaming water massaged away the tension that had built up in his arms and shoulders during the workout. He heard Kipp's shower shut off and the clinking of metal shower-curtain rings. He sighed and tilted his head back, letting the luxuriant heat penetrate to his scalp, cling to his hair, and stream down his face and neck once more before twisting the knob to the off position. He drew back the first curtain, grabbed his towel off the hook, and began to dry off as the steam dissipated. He stopped when Kipp asked, "So, have you talked to Isobel lately?"

Grant wrapped the towel around his waist and drew back the second curtain. Kipp sat on a bench, facing him, his light brown hair turned dark and curling over his forehead. He was already pulling on his socks. Grant ran his hands through his hair, shaking out the excess water.

"And why would I do that?" he asked nonchalantly.

Kipp shrugged. "I don't know. Just thought maybe you had." He didn't say anything for a moment as Grant started to dress. "You seemed really happy when you were with her. Have you ever thought of trying to get back together?"

Grant pulled a T-shirt over his head and turned to face Kipp. "Yeah, briefly, but I'm happy with the way things are." His look did not invite further discussion.

"Sorry, I won't bring it up again," Kipp mumbled.

"No, it's…I'm not mad. I'd just like to leave it behind—move on, you know. Isobel and I are…amicable. That's enough."

They finished dressing and walked through the lobby to the parking lot, where they found Grant's car with its lights still on. Muttering a curse under his breath, Grant jogged to the old Chevy to see if the engine would still turn over.

"Isn't this like the third week in a row?" Kipp asked, leaning on the open driver's door. Grant turned the key in the ignition, and the engine growled heartily in response.

"Don't remind me. It's dark enough in the morning for me to use my lights but not dark enough that I see they're still on when I park. You'd think as overcast as it is today, I would've noticed. You know the ring I wear on this hand?"

Kipp shrugged. "Not really."

"I wear it all the time." Grant shook his head. "Anyway, I usually switch it to another finger when I turn my lights on, as a reminder. But I don't like wearing it when I'm using a racquet. I guess I need to since I can't seem to remember without it."

"Doesn't your car ding when you leave the lights on?"

"No, it doesn't have a dinger, or if it does, it was broken when I bought it."

"Speaking of, now that you've got this big promotion, when are you gonna upgrade?"

"Hey, this old girl has seen me through a lot." Grant ran his hand appreciatively around the leather steering wheel.

"Just thinking of your image, now that you're a bigwig. What you need is a sexy little sports car." Kipp started toward his silver BMW. He called over his shoulder, "See you next week. Hey, you want to go out Friday? Hit a club or two?"

"Maybe. My schedule's not firm yet. I'll call you." Grant shut the door and looked around the front seat of the car. Maybe Kipp was right. Maybe he needed something classier, more posh, but Grant was not a man above sentimental attachments. This was his first car, and he'd done much to keep her running. They had a lot of history.

His right hand felt strange. He looked at where the ring should've been. Without it, his hand felt naked, exposed. He hadn't noticed it was missing a few moments ago, but now that he was aware of its absence, he couldn't shake the feeling. He flexed his hand a few times as if that would help.

He turned his mind back to the car. On the drive to work he reminisced about the places she had taken him, things that had transpired inside her. No, he wasn't ready to give her up.

"C'MON," KATE urged as Danny wheezed beside her. "We're almost done. Finish strong." They pushed on up the hill. The two friends ran together, fairly consistently, at a park midway between Danny's apartment and Kate's house.

"Have I told you lately that I hate you?" he gasped.

"No pity. You're the one who wants to run the mini-marathon." They finished the five-mile run in front of the playground equipment. To be honest with herself, Kate had to admit she found the run a bit more challenging than she let on. She attributed that to a late night working on the case, but in the back of her mind a thought nagged that it had to do more with the half-empty pack of cigarettes sitting on her bedroom dresser. She knew it was psychological. She hadn't started back up recently enough to make a difference. Of course, she also hadn't quit long enough ago for *that* to have made a difference either. She resolved to toss the cigarettes as soon as she got home. Danny sprawled out on the grass as Kate restretched.

"Why? Why do I want to run in the race? I'm insane," he babbled.

"Hey, you better stretch out, walk a bit. You need to cool down."

Danny kicked a leg up in the air, grabbed it, and pulled it toward him, stretching his hamstring. "I'm already cool enough. I think my lungs are frosted."

Kate rolled her eyes. "Don't be a pansy. It's just nippy. If you're cold, you should've worn more clothes."

While the days had shortened, the autumn had remained relatively warm for the Midwest, but Kate had still opted for warm-up pants and a thin sweatshirt. Danny wore basketball shorts and a long-sleeve T-shirt. He rolled himself over and began stretching in earnest.

"It's not my outside that's cold; it's the inside. Oh, the price I pay to maintain this manly physique."

Kate tried to suppress the laugh, but she could rarely help it with Danny. That was one of the reasons she appreciated him so much; she needed someone to make her laugh. Maybe that's why she had latched onto him so quickly when Spence introduced them, shortly after Kate had moved to town. After a brief cool down, the two parted company, and Kate walked home.

A quick shower, a change of clothes, and a bite to eat, and then Kate headed to the station. Noticing her gas tank was almost empty, she stopped at the fuel station on the outskirts of her neighborhood. It had the cheapest gas around, and the local owners fostered a small-town feeling not often found around Fulton Springs.

"Hey, Frank, how you doing?" she called to the middle-aged owner as she got a cup of coffee.

"Great! Good to see ya, Detective. Ya haven't been in a while."

She handed him her credit card. "With the price of gas nowadays, I only fill up when I have to."

"I hear that." He ran her card through and handed her the receipt. She hunched over as she signed it and thus didn't see the pack of cigarettes until he laid them down gently next to the foam cup of coffee. She quickly looked up.

"On the house." He winked with a smile.

"Oh, I can't—"

"C'mon," he insisted. "You do your part for the community. It's a thank-you."

She stood looking at it. She'd thrown out the pack at home. Why was she even thinking about this? Why didn't she just say, "I quit"? Why hadn't she said that as soon as he put them on the counter?

The bell above the door jangled. She turned. Ray Willinger, one of the deacons from her church, entered. She picked up the coffee and with a fluid motion swiped the cigarettes off the counter and into the pocket of her trench coat.

"Thanks, Frank. That's kind of you." She greeted Ray as they brushed by each other. She got in the car and drove toward the station. Now she was all nerved up. Maybe a smoke would help.

Chapter Seventeen

s Kate walked by Potter's desk, she dropped a manila folder in front of him.

"What's this?"

"Take a look." She leaned against the front of her desk, facing him.

Out of the folder he pulled a few pasted-together letters and the photographs of the threats Nathanael Carver had received. It took him only a moment to conclude, "These aren't the originals." He gestured at her with the letters. "Where'd you get them?"

"I made them. Last night."

"You may want to think about getting a hobby." He raised his eyebrows and then looked back at the papers. "But I'm guessing your trip to Roving House turned something up."

"Whoever's sending these threats is using copies of *Truth Will Out,* and it looks like exclusively. I put those three together using the last three issues, one issue per letter. The order of the issues matches the chronology of the letters."

"Looks like we have a pattern."

"And good reason to think the writer's motivation has something to do with the magazine. Did you turn up anything on Mya Duritz?"

"Nothing of note. She does live on the Olivet side of Fulton Springs, though, if that means anything. How does she look to you?"

"She definitely wouldn't mind having Carver's job, but I'm not sure that's enough motive. I do know I wouldn't want to be on her bad side."

"I checked on our other Olivet suspect. He's working nights at a radio station in Chicago, so with commute and all, he may not even be in yet, and by the time we got into the city, he'd be gone. I'm thinking we should check out some of the other suspects this morning and head over there this afternoon."

"You have a suggestion?"

Potter pulled out his notes. "Eloise Stein."

Kate frowned. "Name rings a bell, but I don't know why."

"You don't follow local politics, do you?"

"Try not to."

"She's a prominent businesswoman. Owns several high-end restaurants and shops in Fulton Springs and Chicago. She has her hands in several other business ventures too. She was also on city council here. Until *Truth Will Out* ran an article on her. Not only did she have to resign, but she also faced charges of bribery, fraud, and intimidation. The DA's office in Chicago was pretty ticked because the article ran before they were done building their case."

"I'm guessing the story was pretty juicy since she's not really a national figure?"

"Not particularly. It did paint her in pretty vivid terms though."

"So what makes a national magazine target a regional bigwig?"

"They go where the corruption flows, slow news day." Potter shrugged. "Or maybe it was personal."

"Let's find out. Where are we to find Ms. Stein?"

"She'll be in the city," Potter answered. "We should be able to hit another suspect while we're there. Austin Hetherwick, former congressman. I figured we could stop in Olivet on the way back."

"You've got everything planned out. So where will we be eating lunch?"

"Uno's," he said. And then he gave her the barest trace of a smile.

Chapter Eighteen

"Lenkov!"

Mason slowly turned his blood-shot eyes in Ricky's direction. From the intensity in Ricky's voice, Mason gathered he'd been standing there at the corner of his desk for a while. Mason removed his earbuds and tossed them on the desk, where they emanated the thunder of classic hard rock. He pivoted his chair slightly in Ricky's direction to imply he was listening.

Mason figured Ricky had to be queer. After all, the older man highlighted his hair and dressed like a peacock, and the crappy music he played in his office sounded like the soundtrack for a day spa. Also, his voice was kind of high. While Mason found all this completely lame, he didn't really hate Ricky because of it—he hated Ricky for completely different reasons. Like Ricky's insistence on talking to him, usually nagging. Ricky was his boss; that was reason enough.

"You might try cranking the volume down a notch."

Mason stared blankly at him. "Is that it?"

Kassie, seated at her desk behind Ricky, giggled. She'd been acting self-conscious since she came in, late, and they hadn't yet spoken. Mason wasn't looking forward to that, but he appreciated her laughter at Ricky's expense.

Ricky put on a martyred expression. "No, that's not it. The big cheese on third floor wants to talk to you. Do me a favor—don't embarrass me. Try to act like a human." Ricky walked away. There were two more reasons Mason hated him. He used phrases like "big cheese" and was a condescending jackass.

Mason didn't move right away. His heartbeat had picked up at the thought of going to the third floor. He took the stairs as a method of delay, but the sense of dread built with each trudging step.

NATHANAEL WAS poring over what he hoped would be the final draft of Eirik Boudreau's book. It didn't matter how hard he tried to make the manuscript adhere to itself, Boudreau insisted on introducing stylistic inconsistencies. The little rat was verbose too. Nathanael had cut the original rough draft by thirty pages, twenty-one of which Boudreau had either reinserted or compensated for by expanding other material. Nathanael flipped a page to reveal more stetted edits and inflamed responses to simple queries. His use of exclamation marks constituted punctuation abuse. What in the world made him so defensive? Face-to-face meetings usually turned into heated confrontations. Nathanael had at least six inches on him, and despite the twenty-year gap between them, the editor believed he could easily pile-drive the author. It was a recurring temptation.

Nathanael sighed. He couldn't even convince himself this was good writing. Not that it was outright bad, just mediocre. Mediocre sensationalism, and it would sell. At this point, that was what was important. The next book, he reassured himself, would have meritorious writing, resonation of a poetic soul. But now, he needed financial success so that Roving House wouldn't close his division. Boudreau's book was a sure thing. Nathanael had to give him some credit, for the writer definitely had a knack for vivid detail, which he employed to make the seedier elements come alive on paper. Drugs, sex, and a little violence—sensationalized so as to be fascinating and repugnant at the same time. Give the people what they want.

He looked up to see a kid standing in the doorway of his office. Speaking of the seedier elements. He had a hoop in his upper left ear and a post in his eyebrow, which was swollen. His black hair was cropped almost as short as the thick stubble that covered his jaw. He had pushed up the long sleeves of his black T-shirt, which bore a blast of gray screen printing, of what

Nathanael couldn't tell. A tattoo of a red-eyed dragon coiled around one of his forearms. His hands were stuffed in the front pockets of grungy jeans.

"Mason?"

The kid nodded without making eye contact.

"Have a seat."

Mason sat down. Nathanael felt a flash of recognition but retained nothing from it.

"I don't think we've met before, have we?" The young man shook his head. "How long have you been at Roving House?"

"Couple years."

"You look familiar. I've probably seen you around." This was precisely why Nathanael didn't frequent the design department. Aside from Ricky, Schuppert, and Lareina, they all looked like rock-concert refugees. "Ricky said you did the layout for *International*'s Day of the Dead article last year."

"Yeah."

"It was good work. I want you to design the jacket for our next book." Mason actually looked at him. "I'm counting on this being a bestseller, so I need a best-selling cover. Understood?"

"Yeah. Cool."

"We're in the final stages of editing." At least he hoped so. "I'll email you some files from the book and the marketing campaign, so you can get an idea of where we're going and work up some ideas. The text files don't leave this building." Mason nodded. "I want to see some mock-ups for at least two ideas by the end of the week. This is priority."

MASON HAD his own priorities, and this…this might actually help. As he descended the stairs, he reflected that perhaps his trip upstairs had been a turn of good fortune. Somehow…yeah, he could use this.

Chapter Nineteen

The traffic in Chicago was horrible. It was always horrible. Potter maneuvered expertly, however, and he and Kate eventually found refuge in a parking garage close to Eloise Stein's building. When they arrived at her plush outer office, they found they weren't alone in wanting to speak with her. Several people in various stages of boredom, frustration, and nervousness already sat across from the receptionist, a stone-faced woman with a glossy red manicure and an elaborate weave. Potter stepped up to the desk.

"Excuse me. We'd like to speak with Ms. Stein." He kept his voice low.

"Do you have an appointment?" she inquired without looking up.

"No, but we're—"

"Then you're welcome to wait over there"—she pointed, still without looking—"but I can't promise you anything."

Potter showed his badge. "We're with the police."

The woman looked Potter in the face, ignoring the badge. Her words were slow and deliberate. "But you don't have an appointment."

Kate shook her head. This was going to be ugly.

"We need to speak with Ms. Stein concerning an official police investigation." Potter wasn't bothering to keep his voice down now, but he was still temperate. Kate couldn't fathom how he did it.

"Ms. Stein is unavailable. Unless you have a warrant or some such official document, I suggest you wait over there."

"We don't need a warrant to talk to her. Is she in there?" He pointed at the polished oak door.

"I can't tell you that."

The other people in the waiting area began to stir, exchanging glances and whispers. Kate noticed that one, a short stocky young man, had a large camera. He was the only one not in business attire and looked rather forlorn.

"Hey, you!" she called to him. His head jerked toward her, his eyes big. "You a reporter?"

He nodded enthusiastically.

Kate turned to the receptionist. "We talk to Stein or we talk to him; choice is yours."

The woman narrowed her eyes and picked up the phone. After a hushed interchange, she hung up and said, "Ms. Stein can see you now."

As they walked past, the junior reporter's face fell. Kate gave him a conciliatory pat on the shoulder. "Sorry, buddy. Next time."

A slight, graying blonde in a cream-colored suit sat behind a large oak desk. She glanced at them over the top of designer glasses.

"What do you want?" she asked and immediately went back to examining the papers spread before her.

"I'm Detective Baxter, and this is Detective Davis. We're with the Fulton Springs Police Department. We're investigating a case related to Roving House Publishers."

Stein's wrinkled features conveyed boredom. "And?"

There were no chairs to sit in, an intentional power play. If there had been, Kate would have plopped herself down right then, unbidden. Instead, she walked up to the desk and leaned across it, putting her hands in the middle of Stein's paperwork.

"And we are wondering why you've been harassing Nathanael Carver."

Eloise Stein didn't even blink. "Who?"

"Nathanael Carver," Kate repeated. "Former editor of *Truth Will Out*. They ran an article that told everyone what a crook you are. I believe it caused quite a bit of trouble for you."

A bit of steel came into Stein's eyes, but her face remained impassive. "Does it look like I'm having trouble?" She waved a manicured, age-spotted hand toward the elegant trappings of her office. Kate didn't bother to look. She'd seen it all when she came in, the expensive draperies, imported furniture, Persian carpets on the hardwood floors. She kept her eyes on Stein.

"That was ages ago," the older woman continued. Her condescending smile revealed fanglike canines. "If you'd bothered to do your research, you'd have found that that little article, with its gross exaggerations, was no more than a bump in the road—"

"You were arrested," Kate interrupted. "That's just a bump in the road?"

The woman's smile dropped into a pinched grimace. "I land on my feet. Regardless, none of that had anything to do with this Carver fellow. That article ran because Edward Hampton, one of the owners of Roving House, was furious that I beat him out of a deal in the downtown renovation in Fulton Springs. I'm sure Carver, whoever he is or was, had very little say in the matter."

"How forgiving of you," said Kate.

Stein leaned forward, her elbows on the desk, hands clasped in front of her. The overpowering smell of cigarettes and coffee on her breath mingled with sweet perfume. Kate fought the urge to give ground. "When I take my revenge—and I will—it'll be against Hampton. I can ruin him without breaking the law, but right now, I've got other work to do. Henry will show you out."

Kate and Potter turned, and standing against the back wall, was a large muscular man in a dark tailored suit.

Potter turned back to Stein, who had already returned to her papers. "Thank you for your time." She didn't look up.

Kate couldn't resist a final jab. "Try to keep it clean, Eloise. We'll be checking up on you."

When Henry left them back out on the street, Potter pulled out his phone to review his notes.

"Well, I think that went rather well," Kate said.

"'Keep it clean'?"

"Shut up."

"She was a tough old bird," said Potter.

"More like a hyena. You get a load of those teeth? When we get back to the office, we'll see if her line about Hampton checks out. For now, I'm thinking—"

Potter pocketed his phone. "Lunch."

Chapter Twenty

"Had any unusual visits lately?"

Grant looked up from his computer to see Mya Duritz standing in his office doorway, her thick arms folded in front of her.

"You mean besides this one?" he teased.

"Your buddy Carver came by yesterday. Had some woman with him." Grant recalled the blonde he had spied Carver with. "When he stepped out, she started asking me about how the book division was doing."

Grant leaned back in his chair. "That's interesting."

"Yeah," Mya agreed. "You know anything about that?"

Grant shook his head. The other editor had a hungry look about her.

"So everything's going okay upstairs?"

"As far as I know." Grant wasn't sure which he found more revelatory, that Mya was fishing for news on Nate's division or that the blonde was a business, not personal, associate of Nate's.

"Well, I'd hate to be the last to know if things were changing up again," Mya said.

"Of course," Grant agreed. "I'll keep my ear to the ground." He would do just that, but he had no intention of volunteering any intel to her. The savvy look in her eyes said she guessed as much. The phone rang, and Mya excused herself.

It was Joyce on the line. "Grant, the representative from Oceanic Travel just phoned. He's sorry to give you such late notice, but he has to cancel your meeting. He said he'd be in touch about meeting sometime next week."

Grant wrinkled his nose but was careful to keep his tone light. "Thanks, Joyce. When they call back, go ahead and re-schedule the meeting for any time I've got free."

Grant hung up and looked at the time on his computer: 12:27. The meeting had been schedule for 12:45. Cutting it pretty close, wasn't he? Grant normally enjoyed working with advertisers, the first task that Nate had handed off to him. But sometimes, as today, they could be a pain. He'd canceled lunch with Nate at Marcadé's to attend to this client. Maybe Nate was still up for it.

Grant bounded up the back stairs but found the older man's office was dark. Grant went to Cynthia's desk and asked if Nate had already left for lunch. She eyed his dark jeans and crew neck with open disapproval.

"Yes, Mr. Carver went home for lunch," she informed him.

"Really?"

"Yes, really. He told me of his intention to do so shortly after you came up an hour ago. Would you like me to relay a message when he gets back?"

"No thanks. It's no longer relevant." As Grant walked away from Cynthia's desk, he swore he could feel the condescending arch of an eyebrow above her gigantic glasses.

He decided to have lunch at home himself. Of course, he didn't have a beautiful wife waiting at home to eat with him; if he did, he probably wouldn't get much lunch eaten. He did, however, have some errands that he could run on the way. He stopped by Joyce's desk and notified her that he'd be taking a long lunch.

A half-hour later, he walked into his apartment with his mail and dry-cleaning in hand. He needed the black suit for the reception tonight. He hung it on the back of his bedroom door before starting some soup on the stove. He went back to the bedroom and selected an eye-catching shirt and coordinating tie to complete the evening's ensemble and then returned to the kitchen to finish the soup and grill a panini.

He stood eating in the kitchen when he noticed his right hand was still devoid of flash. He must've gotten lost enough in his work to overpower the feeling of nakedness from his absent ring. He took an enormous bite of sandwich, dusted the crumbs off his hand over the plate, and retrieved the ring from the dresser in his room. Comforting familiarity slid over him as the silver band slipped down his finger.

He carried the rest of his lunch from the kitchen into the living room, where he sat at his desk and read through the rough draft of the crocodile poem he had written the night before. It had an Aesopian flavor. Grant usually didn't view poetry as a storytelling medium, opting instead for an emphasis on human connection and shared emotion or experience. Every once in a while, though, he produced a piece like this, a little narrative with an evident theme. Well, sometimes the theme was evident, but he always layered the piece for possible interpretations, all of them valid in his own mind.

Grant felt he had a good start on this one. In fact, he thought it might not need much revision. It was a sensory feast, especially strong in visuals. Grant leaned over his bowl for a spoonful of soup and caught a reflection of his eye in the yellow broth, like the crocodile's eye differing only in its shape of pupil. For a moment he saw himself face to face, as it were, with the adversarial beast. It unnerved him a little, and he willed himself to see the human eye again.

Grant contemplated the poem's end, where the young villager was lured into the crocodile's jaws. Why did the crocodile win? Grant felt no responsibility for how the tale ended. He wrote things as they came to him. He did wonder, though, why the young man failed to sense the trap, how man did not triumph over "nature," and what exactly it could all mean depending on the perspective of the reader.

He glanced at his watch. He would have to deal with rewriting later, for time was passing rapidly. He should call Joyce to see if he had any messages. He reached for his phone only to realize he'd left it at the office. He quickly finished his lunch and headed back to the office, but on his way out of Olivet, he stopped at a florist to pick up a handsome arrangement of flowers.

Chapter Twenty-one

The morning had stretched on for Amelie, as it was wont to do when she had no committee functions or social engagements. And so she took the chair from her bedroom vanity, placed it in front of the closet, climbed up, and shifted boxes around on the top shelf until she uncovered a pink one hidden toward the back. It was an inexpensive lockbox, little bigger than the one containing her last pair of Jimmy Choos, made of a lightweight wood and stenciled with burgundy. The tiny brass lock would provide little impediment to a serious interloper.

She set the box on the bed and pulled out the drawer of her nightstand. She removed a small brass key taped to its underneath. Sitting on the bed, she opened the box and plunged her hands into its letters and photographs. She clasped several between her hands and held them to her face. She wanted to believe that she could still smell the cologne clinging to them, but it was more likely memory than olfactory that captured the scent.

She laid the mementos on the bed. From the box, she selected a yellowing snapshot of a young couple in bathing suits on the bow of a yacht. The dark-haired man, with goatee and wind-blown curls, leaned over the bare shoulder of his young blonde companion, one arm around her bare waist. They squinted into the sun, smiling at the camera. Who had taken the picture? She couldn't remember. The photo's color had faded, but if she closed her eyes, she could conjure the brilliant blue of the Mediterranean in her mind.

She picked up a letter and read it. Her French comprehension was not what it once was, but these words were familiar.

She may have even known them by heart at one time. She stretched out on the bed. The declarations of passion might have seemed maudlin to an outsider, but to Amelie, who had lived their proof, they were pure romance, poignancies that now simultaneously thrilled and ached.

She put the letter in the box and pulled out a black-and-white photograph. This was no snapshot. Stark against flowing backdrops of dark satin sat the same young blonde, free of clothing, artfully posed to maintain the barest semblance of propriety. Amelie wondered at it. She had been stunning.

She turned the photograph over. In faded pencil, it read, *de tous mon coeur, Alain.*

Amelie started at a thump on the stairway. Nate called her name.

"Just a minute!" she shouted back. As she quickly placed everything back into the box, footfalls thudded on the stairs.

"Where are you?" Nate called. She didn't answer but locked the box, slipped the key into her pocket, and rushed to the closet. "Amelie?" he called again.

"In the bedroom." She lifted the box over her head and shoved it to the back of the shelf. She moved the other boxes back in place. The door opened.

"What are you doing up there?"

She got down off the chair and moved it back to the vanity. "Just...organizing things. We've got too much junk around here. Your closet's next, so be prepared."

Nate looked around the uncluttered room. "Okay," he said with a hint of humor in his voice. His eyes stopped on the drawer of her nightstand.

"What are you doing home?" Amelie asked.

"I came home so we could have lunch together. You haven't made plans with anyone, have you?"

"No, not at all, but you should have called. I could have had it ready."

"Then it wouldn't be a surprise, would it?" He crossed to her and wrapped his arms around her.

"Well, what a pleasant one." She smiled up at him, and they exchanged a kiss.

"I just might have some more up my sleeve," he said.

AFTER LUNCH, Amelie watched Nate drive away, wondering if she should have told him—left the box out, showed him the letters, the pictures. But she couldn't have. After so many years of marriage, they already knew each other, foundationally. She couldn't ask him to redefine her in his mind, not now. Talitha had said that everyone had secrets. Maybe these were ones she was meant to keep, at least from him.

Amelie sighed and turned away from the front window. She was chairing a meeting for the children's hospital fundraiser that afternoon. She needed to get ready. She didn't have more time to spend in the past, but she did have time to make a call. After several rings she received an automated voicemail welcome.

"It's me," she said. "Tomorrow's no good. Let's make it Thursday."

Chapter Twenty-two

"Well, that was a complete waste of time," said Kate. She and Potter were walking back to the car from Austin Hetherwick's three-story home.

"Not a complete waste," Potter corrected. "At least now we know Hetherwick's not a viable suspect."

"That's not exactly what I'd call a break in the case."

Austin Hetherwick had been a senator until *Truth Will Out* published his expense account, cataloging his gross misman-agement of taxpayers' dollars as well as some unsavory professional and personal asides. Kate had little faith in politicians but still had to wonder at the gall of one who would claim strippers on his expense account, regardless of how he camouflaged them on the ledger. Hetherwick, however, had been out of state for most of the last year, so Potter was correct. In fact, Hetherwick had spent most of his retirement traveling. Rather than being vengeful or dismissive, Hetherwick had actually seemed contrite. He had turned out to be a charming and extremely elderly gentleman, until he goosed Kate as she exited past him. Then he turned out to be a typical dirty old man.

"I'm just trying to be positive." Potter gave her a look. He pretty much only had one look, but Kate knew its many translations well enough.

"Mmm. Kind of having a bad attitude, aren't I?"

"You do seem a little…on edge."

"I'd like to see your reaction when an old man grabs your behind."

"I'm not referencing that, although for a moment, I did think you were going to snap his hand off."

"I thought that would leave more of an impression than pressing charges."

"You kind of took the 'back door' approach at Stein's office—"

"You call that 'back door'? And people call *me* square." Potter gave her the look again. How could he say so much without saying anything? "It worked, didn't it?"

Potter nodded. "Yes, it did, and to that point we hadn't been getting anywhere. I'm not criticizing that point. But the cattiness? And you went into Hetherwick's like the proverbial bull in a china shop, and he's turned out to be our least likely suspect. I'm sensing an undercurrent of tension. More than usual."

"Could be." Kate refastened her ponytail. Surely she wasn't letting the grief with her parents seep into her job performance. Maybe, but it was more than that. "I feel like we're spinning our wheels, or at least I am. And then I ask myself if there's even a case here. I'm not saying the Carvers are making this up; we've seen the letters. But nearly everybody gets a little hate mail now and then. I've gotten some."

"Everybody gets death threats?"

"No, not everyone gets death threats," Kate conceded. She opened the door and slid into the car. Potter followed suit. "But I'm not convinced we're dealing with a homicidal person here. Look at the letters." She pulled out her copies as well as her notes. "*You need to die, Carver. Death comes to everyone, Natty. Carving you up will be a pleasure. It won't be much longer now.* If there were really an intense hatred here, you'd expect harsher language, more venom, more—words, for pity's sake. These things are as brief as my last date. And as for the psycho factor, a pun on Carver's last name is as twisted as they get." She looked at Potter, who was staring out the windshield, a thoughtful frown on his face.

"Well," he said at length. "The letters weren't meant to scare you. They were meant to scare Carver, and it seems like they're doing the job. Maybe the writing tells us something. That we're not looking for a psycho. Maybe somebody more like—"

"The boy next door?"

"Yeah," Potter said. "The threats *are* escalating."

"That's true. Do we have any other leads besides the list?"

"We know the letters were made out of copies of *Truth Will Out*, and we know at least some of them went through the Olivet post office."

"So, let's visit our last suspect in Olivet and see if he's the boy-next-door type or the psycho type."

Potter tilted his head back. "You know…"

"Yeah," Kate finished. "Sometime it's the same thing."

Chapter Twenty-three

William McGlynn seemed surprised when he answered his door to find the two Fulton Springs detectives on his front step. Kate took note because, contrary to what one might think, she'd found many people weren't surprised at all when the police showed up at their door. For those in the middle of an investigation, whether as witness or suspect, it's a latent expectation. For the guilty, it's a fear. For some neighborhoods, it's a routine. Eloise Stein had not been surprised, and for that matter, neither had Austin Hetherwick. But Will McGlynn was.

Kate herself was mildly surprised at McGlynn. After Potter's introduction, he graciously invited them in. Unlike most of the gay men she'd met, he was devoid of the stereotypical affectations. He wasn't camp in speech, dress, or gesture. He also looked more like someone you'd find shopping in the aisle next to you at the grocery store than someone named Dr. Love, which had been his former radio moniker. He carried his extra weight as well as he could and wore loose fitting layers of dark clothing to camouflage it. Gray streaked his temples and striped the full beard he kept trimmed short.

He yawned, revealing a cavernous mouth, and then apologized. "Sorry. I haven't been up long. I work nights." He may have looked unremarkable, but when he spoke, Kate could discern the sensual pull of his deep, smoky voice. It somehow evoked images of candles and firelight. She could understand how it had turned him into a radio celebrity with a huge female fan base.

Kate looked around the room as Potter explained to McGlynn why they were there. The small house was well kept but with very little in the way of decoration. There was a sparseness of pictures on the walls, but the mantel was full of framed photographs.

"Do you mind if I look at your photographs?"

"No, go ahead."

"As I was saying," Potter continued. "We know you lost your job because of an article *Truth Will Out* published revealing your sexuality, and we know you originally sued the radio network and the magazine. You even named Carver in the suit. One thing we don't know is why you dropped it."

McGlynn chewed momentarily on his lower lip. "I didn't even want to file in the first place. It was really a rough time. I went from being radio's dream voice with stacks and stacks of fan mail to being the butt of Jimmy Kimmel's jokes. I understood why they canceled my program. I couldn't get through a show without inflammatory phone calls sneaking through my screener. The station was flooded with negative mail and email. Homophobes, women calling me a fraud, even gays accusing me of selling out."

"Don't celebrities come out every day, like literally every day?" Kate asked. "What provoked such a reaction?"

McGylnn flushed slightly. "You never listened to the program, did you?"

"I'm not much of a radio listener."

Potter stepped in. "The Dr. Love persona was very much a ladies' man."

"I see."

"Yeah, I spent nearly eight years romancing women over the airwaves. As he said, it was a persona. I was playing a part. Anyway, when it all blew up, I needed money. I was out of a job, nobody would hire me, and I needed the money. I had lawyers knocking down my door offering to help, so I picked one. He took care of all the details, who to sue, everything."

"And you dropped the suit because—?" Potter pressed.

"The network settled out of court, and that was enough. I'm not greedy. Frankly, I was sick of the whole business. So I dropped the suit against the magazine. About that time, I got a job offer for a show on a satellite station. Money wasn't an issue anymore. That was the only reason I filed in the first place."

Kate had worked her way through most of the photographs, which were either group shots of friends or what appeared to be old family portraits. She found one, though, of McGlynn and a slender Hispanic male in an affectionate embrace, both smiling. Kate picked up the photo and held it out to McGlynn.

"Is this your boyfriend?"

"Yeah. Julio Ambris."

"Were you and he together when all this happened?"

"Actually, no. I kind of met him because of all of it. He read about it and wrote me. Things kind of went from there. He helped me through the mess. I know I made it all sound horrible, and it was (don't get me wrong), but I had my share of supporters too. They weren't all laywers either. Good things eventually came out of it. I'm financially secure again, more than before, really. I've got a great job…a great boyfriend." Kate found it interesting that Julio barely made the list. "I don't fault Carver or his magazine," McGlynn continued. "If it hadn't been them, it would've been someone else. The truth has a way of coming out. They only printed the truth. I guess it was time for me to live up to it."

Kate and Potter exchanged a look.

"That's awfully forgiving of you, Mr. McGlynn," Potter commented.

McGlynn laughed and then bit his lip as he fought for the right words. "I'm not saying that I don't wish it hadn't come out differently. I would've liked to have come out on my own terms and not in the middle of some three-ring circus. What I'm saying is that it doesn't do me any good to hold on to it. Hate is baggage, and I don't need it."

"Sounds smart to me, Mr. McGlynn," Kate said. "Thank you for your time. If we need anything else, we'll be in touch."

JULIO, A BAG of groceries in each arm, watched from the corner of the house as the white couple walked to their car. They were obviously cops. He could have spotted that a mile away. Before the woman turned in his direction, he ducked back under the carport where he had parked his Firebird. The sweat from a thawing bag of vegetables seeped through the bag into his shirt, cutting short the temptation to watch them further.

As he set the bags down on the kitchen island, he called out, "Hey, babe, I'm home." When there was no answer, he peeked into the living room. Willy was sitting on the couch. Not doing anything, just sitting. Julio gave his shoulder a playful shove. "Hey, *papito*, didn't you hear me?"

"Sorry, I was thinking."

Julio sauntered over to the window, showing off his new designer skinny jeans, but he could see in the window's reflection that Willy wasn't paying any attention. "So who were those people that were just here?" he asked nonchalantly.

"The police."

"Oh?" He made his voice go up in surprise. "What'd they want?" He walked back into the kitchen to put the groceries away.

"I guess somebody's been threatening the editor of *Truth Will Out* or at least the guy who was editor when they published the article about me."

"Carver."

Willy turned to look at Julio. "Yeah. I'm surprised you remember his name."

"Like I could forget that—" Julio broke into a short litany of bilingual expletives and flipped a cabinet door closed more violently than necessary. "What he did to you, man."

"Yeah, well, someone's been mailing him threats, and they think it might be me."

Julio laughed. "You? They don't know you so well, eh?"

"Yeah." Willy sprawled back on the couch to stare at the ceiling.

"Why do they think it's you?"

"I don't know. The guy said something about an Olivet postmark." Willy covered his face with his hands. "Just when I think I've left this behind me, it all comes back."

Julio leaned on the back of the couch and pulled Willy's hands from his face. "It's gonna be okay, *papito*."

Willy looked at him coldly. "I just want it to be done." Then he stood up and walked away.

Chapter Twenty-four

ate stood in the ladies' room at the precinct, adding the finishing touches to her lipstick contour. One of her roommates in college, Polly, had gone to beauty school prior to university and had worked at a shop to pay for her four-year business degree. Polly had made sure that in between studying for Intro to Criminology exams and kickboxing lessons, Kate learned at least a few of the finer points of a beauty makeup. Not that she had many occasions in which to deploy such an arsenal. That stuff was a bit showy for a casual date. For her last date, she had barely bothered to apply any makeup at all, and the date hadn't been worth even that. She shook her head at the memory.

Kate set down the makeup brush and picked up the cigarette smoldering on the edge of the sink, knowing it would likely spoil the effect she had just created. But she needed it to psych herself up for the walk through the station. The way she dressed at work and the amount of makeup she wore there intentionally expressed a down-to-business attitude. Every birthday and Christmas, her mother bought her overly feminine clothing, articles Kate either relegated to off-duty wear, which meant they rarely got worn, or donated to Heidi's annual garage sale. She got enough unwelcome advances as it was.

And now she was about to parade through the station in a sleeveless red dress and heels. She tugged at the front, feeling that it was cut too low. Who was she kidding? The only person who would consider this low cut would be her father. Even her mother would approve. It was just that she was at the station.

She turned to get a different angle in the mirror. She did look good. Maybe she could let that self-confidence carry her through the bastion of chauvinistic testosterone waiting outside. That confidence and nicotine. She took another drag. She thought about praying her way through it, but that seemed a bit hypocritical as she sucked on her cigarette. *Whatsoever is not of faith is sin.* If she could just convince herself that there wasn't anything wrong with her smoking, she'd be okay. Right. That's what she kept telling herself, but she'd given up on that the first time she'd quit. Her conscience had been pricked. She exhaled another cloud. She didn't look as good now. She felt tawdry, like a prom girl smoking in the lavatory.

As she extinguished the butt under the tap, the door opened. Kate made a couple of futile swipes at the smoky air but relaxed when she saw it was Sanchez, who was no great fan of the rules as evidenced by the three undone buttons on her uniform's shirt.

"Baxter, look at you, *chica*! You look gorgeous! You got a hot date tonight?"

"Not quite." Kate smiled. "I'm going to this fancy reception but just with a friend."

Sanchez gasped and then sidled up to Kate. "Tell me," she said under her breath, despite there being no one else present, "That your *friend* is not that hunk of jungle fever out in the lobby."

The laugh sneaked up on Kate so violently that she choked. After she got through sputtering, she finally gasped out, "He's not black."

"I don't care what he is. I'd take him home in a heartbeat."

"And what would your boyfriend say about that?"

"Nothing. If I snagged a hunk like your friend out there, Marcos would be out on his lazy, good-for-nothing butt," Sanchez replied with a snap of her fingers. "So what is he? Your friend, is he like Middle Eastern or what?"

"Indian, half Indian." Kate pulled her hair up, leaving a couple of curls on either side of her face.

"Hey, they got jungles in India, right? It's always the mixed ones that are gorgeous. I should be dating a white guy. Or a black guy. Or Asian. Or anybody but Marcos. At least we'd have cute kids. If our kids look anything like Marcos' family, they'll be butt-ugly. So there's nothing going on between you two? You don't have a little somethin'-somethin' going on?"

Kate laughed around the bobby pin in her mouth. "No, just friends. Old friends, actually. We went to college together."

"You think he might go for a Latina?" Sanchez asked with a big wink and smile.

"He might..." Kate said delicately, knowing that her friend and coworker were worldviews apart. "But I really can't see it working out between you."

"You can't blame a girl for asking."

Kate threw her cosmetics back in their bag and made one last attempt to steel herself against what would be on the other side of the door. She actually had her hand pressed against the door to push it open when she told herself she was being stupider than usual. Why did this have to be such a big deal? The answer came back clear—it didn't. And by the time she pushed the door open, Kate had moved into something between apathy and eat-your-heart-out mode.

A beat of silence followed Kate's entrance as several masculine jaws dropped. Then came the whirlwind of whistles and catcalls. Kate plastered on a condescending smile as she walked to her desk and retrieved her coat. Sergeant Polanski met her there.

"Cool it, guys!" he barked. He offered Kate his arm. "You look stunning. Truly a rose among thorns."

"Thank you." She took his arm, and they walked out to the lobby, where a tall broad-shouldered man stood talking on his phone. His brown skin was just a shade or two lighter than his eyes, pointing up their rich warmth, even behind the thin frames of his eyeglasses. The short black hair was slicked back from his narrow, aristocratic face, but it waved nonetheless. His brown suit, crisp white shirt, and gold tie accentuated his coloring. When he saw Kate approach, he pocketed his phone, the hand glinting gold from a large ring that Kate knew had belonged to his grandfather. They greeted each other with a hug, where Kate caught a whiff of heady aftershave.

"Looking good, Katherine."

"Not bad yourself." She turned to Polanski. "Sergeant

Polanski, this is Darshan Spence. Spence, this is Karl Polanski."

Polanski squinted at Spence as they shook hands. "I believe I've seen your byline. You write for the *Tribune*, correct?"

"That's right, sir."

"Well, keep up the good work, and you two have fun." Polanski looked Kate in the eye. "Unlike those yahoos in there, I don't need to remind you that you're on duty tomorrow."

"And yet you are." Kate smiled.

"And yet I am." He winked back. "Have fun."

As they walked out, Spence asked, "So is Sergeant Polanski your guardian angel?"

"Today, for the moment. But now you get to take over."

"Ah." He took her arm. "Gladly, but I fully intend to defer to your kickboxing expertise should ruffians attempt to mug us."

"Oh, please, in these heels? You're on your own. It's good to finally see you after all the phone tag. It's been a couple weeks."

"Yes, it has been, and yes, it's good to see you." He opened the car door for her.

"By the way, I'd consider switching colognes if I were you."

Spence just shook his head. "Not working for me, huh?"

"Not so much. Smells too much like an old man."

"Well, you smell like smoke."

"Oh, somebody was smoking in the restroom," Kate deflected. So the perfume hadn't covered it. Spence shut the door and walked around to the driver's side. His unresponsiveness to her excuse was hard to read. He was like that. Kate tried soothing her conscience with the facts that it wasn't a lie, merely an equivocation, and that she was really quitting this time. It didn't quite work.

"So what's this reception for, and am I underdressed?" she asked as soon as he was behind the wheel.

Spence laughed. "You'll be fine. Obviously, it's not black tie, or I would be sorely in trouble. Chapman Books is launching a new imprint for kiddy lit, Chapboy—"

"You're kidding me?"

"No, it's called Chapboy. This is just their way of getting a bit of attention; hence, the reason I'll be there."

"So it doesn't have anything to do with this story you're working on that you won't tell us about?"

"No." Spence drew the word out. "But it has to do with this circle of people, so who knows? I might find out something useful while we're there."

"What do you know?" Kate elbowed him in the arm. "I'm hoping the same thing."

Chapter Twenty-five

"Well, well. The veil has lifted," Kate said as she took another sip of Perrier.

"And you've seen the glory of the Lord?" Spence replied, not looking up from his smart phone on which he was making notes for his article on the reception.

"More like the favoritism of the well-to-do. On Saturday I wondered why in the world I got called in to take a report. Now I know. *That* is my case." She discreetly indicated the Carvers, whom she had spotted almost immediately. "And it's talking to the chief of police. Should've figured."

"Another mystery solved. It's all about connections. Nathanael Carver, huh?"

"Yeah. What do you know about him?"

"Probably less than you at this point," Spence said, scanning the room. "I know he's publishing Eirik Boudreau's new book."

"Do you know much about Boudreau?"

"Kind of. I thought he'd be here tonight, but I haven't seen him. So is the case interesting?"

Kate reflected briefly. "No. Not yet, at least." She looked at Amelie Carver, who was laughing in the most charming way at something the police chief's wife had just said. "Except…something's going on in the Carver household—somebody's got a secret. I don't even know if it has to do with the case, though. There's that and I got goosed today. That was interesting."

Spence's eyebrows shot well above his glasses. "By Carver?"

Kate laughed. "No, silly boy. Some old perv in the city we were interviewing as a possible suspect."

"Hey!" Spence exclaimed in a hushed tone. "There's Boudreau." He indicated a small, bespectacled man with a receding crew cut and blond goatee. He held two or three hors d'oeuvres in one hand and with the other was taking a glass of wine from a waiter.

"Why would he be here?" Kate asked. "I thought he left Chapman Books for Roving House."

"Oh, he did. But all the local bigwigs are here. It would be like him to show up uninvited, regardless. He has a reputation for reckless abandon. Have you read his book?"

"No. I've heard about it, though."

"It's pretty heady stuff and not at all kind to Christianity. Apparently, he was raised Presbyterian before delving into a life of drugs and debauchery. I wouldn't recommend reading it; it would just make you mad, or sick alternately. But it's earned him a reputation. He's allegedly reformed from his less savory habits, but from the way he acts, I wouldn't be surprised if he still takes an occasional snort. Even if he is clean, if he keeps pushing people's buttons the way he does, he's going to kill himself professionally. Rumor has it that Chapman's trying to win him back. I don't believe it, but if it were true, that could explain why he's here."

"Sounds like you've been following up on him."

"Let's just say I've found him to be a person of interest."

"Can you introduce me?"

Spence grimaced. "We've only met once, and oddly he doesn't seem to like the press much. You may be better off on your own, and you may want to catch him sooner than later. I think that's his second glass of wine, and he doesn't look like he's slowing down."

"He definitely didn't give up booze. I'll catch you later."

Kate drifted around the room until she stood on the other side of a display table from Boudreau. She had noticed he was sticking close to the path the servers were making with the refreshments, so she counted on his not drifting far. She made a pretense of looking at the books on the table, slowly walking around. He was shorter than she'd realized from across the room. Kate didn't consider herself tall, but she had a good three or four inches on him. When she had circled to his side of the table, she glanced up. He was staring at her. She smiled, as Danny would put it, "with lights."

He cocked his head slightly. "I don't know you," he said abruptly. Obviously not a charmer.

"No, I'm Kate Baxter." She offered her hand, which he took in his small, exceptionally soft one. "Aren't you—"

"Yes, I am. Eirik Boudreau." It was then that he finally smiled as he slowly and gently squeezed her hand. Kate resisted the urge to vomit and kept on smiling.

"Wow, I've never met somebody so famous before!"

"You're not likely to out here in Fulton Springs." A smug smile squatted underneath his pointed little nose and trim mustache. "I moved out here because it was close to Chicago, but there's more of a sense of privacy, which is so important to a writer."

"Wow, really?" Kate instinctually adopted an uptalk inflection. Dumb blonde seemed to be the part to play with this guy.

"Yes, especially once you become famous. People are always after you for interviews. Would-be writers want your advice or help. It can be hard to find the time to write, which is what made you famous in the first place." He chuckled and downed the rest of his wine.

"You're still writing, though, aren't you? I thought your first book was so—" Kate paused dramatically. "Tragic."

Boudreau smirked. But he sobered almost immediately and turned a disquieting gaze on her. "Yes, it was, but I trust you found the ending uplifting." Kate just smiled bigger. Boudreau ran a finger around the rim of his empty glass then finally said, "I've actually just finished another book. It's with the publisher right now, coming out this winter."

"Is it a true story, like your first book? Can you tell me about it?"

Boudreau sucked his teeth. "I wish I could. The publisher won't let me say much. Doesn't want me to give too much away too early, you understand. All I can say is that it's another tragic story. It's called *My Girl Leona*. It's about a lover of mine, who—" He broke off, seemingly overcome with emotion. He put his hot little hand on her upper arm. "Well, you'll just have to read it when it comes out. I'd be happy to autograph your copy."

"Oh, wow. That would be great." Kate looked to where Linley Chapman was conversing with some reporters, including Spence. "Is that why you're here tonight? To talk to the publisher about your book? It's not a kid's book, right?"

"Um, no. I'm just here tonight because I'm a key figure in the industry. Besides, my new book isn't being published by Chapman Books."

"Didn't they publish the first one?" Did she look as stupid as she sounded?

"They did." Boudreau signaled a server to bring him more wine. "But they are swine." He took two glasses and began to hand one to Kate, which she declined as innocuously as possible.

"So you like the new publisher better?"

"Katie—you said your name was Katie, right?—all publishers are swine. They just use writers like me to make money for themselves. I owe no one but my readership. Readers need to hear what I have to say, and that's why I write. I do it for them, not for the money."

Kate nodded. His little sermon seemed impassioned. It seemed motivated. It seemed prepared. She wondered how many times he'd given it. She then realized he was waiting for more of a response than her bobbing head. "Wow…Thank you so much."

Again with the hand on her arm, this time it slid down to her elbow. "You're welcome. Why don't we—"

"So who's publishing the new book?"

"Uh, Roving House. Perhaps we could talk about this somewhere more private."

And so it went, Kate trying to steer the conversation toward Carver and Boudreau trying to steer her toward the door. Once she realized she wasn't getting anywhere useful, Kate begged off, saying that she couldn't leave without her friend but promising "another time." He slipped her a calling card before she excused herself to the ladies' room.

When she came back, she set her sights on Linley Chapman. Thus far, the distinguished silver-haired man had been continually surrounded by the press, his staff, or the authors promoted by his new imprint. Right now he was bridging the gap between the mousy waif who had written the verse book *Sonnet in My Bonnet* and a polished female news anchor from a regional station. Spence wasn't too far away from them, talking to another reporter, so Kate went over and slipped her hand into the crook of his arm.

"How did it go?" Spence asked when the other man finally left them. "You guys chatted for quite a bit."

"Well, we were talking about one of his favorite subjects—him. He certainly is a character, a bit of a pompous sleaze, but he didn't seem all that unstable. His reputation seems a little large for such a *small* man. Pun intended."

"Time will tell, I suppose."

"I'd like to talk to Chapman. Find out how angry he was about losing Boudreau to Carver."

"Hmm." Spence rocked back on his heels. "That is an interesting question. I've heard mixed reports."

Kate jostled Spence's arm. "I saw you talking to him earlier. Can you hook me up, or am I going to have to do this one myself too?"

Spence snorted. "I'm the one who got you here, aren't I? I don't see Chapman being willing to spill that kind of info on the journalistic record. He's a pretty class individual."

"He looks the part at any rate."

"But maybe…"

"Maybe what?" Kate prompted when Spence never finished, his eyes riveted on the publisher.

"It's all about how you ask and where." He looked at Kate. "He's not going to talk about it in the open here, especially if you broach it as if it's about him."

"But if he's the victim?"

"That might work, but as I said, he's not going to dish dirt on someone else, not really his style." Spence chuckled. "But now may be the time to try."

Chapman had begun heading for the door, and Spence moved, with Kate in tow, to intercept him.

"Do you know where he's going?" Kate asked in a whisper as they rounded a fat woman in a gaudy dress.

"Pretty good idea," was all the response she got.

Chapman managed to get through the crowd without being waylaid by anyone, but the number of greetings he received in passing slowed him down. When he hit the doorway to the lobby, he picked up his pace.

Spence made his move, dashing the last few steps into the lobby. "Mr. Chapman!" he called.

Chapman turned. "Yes?"

"Darshan Spence, with the *Tribune*. We talked a bit earlier. This is Katherine Baxter." Kate smiled. "I'm sorry to hunt you down like this, but I was wondering if I could ask you just a few more questions."

Chapman shifted his weight. "About the launch?"

"Actually, no. About Eirik Boudreau."

Chapman stopped in midshift, his mouth in a little *o*.

Spence rushed on, "I'm interested in doing a profile on him, but I understand his new book isn't being published by your company."

"Yes, that's true." Chapman nodded. "You'd want to speak with Nathanael Carver of Roving House." He started to turn away.

"Well, I was actually wondering why he left your house. I mean, you made his first book a bestseller, right?"

"We did. If you want to know his reasons for leaving, perhaps you should ask him. If you'll—"

"What if I have, Mr. Chapman?" Spence ventured.

"Excuse me?" the older man asked politely.

"There are two sides to every story. I'm just trying to get the whole picture. You were making money for him; he was making money for you. Who upset the cart?"

Chapman clasped his hands in front of him and jutted out his jaw. After a brief delay, he said, "If you've ever met Eirik, I'm sure you can guess the answer to that yourself."

Spence smiled. "I understand that. But what about Carver?"

"I don't believe Eirik was seduced from our house if that's what you're asking. He ran out, waving his arms, so to speak."

"Any truth to the rumor that you're trying to win him back?" Spence asked.

Chapman gave a tight smile as he suppressed a laugh. "None whatsoever."

"So there's no ill will between the two houses?" Spence depersonalized the question.

Chapman tilted his head back as he once again shifted his weight. Kate wondered if he realized that he was literally sticking his nose in the air. "Not now," he said. "Carver's welcome to him."

"People have been saying that Chapman Books really took a hit losing Boudreau."

Chapman grimaced a bit and swayed. "Well, as you can see from tonight, Chapman Books is branching out into a new market. Also, we've signed a very promising author recently. With Eirik gone, we can give her the attention she needs to be a bestseller. I wouldn't say we've suffered much." He paused.

Spence held his hands up questioningly. "Off the record?" he prompted.

Chapman gave a small smile that almost reached his small, dark eyes. "I was going to say, for many of our staff, the recent changes have actually been a relief." He cleared his throat. "Now, I really must excuse myself." He turned and left.

Spence called out his thanks and then turned to Kate. "So?"

"What I'm really curious about is how you knew he was heading to the john," Kate said, watching Chapman disappear into the men's room.

"I think he gets dry mouth. I'd been watching him, and he was drinking like a camel. He hadn't left the room yet this evening, so when he headed for the door, it was a simple deduction. And often people are more likely to let things slip out under pressure."

"Maybe you should be the detective."

Spence laughed. "So was it any help to you?"

Kate shrugged. "He doesn't seem like a likely candidate. Unfortunately, we've been wracking those up. We have far fewer in the 'looks guilty' column. You really think losing Boudreau didn't hurt his company?"

Spence sat on one of the many circular couches that populated the lobby, and Kate joined him. "It certainly wasn't a financial move up," he said. "But if the new signee he's talking about is Elena Hidalgo, he may not be blowing smoke. She's a prof at Stanford, and she's published several historical studies, some popular and some scholarly. She's been working on a novel, so she might be in the market for a new publisher. She was in Chicago last week for a lecture, but she's stuck around. I saw her yesterday."

Kate shook her head in mock amazement. "How do you know so much?"

"Well, for one thing, I read." He looked at her over the top of his glasses.

"I read," she said.

"Yes, things written a hundred years ago."

"I say, if it lasts a hundred years, then it's worth reading."

KATE WANDERED back into the convention room. Spence had taken a call on his cell and said he would catch up with her later. She spotted Boudreau. He had cornered Carver, who was patiently nodding at whatever the smaller man was saying. Kate could see a strain in Carver's neck and face. She smiled. The interchange didn't prove to her that the author was as erratic as Carver had indicated; rather, it highlighted how longsuffering the editor was. She laughed to herself.

"What a pretty sound."

A man about her age stood on the other side of the poetry lady's display table looking at her. A palpable sensuality undercut his almost boyish features. One hand held a glass of red wine. With the other, he brushed long dark bangs from his face, drawing attention to rich brown eyes, full of invitation. Kate felt a tug but retreated slightly.

"I don't believe we've met," she said.

"No, we haven't. I wondered if we'd get the chance. You seem to know most of the men here." His voice was light and mocking.

Kate crossed her arms. "Meaning?"

The stranger circled to her side of the table. "Well, you came in with that man—" He indicated Spence, who was visible through the open doorway. "Then for some incomprehensible reason, you suffered through a long conversation with Eirik Boudreau."

"You were watching, hmm?"

"Yes." He put on an exaggerated frown. "I'd be hard-pressed to say who was putting on whom?" He raised an eyebrow at her.

She laughed. "You're quite observant."

"We editors are supposed to be. Returning to your list of male acquaintances, I believe I saw you walking through Roving House the other day with Nathanael Carver."

Kate didn't let the surprise read on her face. "I don't remember seeing you there."

"I don't suppose you saw me." He took a sip of wine.

"I don't suppose that *you* are Grant Innerst?"

He broke into a broad smile. "Well done. And how is it that you know my name but I don't know yours?"

"Nathanael. He actually brought me by your office to meet you, but you'd already left."

"Really?" Innerst looked surprise. "You must have just missed me, Ms…?"

"Miss Baxter. Kate Baxter."

"So, Miss Baxter, what were you doing at Roving House?"

"Nathanael was just giving me a tour."

"Nate's never mentioned you before. What exactly is your relationship? If you don't mind my asking." He looked at her intently.

"It's a working relationship," she answered.

"Did the board hire you? Some kind of consultant?"

"No, nothing like that. Nathanael's just helping me gather some information."

"Vague and terribly mysterious."

"Said the man who's been spying on me the whole evening."

"*Spying*, what an ugly word. I would say I was merely appreciating your beauty."

Kate did not want to blush at his comment, but she could feel a mild heat rise in her cheeks. It quickly dissipated as she shook her head and looked out across the room. Still, she would have liked very much to forget that this man was a suspect.

"Are you all settled in as editor-in-chief or whatever your title is?" she asked without looking back at him.

"Oh, yes. Nate's a good mentor, and if I ever run into any problems, he's just upstairs to help me out of them."

"Then you like the new position?"

"Of course; it's a step up."

Kate scrutinized him as he took a turn looking out over the room. "You wouldn't have rather taken the book division?"

Innerst looked at her, bemused. "No," he said. "Is that what Nate thinks?"

Kate shrugged. "Not necessarily. I did get the vibe that some people around Roving House were a tad...envious, shall we say?"

Innerst gave a little laugh. "You must mean Mya. She came by and told me about your little visit. She wanted to know if I knew anything."

"Did she?"

"Oh, yeah, but I don't really envy Nate, at least not his job. It seems a bit slow paced for me. And—" He gave Kate a wry look. "—I'd have to deal with Eirik Boudreau."

Kate smiled. "Good point."

Kate felt a hand on her shoulder, and there was Spence standing beside her.

"Ah, here's your boyfriend," said Innerst.

"Oh no," Kate said hurriedly. "We're just friends. This is Darshan Spence with the *Fulton Springs Tribune*. Spence, this is Grant Innerst, editor of *Truth Will Out*."

Spence gave her a somewhat dirty look as he reached out to shake Innerst's hand. "Yes," he told the other man. "We're *just* friends."

"I see," said Innerst. "Good to know." He turned to Kate. "I'm afraid I've monopolized enough of your time, but I look forward to talking with you again."

"Likewise."

After Innerst walked away, Kate gave Spence a light backhand on the arm. "What's wrong with you?"

Spence shook his head as if to clear it and replied, "I'm sorry. If I'd realized I was interrupting your throwing yourself at him, I wouldn't have bothered to come over."

Kate's mouth gaped for a moment and then snapped shut. "I was not throwing myself at him," she whispered between gritted teeth.

"My mistake. I'd best go get some more quotes. The ones I have are junk." And he stalked away, or at least it seemed a lot like stalking to Kate. She rolled her eyes. As she debated whether to follow him, Nathanael Carver approached her.

"Miss Baxter," he said softly, extending his hand. "I'm surprised to see you…working here tonight?"

Kate was pleased to find the handshake dry, the first such a one she had received from him.

"Well, I'm full of surprises, but technically I'm off duty right now."

"I see," Carver replied, keeping his voice low. "I hope you're enjoying yourself. I saw you talking to Grant a bit ago."

"He's quite the charmer, isn't he?"

Carver gave a slight laugh and nodded. "That he is. Since you are here socially, I hope it won't be an imposition if I bring up a business matter."

"Not at all."

Carver grimaced. "I feel bad. I'm sure I've already put you through a lot of trouble, but I'm canceling my report or calling off the investigation, whatever you would call that."

Kate realized she needed to close her mouth again or say something. "Are you sure about that, Mr. Carver?"

"Yes. I'm sure it's actually nothing. I let Amelie get me a little worked up. She worries too much."

Kate thought of all the arguments Potter had given her for the case's validity. She tried plying one or two of them to Carver, but he remained happily resigned.

"It's been going on for almost a year," he said. "If this person were actually going to do something hurtful, don't you think he would've tried by now?"

Kate shook her head. "Not necessarily. As I just pointed out, the threats seem to be escalating. That implies the writer is likely becoming more agitated and thus more likely to do something dangerous. Even if the whole thing started out as a prank, this guy could be going mentally south in a hurry."

"I appreciate your concern. Really. But I don't want to waste any more of your time. I'm sure if I ignore it, it will all blow over. Any more unmarked letters from Olivet can go straight into the trash can."

Kate studied him. Carver seemed to honestly believe he wasn't in danger. He was by far the most relaxed she had seen him. She finally shrugged.

"Well, if I can't change your mind, I guess that's it. I trust you'll contact us, though, if anything more threatening happens."

"I promise." He started to walk away.

"Before you go, just tell me that you've had a security system installed."

Carver turned around with a chagrinned expression. "No, but I will call about that tomorrow, I promise. I know it would put Amelie at ease."

"Good," Kate said. "You said you had a gun, right?" Carver nodded. "Till then, keep it handy. Be safe."

"Trust me, I will," Carver promised and then walked over to schmooze with a small group of suits.

Kate tried to relax, but her gut was knotted up. She hated this. Some niggling thought just left of her conscience told her that calling off the case was a bad idea, that she should not let this go. Maybe she could talk to the chief about it. After all, if he was friends with Carver, he'd surely want to ensure his safety, right? Or more likely, he'd side with Carver that the case was really nothing, so why bother? She'd been less than impressed with the current chief, whose political ambitions were blatantly forefront. With any luck, they'd be rid of him in the next election.

She tried to push her concern aside as she made her way to the lobby to call Potter. Potter took the news, as he did most everything, in stride. Kate found it exasperating.

"Don't you think that's a bit odd?"

"Yes," he said.

"Well?"

"I don't know what else to say, Kate. We can talk about it tomorrow. You need a night off. Why don't you try to enjoy the rest of your evening?"

Kate made a face. Fat chance of that happening. "Okay, I'll see you tomorrow." She hung up. Why was she dwelling on this? She'd been tempted to call things off herself that afternoon. Maybe it was just pride. Maybe she had been right about the case before and Potter had been wrong.

Kate looked around the rather empty second-floor lobby. The reception was being held in a convention room in the Peacock Hotel, one of the more elegant buildings in downtown Fulton Springs. Kate peeked into the room, wondering if she should find Spence and whether he was still in a snit. Someone was making a speech about Chapboy, which she found a less-than-enticing prospect. She opted instead for some fresh air. Perhaps it would distill her jittery feeling. The night seemed to be taking one turn after another for the worse.

Two large doors propped open at one end of the lobby led outside to a terrace. Even before she stepped out, a rush of cool air tingled against her bare arms, face, and neck. Autumn was finally starting to cool down. Thoughts of football, bonfires, and cider ran through her mind. Last year, she and her friends had gone apple picking. Maybe they could do that again. Looking out at the city lights, she leaned against the thick balustrade and felt the cold stone draw her body heat through her dress. She released some of her stress in an elongated exhalation, its sound obscured by the noise of taxis pulling up and then away from the hotel's front entrance on the street below.

It wasn't long before her thoughts on autumn led her to calculate the number of weeks until Thanksgiving. Thanksgiving with her parents and sundry other well-intentioned but meddlesome relatives who would prod her with questions like: Why was she still single? Was she still doing that police "thing"? And had she thought of doing something different with her hair? Kate groaned. Perhaps she would stay in Fulton Springs this year. But it had been a long time since she had seen her brother, Robbie, who lived near their parents in Indiana. Of course his wife tended to be jealous of his time with Kate, which Kate found insane, but her sister-in-law's attitude could sap the fun out of visiting her brother and nieces.

She closed her eyes. It was then that she heard a rustle, the pulling of fabric away from stone. She opened her eyes and looked to the left. The terrace ran the length of the building, and large patches of light from the convention room's French doors illuminated most of it, but in between, shadows congregated. In those shadows Kate made out a figure standing two sets of doors down, betrayed by the glowing tip of a cigarette. Smoke wafted into the light.

"You doing okay?" It was a woman's voice, on the husky side.

"Yeah. Thanks." Kate's eyes followed the smoke until it disappeared.

"Just checking, honey." Another plume streamed into the air. Kate could feel something dancing in her middle. She looked away and gripped her temples with one hand, as if the pressure would somehow help. "You look like you're having a rough night," the other woman commented.

"Just a little and mostly in the last twenty minutes," Kate replied.

The woman laughed and moved into the light, revealing herself as a full-figured, middle-aged woman with rich brown skin and a head of magnificent glossy curls. In her right hand, she held a red rhinestone-studded cigarette holder away from her tailored suit and flicked the ashes over the ledge. Then deftly with her left hand, she drew a gold cigarette case out of an inside pocket and held it in Kate's direction. "Smoke?"

Kate hesitated for a moment. "No, thank you. I'm quitting."

The other woman nodded and smiled, the lips of her large mouth remaining tight. "Hmm. Interesting choice of words. *Quitting*, meaning that you haven't quite, I suppose."

"Perceptive."

The woman gave a grunt of laughter as she replaced the case. "Well, I won't tempt you, but if you change your mind."

"Thanks." Kate looked back out at the lights, yellow, white, and red, and tried to ignore the other woman as she released another stream of smoke into the air, which Kate now found a bit chilly. She wondered what time it was. "Are you here for the Chapman reception?" she asked, more out of compulsion than curiosity.

The woman grimaced. "Yes."

Now it was Kate's turn to laugh. "Not enjoying it much either?"

"No, I'm not really a reader, and I can only make nice for so long. At least not without a cigarette or a proper drink, neither of which was happening in there."

"I take it you're not in the industry."

"No. My husband is, barely. He's a lawyer. Did you know there's such a thing as a literary lawyer?" Kate shook her head. "Well, there is, and it's my husband. He started specializing in that a few years ago. He should've stayed with estate law. The money was better; that's for sure."

"What do you do?"

"At the moment, I play tennis…and spend money." She looked at Kate with hooded eyes. "And you?"

"I'm a detective."

The woman raised her eyebrows. "Well now. That's something."

Kate held her hand out toward the woman. "Kate Baxter."

The woman slowly moved closer to Kate and shook Kate's hand firmly with her heavily ornamented one. "Talitha Banks."

And at that moment, shouts broke out on the sidewalk

below. Kate leaned over the stone railing for a better view. The loudest voice, the one shouting profanity, sounded familiar. She caught sight of a balding head. It was Boudreau, screaming at a valet. The doorman and concierge stood on either side trying to calm him. From what Kate could make out, the problem had something to do with a keychain.

Talitha muttered a few choice words about the writer.

"You know him?" Kate asked.

"More than I care to."

Kate looked back down in time to see Boudreau take a swing at one of the men, after which things turned into a bit of a free-for-all for a moment or two.

Kate whistled. "He really does have a screw loose."

"Oh, honey, I could've told you that. But knowing him, he's probably just smashed."

Kate watched security escort the inflamed writer to a taxicab. She wondered how dangerous he could actually be.

She pushed herself away from the railing and felt the front of her dress cling to the granite. She looked down to see countless little snags across the midsection. Looking at Talitha, who already had the case in hand, she asked for a cigarette.

Kate stood, a short time later, in front of a mirror in the ladies' room, checking her hair and makeup and hoping that Spence was ready to leave. The fun part of the evening had been short lived. She was about to go find him when Amelie Carver walked in. They greeted each other cordially, and Amelie began her own primp.

Kate dawdled in front of her mirror, arguing with herself as to whether she should butt in or butt out. No one else was present. Perhaps that was a sign. With an inward groan, she faced the other woman. "Mrs. Carver?"

"Yes?" Amelie asked as she stowed her lipstick in a small handbag.

"Your husband's asked me to stop the investigation." Amelie Carver became the poster girl for eloquent surprise. Kate continued, keeping her tone flat, "So this may be the last time I talk to you about the subject." She took a breath. "I don't know what is going on with you and Olivet—" Amelie tried to protest, but Kate plowed on. "—but if it has anything to do with these letters your husband is getting, stop it whatever it is."

Amelie shook her head and swallowed. "I'm afraid I don't know what you're talking about."

"Please, Mrs. Carver. When we mentioned Olivet in our conversation on Saturday, you might as well have had *guilt* tattooed on your forehead. Whatever it is, you'd best take care of it. That's all I have to say. Good evening."

She walked out, leaving Amelie Carver shell-shocked. When Kate walked into the convention room, she could see that things were winding down, although plenty of people still loitered, conversing. She spotted Spence as he made his way toward her.

"You got everything you need?" she asked.

"Yeah, let's go."

They sustained an awkward silence for most of the car ride. As they neared the station, Kate realized if she was going to mend things tonight, she'd better start.

"Can I ask why you got mad?"

Spence sighed and after a moment said, "It's the way you answered that guy."

Kate was a little leery of where this was going. "I just told him that we were friends. That's right, isn't it?"

"Yes," Spence said tensely. "But it's the way you say it. The rapidity with which you hurriedly push forth that fact—as if you're desperately afraid someone will get the wrong idea about us. As if I'm the last guy on earth you'd be willing to date. It makes me feel a little leprous."

"I didn't say it like that—"

"Yes, Kate, you did—and do every time someone asks."

Kate tried to remember the last time the issue had come up, as it often did when they were together and would run into someone from either's circle. She couldn't guarantee the speed with which she'd answered, but after thinking about it, she did realize that she was always the one to answer. She was suddenly very glad that she had not told Spence about her reaction to Sanchez's inquiry.

"I'm sorry. I don't mean to sound like that…or imply that." She limped through an apology as Spence pulled up alongside her car at the police station.

"Well, it makes me feel as if you're ashamed of me somehow. And tonight—" His voice rose slightly. "I know that we're just friends, but still you were supposed to be there with me, and you start flirting with this other guy."

Once again Kate wasn't sure what to say. He wasn't putting the car in park, which meant he didn't intend to discuss this much longer.

"I'm sorry," she said again. "You know I'm not ashamed of you in any way, and I'm sorry if I give that impression. You know I think you're a great guy, and you're my oldest friend here. I'll try to be more…aware of my response to that kind of situation in the future. Grant Innerst is—or was—part of my case."

"Yeah, but there was a difference between the way you were flirting with him and the way you flirted with Boudreau."

"There was?"

Spence gave her a look. "Katherine, I know you." He held up his hand, showing her the back and tapping it, a sign he had created back in their college days indicating that he knew her like the back of his hand. "When you were flirting with Innerst, it wasn't…pretense."

Kate suddenly felt a little overheated. "Well, I wouldn't hurt your feelings on purpose. I'm sorry if I did."

"Thanks. I appreciate that," he said. "And I'm sorry for being stupid about all this and being too sensitive." Before she could reply, he rushed on. "I've got an early morning tomorrow, so I'd better let you go."

"All right, but don't be a stranger."

Spence waited for her as she got out her keys, but she waved him on. Kate leaned against her car and watched him drive away. She hated hurting any of her friends, but Spence had a point. He could be so sensitive sometimes. As she drove home, her thoughts turned toward other matters. What in the world would she do tomorrow since the case was dead? And had she remembered to put food out for the cats?

Chapter Twenty-six

"Did you see the beautiful flowers on my desk?" Joyce had waited all through lunch for Cynthia to ask about them, but now that they were returning to the office, she figured she would have to direct the conversation that way herself.

Cynthia only murmured an affirmative. The clicking of Joyce's heels echoed in the parking garage in contrast to the *thwump* of Cynthia's sensible shoes.

"You probably thought they were from my husband, but they weren't," Joyce bubbled on. "Guess who gave them to me!"

Cynthia seemed unintrigued but asked, nonetheless.

"Mr. Innerst—Grant," Joyce corrected herself. "He brought them back for me on his lunch break yesterday. He said he felt awful about hurting my feelings the other day—but it wasn't anything, just a misunderstanding. Wasn't that so sweet of him?"

Cynthia sniffed.

"I told him he didn't need to do that but I appreciated it so much. To tell the truth, I've been a little worried that he might want someone younger for his assistant. You know, someone who—"

Joyce broke off as they neared the entrance to Roving House. A young Hispanic man stood on the curb, swaying slightly as the wind pushed against him. He just stood there staring at the front door, his hands thrust into the pockets of his leather jacket.

"I wonder if he needs help?" she asked Cynthia.

"I wouldn't know, but I—" Cynthia started to say, but Joyce was already approaching him.

"Excuse me, sir." The man jerked. "Do you need something? We work inside, if you're needing to meet with someone or…"

He shook his head. "No, I'm fine," he said and strode away.

"Well, that was a little odd," Joyce said.

"You ought to be more careful," Cynthia reproached in her fluty voice. "He could have been dangerous. A mugger."

Joyce pursed her lips but held her tongue. She didn't like it when Cynthia lectured her, but she also didn't like to argue, even when she felt she was right. If he had wanted to mug them, he would have attacked them whether she had talked to him or not. Joyce also figured that most muggers didn't wear fancy leather shoes.

JULIO ROUNDED the corner from Roving House, embarrassed at how unaware he'd been of his surroundings, how conspicuous he'd been. He was getting soft, getting sloppy. He hadn't cared much before, but this was different. He needed to slide back into the old skin, get his rhythm back.

At an empty bus stop he quit walking. He'd gone the wrong direction from where he'd parked. He had meant to go inside the building, but for some reason, his mind had begun to replay the fight he'd had with Willy that morning.

Julio was losing him. He was almost sure of it but didn't know why. It had been going downhill ever so slowly for a while, but since those cops had been by yesterday, everything was pulling apart faster. It was like Willy had gone off the hook. He was irritable, restless. He hadn't even gone to work last night, told them he was sick.

Unable to take the tension anymore, Julio had escaped the house for a few hours only to come back and find Will worse. Accusations filled his eyes and lurked beneath his words. Julio punched the plastic side of the bus stop. He hadn't cheated on Willy once since they hooked up, and he'd had chances. He got the look—and more—all the time from guys who came into the men's store where he worked. Still he hadn't done it. The New Year's party didn't count. He'd been so smashed he didn't know what he was doing. It'd been the same for Willy. The pressure was so real, Julio could feel it pinning him down. Then he thought about what Willy had said to him after the cops left, and he knew what Willy was asking him to do, what he should have done a long time ago. If Willy wanted him to prove his love, he'd do it.

Julio checked his watch. Almost twelve-thirty. He had to be at work at one. He walked back toward Roving House, dialing the company's number on his cell phone. Using what he called his "store voice," he asked for Nathanael Carver, and the receptionist transferred him. Another woman, the *gorda* from the sidewalk, answered. He'd heard her voice, really high, as he walked away. He asked for Carver again.

"He's unavailable. May I take a message?"

Julio gambled. "Can you tell me when he'll be back? I need to speak with him personally."

"I can't say for certain, but he should be back shortly. Would you like me to have him call you?"

"No, I'll get him later." Julio hung up. He had parked in a thirty-minute spot on the street where he could see the front of the building and the parking garage next door. For the next twenty-five minutes, he sat in the Firebird and watched every car that went in to the garage and then who came out. While he waited, he phoned an old friend.

"Hey, *ese*, I need my knuckles back…Just to borrow, you'll get them back. Shut your hole and bring them to me at work today. At the store. You're not doing jack. Three o'clock." He hung up without waiting for further objection. He leaned over and pulled a leather sheath from under the passenger's seat. A souvenir from a past life but something worth hanging on to.

Finally, the person walking out of the garage was Nathanael Carver. Julio had no problem recognizing him. Julio drove through the parking garage until he found the last car that had gone in, a silver Saab on the third level.

He was late to work, but it was worth it. He'd already decided his plan couldn't wait another day.

Chapter Twenty-seven

Seated at a folding table in a convention hall, Kate did her best to block out the ambient noise. Nash and two junior commando types stood conversing at the other end of the table in front of the police department's display. With her case canceled, she'd been sent along to a countywide job fair. Potter had the luck of being behind in his paperwork and had thus escaped a similar sentence. She'd hinted strongly before leaving that he should do more poking around if possible, regardless of what Carver and the sergeant had said. Meanwhile, stuck amid a crowd of adolescents, unemployed college grads, and dissatisfied blue-collar workers, Kate reviewed her own case notes. After all, she had to occupy her time some way.

They'd investigated nearly everyone on the list Carver had given them, all except one—Irwin Kennedy, a university president deposed for embezzling a small fortune from his school. Kate had with her the exposé from *Truth Will Out*. Like most of the others she had read in the passing days, it stirred a loathing of its subject. Easy to see how such publicity could sink a person's career or public life. Of course, some, such as Eloise Stein, seemed to rise above. Their most likely candidate would be someone less resilient.

Then there were the people Carver hadn't listed—his protégé, Grant Innerst; Mya Duritz, the *International* editor; and his wife, who was definitely hiding something. Kate grunted. Some people looked more suspicious than others, but she still had no clear leads.

Amelie Carver had persuaded her husband to go to the police. Why would she have done that if she were involved? To throw suspicion elsewhere? Kate wouldn't be surprised if somehow, some way, Amelie was at the center of all this, but for the present, she turned her attention back to Irwin Kennedy, the last name on the list. What if they had stopped one name too soon? She wished she'd had more time to investigate Roving House without having to pussyfoot around for Carver's comfort.

Kate became aware of someone standing in front of the table. As she looked up, that someone said, "I'd like to be a police officer. Am I tall enough?"

Kate laughed. "Heidi, what are you doing here?"

"Field trip. All the eighth graders do job shadowing, so we bring them here to get ideas, contacts, all that. You?"

Kate shook her head. "Long story."

As soon as the surprise of seeing Heidi wore off, guilt settled in. Upon seeing her friend, Kate had immediately scanned the table for the pack of cigarettes she'd picked up that morning. She casually messed about with her coat, which hung on the back of her chair, until she assured herself that's where they were. She hadn't even smoked one yet. She could still throw them out. What a waste of money though. She forced her mind back to the conversation at hand.

The two women were in the middle of making Sunday lunch plans when Nash sidled up.

"So who is this?" he asked, eying Kate's friend up and down.

Kate made a face to Heidi. "This is my friend Heidi. Heidi, this is Nash."

Nash winked and grinned at Heidi. "Well, you're just about bite size, aren't you?"

Heidi absorbed the comment with a stone face. "Wow," she monotoned. "You're kind of sleazy."

"I see why you two are friends," Nash said and took a walk.

"If any teenage girls come over here, do not let them talk to him," Heidi commanded.

"Roger," said Kate. "For the record though, that's pretty demure behavior for him."

"That's hardly comforting. We've got a new a math teacher whose girlfriend lives in South Bend. I said something about that being difficult, not living in the same city. He agreed and then asked if I'd like to keep him company some weekend that she couldn't visit. I told him he was a pig."

A call from Potter rang in on Kate's cell phone, interrupting Heidi's latest account of male depravity. Kate excused herself to answer it.

"What's up?"

"I'm almost finished with my backlog of paperwork."

"But what did you call to tell me?" she pressed.

"How surprised would you be if I told you Will McGlynn's boyfriend has a record?"

"Not terribly. He serve time?"

"For robbery and two charges of assault," Potter answered. "Sounds as if he's prone to violence. Doesn't really seem like McGlynn's type. Will's record is clean."

"Misery can tie a strong knot."

"Meaning?"

"He said Ambris pulled him through. Maybe they hooked up when McGlynn was at his lowest. I don't think McGlynn's happy right now, but he could feel indebted to him."

"Wait a second," Potter said. Kate could hear the clatter of his keyboard. "Ambris was released about a month after McGlynn's story broke. He must have written him from the inside. Maybe they decided to turn over new leaves together."

"Or maybe McGlynn found himself a boyfriend who would carry out his revenge for him."

BY THE time Kate escaped the job fair, Potter had unearthed their most interesting find thus far. Kate knew that if something existed on the Internet, Potter could find it, and while he usually downplayed any of his skills, he did evidence at least a minimum of pride as he prepared to display his latest findings.

"I had to jump through some hoops to get access to this site, and if I get called up on filter violation for this one, you're my witness that it's work related."

Kate leaned against his desk where she could see his monitor. "*What* exactly did you find?"

He raised his eyebrows. "You ready?" He restored the browser window to full size, revealing a nude female figure.

"Potter!"

He picked an envelope up off his desk and held it over most of the woman's body. "Look at the face."

Upon examination, Kate realized it was a young Amelie Carver looking back at her. "You've got to be kidding me. Are you sure that's her?"

"Well, the title of the photograph is *Amelie 3b*. There are two or three others on this site that are definitely her, and a few that it's impossible to tell without more…intimate knowledge. They're all by the same photographer, Alain Guerre."

"Where did you find these?"

"France. You remember I told you she spent time in Europe after she finished school? The dates given for the photographs match the time she was there. Apparently she met up with Guerre. These photos are on loan from his private collection for a retrospective at some gallery. They're listed under the *Amelie series*."

"Do you know if the relationship was more than professional?"

Potter cleared his throat. "I'm going to say yes, on the basis of one of the photographs that was listed under *self portraits*. It's actually of both of them. I can show it to you if you like, but it's along the same lines—"

"That's okay. Really. Do you have a photo of him with his clothes on?"

Potter clicked to the site's home page. It was in French, which was incomprehensible to Kate, but she easily spotted the name Potter had mentioned, Alain Guerre. A large color photo showed a slender, bearded man with salt-and-pepper hair and piercing eyes. He looked vaguely familiar, not as in someone she knew but as in he looked like someone she knew. Kate couldn't place it exactly. His coloring was similar to Nathanael Carver's, but his features were more delicate and his frame slighter.

"Is there anything to tie him to Olivet, by chance?" she asked.

"Not that I've found. In fact, I didn't find any record that he's ever been to the United States. He shoots mostly in France, and he seems to have traveled widely in Africa and the Far East, but not the Americas."

"Do you think it could be blackmail?"

"Could be," Potter said. "If I could find them, somebody else could too. Although I will tell you that Amelie is not an uncommon name in the French-speaking world, so they'd either have to know what they're looking for or have just gotten lucky."

"Or have mad computer skills like you?" Kate offered.

Potter shrugged. "Maybe."

"I'll be sure to recommend you for a commendation. It's not every detective who can dig up porn on the Internet."

"I believe this falls under the category of art."

"Sometimes it's the same thing."

The partners looked back at the monitor and lapsed into silence, mulling over the possible import of Potter's discovery.

Chapter Twenty-eight

"When you were working on the magazine, you never came home for lunch," Amelie said as she arranged dishes on the table. "It's nice. I did appreciate the heads-up this time." She joined him in the kitchen doorway for a hello peck on the cheek.

"Not a problem," Nathanael said. She looked happy. He thought she'd been more at ease since they'd gone to the police. He also knew how quickly that easy grace would evaporate if he told her that he'd called the investigation off.

"Has the mail come yet?" he asked.

"Probably. I was getting lunch together so I didn't check. Why don't you run and see while I toss the salad?"

As Nathanael walked out into the sunlight, the wind beat his hair in all directions. It carried the scent of freshly cut grass. He frowned at the clippings tumbling in the yard. Great clouds spotted the sky, casting large shadows. He entered the chill of one on his way to the mailbox and shivered. The forecaster that morning had said to enjoy the sun because rain was definitely on its way, but then they'd been promising that for days. Despite the mess, it was good the lawn service had come when they did.

The mailbox was full, and despite the wind, Nathanael couldn't keep himself from rifling through the stack of envelopes and advertisements. He stopped when he got to a plain white envelope with his name and address printed in plain type. There was no return address and an Olivet postmark.

He had to push hard against the door to close it. He had hung his suit jacket on the coat tree, and now he slipped the familiar envelope into its interior pocket.

"Anything interesting?" Amelie asked when he returned to the kitchen.

"Not really," he replied. "I left it all on the hall table."

"I'll go through it after lunch. I've been thinking about that trip you mentioned. I think we should do it." They sat down opposite each other. "I found a terrific package for an Alaskan cruise. It leaves this weekend."

"That's a little soon."

"I think it would be good for us," she insisted. "To get away. Right now. To just get out of all this."

"I have things I have to take care of first, but we will, I promise. Soon."

Amelie stared at the tablecloth. "What is there that can't wait?" she demanded.

"The book for one. We're really close to wrapping it up. If I took time off now, Eirik would go into convulsions, plus it would be irresponsible of me. I don't have anyone to hand my work off to. Grant doesn't work for me anymore."

Amelie did not reply. Nathanael pushed at his salad with a fork.

"Could you get some price quotes on a security system?" he asked, breaking the silence.

Amelie's fork clattered against her plate and danced out onto the table. "I thought you already did that."

"I made a list of companies. It's on my desk. I just—I haven't had time to call them. You know how hectic things have been—"

Amelie swore and threw her napkin onto her plate. "It's nice to know how important our safety is to you. You're not the only one who lives in this house."

She tried to leave the room, but Nathanael caught her by the wrist and pulled her to him.

"Hey." He wrapped his other arm around her. "Nothing's going to happen to you."

"You can't promise—"

"Yes, I can. No one is going to hurt you, I promise. I'm

sorry. I should have taken care of the security system immediately. I'll take the info back to the office and set up an appointment.

"My timing is definitely off," he said, trying unsuccessfully to lighten the mood. "I'll get it right, though. Trust me."

They stayed there, her leaning against him in begrudging reconciliation, until the phone rang.

"I should get that." She pulled away, though her voice had softened some.

Nathanael took a deep breath. He would get through this, and then everything would be okay.

NATHANAEL WAITED until he was back in his office with the door closed before he took out the envelope. He debated whether he should take it to the police before opening it, but he knew they wouldn't find anything. They hadn't found anything on the previous ones. He slipped a letter opener beneath the flap, but before he ripped it through, a fist banged at the door.

"Come in," Nathanael called, and in strode Eirik Boudreau.

"I was just in the neighborhood and thought I'd drop by and see how my book is coming," Boudreau said, foregoing any type of civil greeting. Behind him, Cynthia glowered. As Boudreau took a seat unbidden, Nathanael waved at her, at once dismissing her and absolving her of the intrusion.

"I think we're in the home stretch. I have one of our most talented designers working on the cover, and we'll use that to finish up the interior template. All we have to do is finish…polishing the text, and we can start setting up proofs."

"Speaking of, I don't like the cuts to the last chapter. I want you to leave it as I wrote it." That was Boudreau's way. No allowance for discussion, no interest in outside insight except where it mattered the least.

Nathanael suppressed a sigh and said okay, even though the chapter needed trimming and the extra pages would make the projected page count run just over another half signature of paper, which would result in a load of blank pages at the back of the book and increased productions costs. He took a deep breath and told himself that it didn't matter because the book would bring in a handsome profit, regardless. Perhaps they could pad the front matter with a half title page or something to eat up some of the empty pages. Apparently, however, he elongated the word *okay* just enough for Boudreau to perceive attitude.

"Is that a problem?" he asked, his high voice sharp with sarcasm.

"Of course not," Nathanael said with all the false nonchalance he could muster, but he couldn't resist getting a bit of his own back. "But speaking of problems, I understand you had some trouble outside the launch reception last night."

Boudreau narrowed his eyes at Nathanael. "Not a big deal. Trust me."

"I mention it merely because we've already begun promoting the new book. We don't want any bad PR. I hesitate to remind you about the morality clause in—"

"Don't worry about it," Boudreau said as he stood. "I'm not about to get #MeToo'd." He leaned across the desk. His breath smelled of mint. "You just get an advance copy to Oprah, and I'll take care of the rest."

As soon as the author left, Nathanael ripped through the envelope flap with undue force. He pulled the paper out and unfolded it. It held four words.

I'm coming for you.

"I bet," he said.

Chapter Twenty-nine

Julio convinced a coworker to cover for him so that he could sneak out from work early. He then drove back to the parking garage, where the silver Saab still sat on the third level. It wasn't close to any of the pillars. That would've been better. Quite a few people were leaving, though, so Julio was able to pretty much take his pick of spaces. He pulled in kitty-corner to the driver's side of the Saab.

On the seat next to Julio sat a small, brown paper bag. From it, he withdrew a set of brass knuckles. He slipped the fingers of his right hand through the rings and contemplated the feel. It definitely had been a while. He looked over at the passenger seat and after a short deliberation fished out the knife from underneath it. He unfastened the clasp and slid the sheath through his belt at his right hip, where the knife would be concealed by his jacket yet easy to draw. Who knew? The old man might be tougher than he expected.

Then he waited.

"ARE WE still on for dinner?" Grant asked as Nate walked by. Grant had been waiting for him in the small downstairs lobby. "I was about ready to come up and get you."

"I completely forgot." Nate stood there, briefcase in one hand and a couple of books in the other. "Is it all right if we reschedule? I don't think tonight would be such a good idea."

"Sure." Grant sank back down onto the sofa arm he'd been sitting on.

"I'm sorry to cancel last minute. Things have been crazy lately—here and at home. In fact, I think I even forgot to mention to Amelie that I'd invited you. She'd be furious at me if she knew."

"Don't worry about it. I understand."

After Nate left, Grant rolled his eyes, slid off the arm, and sprawled on the sofa. He texted his friend Kipp, asking if he wanted to meet at Marcadé's in a half hour. Then he dialed another number.

"It's me. How are you doing?" He listened to the reply and then answered, "No, tonight's off. I thought I'd let you know...Don't ask me. He just canceled, said things had been crazy...Tomorrow night then." He heard the elevator open. "Gotta go. I'll see you then."

Nate's administrative assistant hurried out of the elevator.

"Did Mr. Carver come this way?"

"Yeah." Grant eyed the file folder in Cynthia's puffy hand. "Did he forget something?"

"Yes, he said he wanted to take these proposals home, but I found them on his desk. I was trying to catch him."

Grant took the folder, but Cynthia didn't release it until Grant finished saying that he could run it out to Nate if he hurried.

"Thank you," she said as stonily as possible and turned back to the elevator.

Grant shook his head as he jogged out the door, holding his leather messenger bag tight so that it didn't bang against him. He couldn't fathom why Cynthia disliked him, but it did, on occasion, amuse him.

He dialed Nate as he hurried out of the dark and into the sickly yellow light of the parking garage. He scanned the first floor but saw no one. On the second floor, he could hear the echoing ring of Nate's phone above him. Why didn't Nate answer? The ringing stopped and the voicemail picked up.

Grant vaulted up the last set of stairs to the third level. He could see Nate at the far end of the garage nearing his car. Only a few cars remained on this level. A man in a black jacket was getting out of a muscle car parked near Nate's.

Grant must have eased his grip on the folder because its

papers spilled out onto the cement. He swore, knelt down, and scooped up the proposals. He glanced toward Nate and, below the fringe of dark hair that fell in his eyes, saw Nate reach for the door handle as the other man approached him. Grant looked back down to ensure he wasn't mutilating the papers as he stuffed them into the folder. He thought perhaps he should call out to Nate to stop him, but Nate would have to drive past him to exit. Grant would catch him then if need be.

The stranger said something to Nate, but Grant couldn't make out what. He looked up to see the narrow arc of the man's glinting fist, Nate raising his arms in defense, and then Nate's briefcase cracking open as the man's fist smashed into it.

For a second time that evening, paper littered the cement. This time soon spotted with blood.

Chapter Thirty

When Kate reached the top level of the parking garage, a few police cars were already there, lights flashing, as well as an ambulance. The doors were opened, and Carver sat on the back end pressing a cold pack to his left eye. Potter and Grant Innerst stood nearby, but Potter split from the group to meet Kate.

"What happened?" she asked. He hadn't told her much on the phone.

"Julio Ambris—" Potter motioned toward a patrol car. "—was waiting up here for Carver to get off work. He jumped him. He said something to Carver right before he swung, but Carver can't remember what exactly." Potter walked Kate over to a broken briefcase and a mass of scattered papers, some of which were spattered with blood. "But he definitely knew who he was going for. Carver said Ambris called him by name. Grant Innerst was down there," Potter pointed toward the stairs. "He had just come out of the stairwell. He was trying to catch Carver before he left."

"So he saw the whole thing?"

"For the most part. He's the one who pulled Ambris off Carver, but he had some distance to cover, as you can see, so Ambris got in some pretty good punches before Innerst got to him. I think he knew Innerst was coming, but he didn't let up on Carver."

"So he was enraged enough that he was more concerned with beating the snot out of Carver than a witness who could ID him?"

"That and he probably figured he could take them both. He took Carver by surprise, so he had that situation pretty well under control. But Innerst's first move was to sling his messenger bag, which has a laptop and some books in it, into Ambris's head, so he got a pretty good lick in before he was ever in range for Ambris to hit him. The attendant on the ground level is pretty skittish. As soon as he heard shouting, he called 911."

"How much damage did our friend do?"

"Well, he was wearing brass knuckles, so Carver's pretty banged up. They want to get him to the hospital for x-rays, think maybe he cracked some ribs, but he wants to give you something first."

Kate shot Potter a questioning look, and he shrugged in reply.

As Kate neared the ambulance, Carver lowered the cold pack. His eye was already darkening, and blood already soaked the bandages on his cheek and forehead.

"I should apologize—" Carver started.

"Mr. Carver, don't. What's important is that you're okay."

An EMT came around the corner of the ambulance. "We really need to get him to the hospital. He needs stitches and might have some fractures."

"Just one minute," Kate said. "You wanted to give me something, Mr. Carver?"

"I should have listened to you." Carver winced as he brought an envelope out from his breast pocket and handed it to Kate.

She noticed the Olivet postmark. "Another threat?"

Carver nodded. "It came today. I should've called you immediately, but I thought it could wait till tomorrow."

"Get yourself taken care of," Kate said. "We'll come by the hospital."

As soon as the ambulance doors shut, Kate turned to Potter, who shrugged as she exclaimed, "Criminy! Wait till tomorrow? He's lucky he's not dead."

Kate heard a snicker and turned to see Grant, a little on the rumpled, dusty side of things from his tussle with Ambris. His lower lip was split, but the blood had already clotted.

"Criminy?" he asked. "I had no idea people actually said that, like after 1950."

"I'm glad you're amused. Your friend was very lucky you were here." She noticed a slash in the front of Grant's leather blazer. "What happened there? Did he have a knife?"

Grant pulled the jacket out to examine it. "Yeah, the lunatic pulled it out when I was tackling him."

"You're very brave."

"Well, I didn't know he had a knife," he said wryly. "I also didn't know you were a police officer. You neglected to mention that when we met last night."

"Yes, I did." Kate smiled back, ignoring the pointed look she was receiving from Potter. She held up the envelope Carver had given her. "Did you know that Nathanael Carver was receiving threats?"

"No," he answered and then shook his head as if his answer warranted clarification. "You think this guy was the one sending them?"

"We can't say for sure," Kate answered. "But at the moment, he looks promising."

Grant watched the squad car containing Ambris pull away. "Make sure he stays locked up, okay?"

"We'll do our best. Has anyone called Mrs. Carver?"

Potter spoke up. "He didn't want us to. He's afraid she'll overreact."

Kate just looked at Potter in response.

"His words, not mine," he said flatly. "Hospital or station?"

"Hospital. You know more about Ambris than I do. I'll catch up with you later."

WHEN KATE walked into the station, Potter was refreshing his cup of coffee. It was nearly ten o'clock, and he looked tired.

"Long day?" Kate asked.

"Considering that it's not over with, yes. How's Carver doing?"

"Not too bad, given the circumstance. He's mostly just bruised up. No broken bones, which is no small miracle. The doctor thought he might have a concussion. The cuts on his face had to be stitched up. They said the one on his cheek bone was actually from his briefcase?"

"Yeah," Potter said. "He told me that he threw his arm up to fend off Ambris. When Ambris connected, the case popped open and caught him in the face. One of the metallic corners was loose so the edge sliced him. I'm guessing you got an official statement."

"From both him and Grant Innerst." Kate nodded toward the interview room. "How's it going here?"

"As we suspected, he's a pretty grade-A punk. He's not saying much. I told him we were charging him with attempted murder, and he said he never intended to kill Carver. Then he said it was actually Carver who attacked him and that he was defending himself."

Kate gave a tired laugh. "People are so stupid. We have physical evidence and an eyewitness, highly credible, and the thug thinks he can lie his way out. It floors me."

"Yeah. After he spun that one, he clammed up. I asked him about the letters, and he wouldn't say anything—admit or deny them."

"Did you ask about the boyfriend's involvement? That might push some buttons."

Potter took a gulp of coffee. "I would have, but he'd already shut down. He's been exercising his right to remain silent for about an hour now. He hasn't asked for a lawyer, so he's still open for questioning. He used his phone call to call McGlynn."

"And?" Kate prompted.

Potter cracked a slim smile. "He'd already left for work. Apparently he turns his cell off when he's at the radio station."

Kate chuckled. "So he won't even get the message till tomorrow morning. I'm tempted to call it a night, but let's see if he'll say anything about McGlynn."

"Maybe you'll have better luck than I did."

In the interview room, Potter hung back as Kate took the chair opposite Julio, who glared at both of them but said nothing.

"Hey, Julio, how's it going?"

Kate couldn't tell whether his response was sarcastic or just insulting since it was in Spanish.

"Do we need a translator?" Kate asked. "My Spanish is a bit rusty. I haven't had any since high school."

Potter spoke up. "Oh no, we went through that little trick. Officer Sanchez even came in to talk with him, but his English is quite good. For all his *Mexicano* bluster, he's American born and bred."

"Good enough to write those threats to Carver I bet."

A muscle twitched in Julio's jaw, but he remained silent.

"You know, those threats show premeditation. No claiming it was a 'crime of passion.'" Kate used finger quotes just to be annoying. "But I don't think you wrote those letters." She let the words sink in as Julio scowled at her. "I think your boyfriend did."

"Will didn't have anything to do with this!"

"Oh, really," Kate laughed. "What connection do you have with Nathanael Carver other than Will?"

Julio clamped his mouth shut and looked away.

"That's what I thought." Kate stood up. "Right now we have you dead to rights. You tell us how much Will was involved—"

"He wasn't involved at all!" Julio shouted.

"Then I guess you'll be taking the rap alone. Maybe we can even get you placed in your old cell block. I'm sure your old neighbors would be glad to see you again." Kate walked to the door. "Think about it."

Outside, Potter asked, "You want to bring McGlynn in?"

"I have a feeling he'll show up soon enough."

LATE AS it was, the day still held surprises for Kate. When she neared her house, she saw a car parked on the road out front. Its lights were off, and she was suspicious until she recognized it as the Purple Mosquito, Danny's Geo Metro. The stars were all hidden, and the moon itself only peeked out from behind the gray blanket of clouds; but enough illumination shone from the light pole outside her storage shed that she could see Danny's lanky form tucked into the shadows on her porch, sitting on the glider.

"What are you doing on my porch?" she called out in mock confrontation as she came up the sidewalk.

Danny didn't reply immediately, and when he did, he lacked his trademark snap and cheer. He pushed himself up from the glider and came forward to lean on the railing, where the cool white of the light spilled across his face. "I don't know," he said with a crooked smile. "It seems like a pretty happenin' place to me."

Kate stopped on the steps and looked up into his face. "What's up, buddy?" she asked, dispensing with her playful tone.

"I just didn't want to go home. I'm more alone there."

"More alone there than on my porch alone?" she asked, mounting the last few steps.

"Yeah. Because I know you'll show up eventually."

Kate grimaced. With her job, that wasn't always guaranteed; however, now wasn't the time to mention that. Danny leaned against a pillar and, pulling his knees up and encircling them with his arms, perched on the railing. Kate took a seat facing him, careful not to disrupt his balance.

"It just seems so amplified at home," he said. "Nobody's stuff but mine. No noise but mine. No one to talk to, be with. Just me and the TV."

Kate nodded. Danny's face was shadowed now, but the ambient light provided enough distinction for her to discern some features once her eyes had adjusted, a dark moving gash for a mouth and deep wells for eyes wherein a speck of light from who-knows-where reflected.

"I've been thinking about Stevie lately."

"That's natural if you're lonely." Stevie had been Danny's girlfriend off and on for about a year and a half until the relationship ended in what Danny referred to as the Post–Valentine's Day Debacle. "Have you seen her lately?"

Danny shook his head. "I hear she's dating somebody now."

Kate wasn't sure what to say, so she said nothing.

After a while, Danny continued. "You know, when we got back together some friends from the singles' group at church told me they thought she was the only one who would be able to put up with me." He chuckled without motivation.

"That's awful," Kate said.

"They were just being funny."

"No, they were just being stupid. It's an awful thing to say."

They let the silence seep around them again.

"What if it's true?" Danny finally asked.

"Daniel Taylor Bohannon, it is not true. You can't think like that. I know it's hard. I'm in the same boat, rowing right next to you practically. I want someone, a family. When I go home to Indiana and see Robbie and Lauren with their girls, I can very easily get jealous. We just have to trust that God's timing is perfect."

"Even when it doesn't feel that way."

"Yeah, even when it doesn't feel that way."

"That's most of the time, you know?" Even in the shadows she could see the cocked eyebrow.

She laughed. "Yeah, I know. That's what faith is for."

"What if it never happens? You know, some people, it never happens."

"I don't think it will be never for you, Danny. You've got a lot to give. But His timing is perfect, even when it's never."

Kate wasn't sure how much comfort there was in that, but she wouldn't be Pollyanna in Christian clothing. She respected Danny too much for that. He didn't say anything for a while, and Kate presumed he was thinking about what she had said. She let him.

"The answers are easy; accepting them is not," he finally said. "My dad used to say that whenever I was struggling with something like this."

"There's a lot of truth in that. Sounds like he was a wise man."

"Yeah. I miss him."

After another moment of silence, Danny groaned and eased off the railing. "My bum hurts." He walked, a little stiffly, to the end of the porch, which wasn't all that far since Kate's house was rather small.

When a few minutes passed with only the sound of a distant dog barking, Kate joined him. She put a hand on his shoulder and just stood there, not saying anything.

Finally, he said, "I don't know if I can forgive her."

After a brief hesitation Kate said, "I thought you were the one who broke things off."

"I was."

"Forgive her for what?"

"For not being the right one," he answered in a thick voice.

Kate had no words for that, so she gave Danny a big hug and he hugged her back tightly, clinging to the knowledge that someone cared.

When he pulled back from the hug, Danny didn't let go. That left eyebrow was cocked again. "So," he said slowly, "when did we start smoking again?"

Kate gently tried to disentangle herself, but Danny held her firmly.

"Busted, huh?"

"Oh, yeah. I could feel the pack in your coat pocket, and your hair smells like smoke."

"I kind of fell off the wagon last night…again. And I haven't made a concentrated effort to get back on. But I only had one today to unwind on the drive home. It was that kind of day."

The eyebrow remained arched. Now the other one went up.

"I don't have to tell you—again—what those things do to your lungs, but as your resident health-care professional, I refuse to let you slowly kill yourself. If anyone was meant for a quick, fantastic demise, dearie, it was you. Give me your cancer sticks. Hand them over."

She deposited the nearly full pack in his open palm and, in truth, found it a relief.

"I don't know why this is so hard for me," she said. "But when I get down or frustrated or have a bad day, the temptation is so strong. It's a little way to make me feel good again."

"Does it?"

"For a little while, but not usually as much as I want."

"It sounds like a coping mechanism." Danny held up the pack. "You turn to these for comfort, instead of turning to God." Kate wanted to defend herself, but what he said smacked of truth. It stung a little. "When I turn to you," he said, "you turn me to God because you're a good friend. I don't think these are gonna do that for you."

"You're not so dumb, you know that."

"Yeah," Danny said. His smile glinted in the dark. "Hey, if you want, I'll keep you accountable on this," he offered.

"Thanks," she said. "I'd appreciate that."

"You'd do the same for me. Actually, you *do* the same for me. What's that called?"

"Reciprocity?"

"I think I was thinking more of 'iron sharpening iron.'"

"You tell Heidi about this and I'll kill you," Kate threatened.

"Ditto," he said, referencing their earlier conversation.

They talked a little longer and promised they would meet in the morning for their run. When Danny left, she could tell he was more at peace. Perhaps her problem had distracted him from focusing on his own, or maybe her encouragement had been enough, for the moment.

When Kate walked into the house, she felt its emptiness as if the sharpness of Danny's loneliness had pricked her own, causing it to bleed afresh. The positive feelings she had experienced on the porch dissipated. Despite what her mind preached, her spirit would not accept the argument that she should be grateful for what she had. She had a good partner in Potter and a dependable tribe in Danny, Heidi, and Spence; and unlike Danny, she had family, albeit not nearby. But she was thirty with no family of her own. The years were running by all too rapidly. She'd recently read an article online detailing the optimal birthing years, and now she tried to remember when they ended, then decided she'd rather not remember.

She tossed her coat onto the couch. The air seemed colder in here than outside, but she didn't bother with the heat. She was on the verge of crying, which was very stupid, she thought. She took some deep breaths and willed her eyes dry. She looked around and called for Louis and St. Joan, but of course neither of them came. She curled up in a recliner to think…and pray. Pray for Danny, for herself, for the future.

It wasn't long, even in the midst of talking to the Almighty, before she found herself wishing she hadn't let Danny take the cigarettes. At that moment, she felt the vibration of little cat feet pouncing onto the chair arm, and there was Joan, looking at her with big amber eyes.

Kate smiled and scooped up the elusive feline. "Where you been, girl?" Kate rubbed the crest of white on Joan's neck, the only contrast in her short black coat. St. Joan craned her neck and purred, offering what reassurance she could.

Chapter Thirty-one

It hadn't been difficult to convince Danny to cut their morning run a bit short. It never was. The long-promised rain sprinkled in to cement the decision, but Kate's motivation stemmed from her desire to get to the station before Will McGlynn did. By the time she arrived, the light rain had dissipated, though the sky remained overcast and heavy.

She checked in with Potter, who told her between yawns that McGlynn was en route. When he arrived, they showed him to an empty interview room.

"What did Julio do?" he asked before his behind even hit the chair.

"Is he in the habit of causing trouble?" Kate asked the smoky-voiced announcer.

"No, he's—he's not been in trouble since he got out of jail. That's why I was floored when I got the message you'd arrested him. I know he doesn't ever want to go back. Did he steal something from the store?"

Kate and Potter exchanged looks.

"Just tell me. What is it?"

"He assaulted someone," Kate said. "He may even be charged with attempted murder."

McGlynn leaned back in his seat, stunned. "Who?"

"Who do you think?" Kate retorted.

"I have no idea. Honestly."

Kate didn't answer. She let her face do the talking as her gaze stayed fixed on McGlynn. After a moment, Potter answered, "He attacked Nathanael Carver in the parking garage next to Roving House Publishers."

McGlynn's mouth fell open. He leaned forward, resting his head in his hand.

"The real question," said Kate, "is how big was your role in all this?"

McGlynn's mouth gaped further. "I didn't have anything to do with this!" His voice lost some of its appeal when he got agitated.

"So Julio had something personal against Mr. Carver?" Potter asked.

"No. Well—" McGlynn faltered. "Julio's talked—in the past, he's talked about how wrong the magazine was, what they did to me, but he never talked about doing something like this."

Kate could read immediately in McGlynn's eyes that as soon as he had said it, his memory reproved him.

"What did he talk about doing?" she pressed.

He looked down. "Nothing, he just talked!"

"You just lied to me, Will. I can't prove it, at least not yet, but I know it as sure as I'm sitting here. So why should I believe anything else you have to say?"

He paused and when he did speak, his words were emphatic. "I never thought he'd do it."

"What about the author of the article? Have you sent him threats too?"

"No! I told you I didn't have anything to do with those."

"You live in Olivet, and that's where the letters were postmarked," Kate pointed out. "Does Julio live with you?"

"Kind of. He stays at my place most of the time, but he shares an apartment with his sister."

Kate slid a photocopy of Julio's license across the table. "Is this the address?"

"Yes." McGlynn sighed. Kate didn't have to point out that Julio's other address was also in Olivet.

"Will," she said, "we're not talking about some bar fight here. We're talking about a premeditated attempt at murder. Your boyfriend had a knife on him, and when somebody tried to stop him, he attacked that person with it. I'm guessing it was his backup plan for Carver. If he couldn't beat him to death, he'd carve him up. The person who wrote the letters threatened to do just that. It'd be best for him and you, if you just tell us everything. You think Julio won't eventually finger you for putting him up to this? I don't think he's the type to go down alone."

Something changed in McGlynn's face. The franticness in the eyes hardened into something else. "Well, he'll have to, because I don't know anything about it. Can I talk to him?"

"Sure." Kate pushed herself back from the table and let McGlynn leave the room before her.

"Have you—" she started to ask Potter.

"I've got the one for Julio's place. Give me a minute to get one for McGlynn's," he said and walked to his desk to call for another search warrant. Kate smiled at the delicious efficiency in her partnership with Potter.

It did not take long for McGlynn and Julio's conversation to turn from fierce whispering to full-out shouting. Standing in the observation room, Kate shook her head.

"I did it for you!"

"I never asked you to! You're going to ruin me all over again!"

After another moment or two of intense whispering, McGlynn barreled through the door.

"I'm calling him a lawyer, and then he's all yours," he said, barreling toward the door. Kate stopped him.

"If you wouldn't mind waiting," she said, feigning politeness, "we've got a warrant on the way. We need to search your house."

McGlynn swayed in agitation. "Don't worry about a warrant. I'll let you in myself. I don't have anything to hide."

Kate was inclined to believe him. Unless he and Julio were better actors than she gave them credit for, their conversation indicated Julio had acted alone. Though she was inclined to believe McGlynn, she wasn't ready to just yet.

"Great," she said. "Let's go."

Chapter Thirty-two

Mason stared at his supervisor. "It'd just be less distracting if I did it at home."

Ricky got a constipated look on his face. "You're not distracted working on your other projects here. What's the diff, big guy?"

Mason sighed. "I told you. I left the flash drive with my files and sketches at home. On accident. It'd be a waste of time to drive out and back when I can just work on them at home."

"But that's not how we roll here, Mason."

"Don't be such—" Mason stopped short, realizing he would damage his case. "Look. I was working on the mockups at home on my own time. Doesn't that show, like, dedication or something?" Ricky nodded slowly, but Mason couldn't tell if he believed him. "I can email you the files from home of what I've got to prove it."

"Okay," Ricky conceded. "You do that *as soon* as you get home, and you can telecommute the rest of the day, but let's not make a habit of this, capiche?"

"Right," Mason muttered and split from Ricky's office.

"Where ya going?" Kassie asked as he pulled on his backpack.

"Home. I'm gonna work from there."

"Oh." She moved behind him as he shut down his computer and, with her forefinger, traced along the characters tattooed on the back of his neck. "I was thinking…maybe we could get together tonight. You could show me more of your drawings for the new book."

He looked around to see if anyone was watching. He hated when she touched him at the office. He stood up as the computer closed. "Can't."

Kassie deflated. She looked away and pulled at the hair at the nape of her neck with a heavily ringed hand.

"I got this book cover design I'm doing. It's really…big. Important, you know."

"Oh, okay," she said but didn't move out of his way.

"Tomorrow though."

"Really?"

He nodded. "I just did some more stuff last night. I should have it finished by then."

Kassie smiled. "Cool."

Mason finally managed to detach himself and get to his car. On the drive home, his eyelids kept sliding down despite the loud music playing on the radio. He had been up most of the night, working on the cover design for Carver as he had told Ricky *and* creating new drawings for his upcoming book as he had told Kassie. The drawings he needed tomorrow; he'd promised Trav the next set would be done before he got back from his vacation. The mockups for Carver he needed this afternoon, if his plan was going to work.

When he arrived home, he went up to his room and used his binoculars to see if *she* was home. The blinds were up and the curtains were drawn, but he didn't see anyone moving around the house. She liked the house full of light. During the day, it was always open like this, inviting him to look inside. So unlike him, who kept his room shut up, preferring the enveloping comfort and anonymity of darkness. They were like opposite parts of a whole, yin and yang. Maybe that's what he'd get for his next tat, with their initials forming the little dots inside. He thought about where he would place it.

He swore when he remembered what he'd promised Ricky. He put the binoculars down and emailed the files. He did need to do some more work on them before evening, but the lack of sleep gnawed at him, fraying his concentration. He kicked off his boots and crashed on the bed.

Mason slept soundly through the midmorning, and in his dream, he held a knife in one hand and a paintbrush in the other. He began to wobble, the ground uneven beneath his feet, but a hand reached out to steady him. It was her. She gazed up at him with wonder, then smiled. He smiled back. Then he looked down to see that he was standing on the body of Nathanael Carver.

Chapter Thirty-three

The search of Will McGlynn's house yielded nothing to tie either of the boyfriends to the threatening letters Carver had received. Kate, Potter, and the two patrolmen that accompanied them searched every closet, cupboard, trash can and drawer with no success. Benny from the crime lab had already reported that the newest letter offered no more evidence of the sender than the previous ones had. Kate held out hope that evidence might exist at Julio's sister's place, but her assumption that they would soon find out was premature.

Before they could pull away from McGlynn's house, a call came for all available units to report to the east side of town, where a meth lab bust had gone awry. The lab was operating in an old warehouse whose various exits proved difficult to secure. An officer had been shot, and two of the five persons in the lab had escaped on foot. Another had started a fire. Whether his intention was to destroy evidence or just cause confusion was unknown—for all they could tell it had been an accident—regardless, it had gone a long way toward making the morning more interesting for the Fulton Springs Police Department.

Kate and Potter spent the next two hours driving the area looking for the escaped, emaciated dealers, although Kate was unsure how to differentiate them physically from the homeless people that inhabited the neighborhood. Many of the homeless were on the hefty side, so some of them could be ruled out, but that was the only sure distinction she could reason. Now that downtown had been given a face-lift, perhaps the city would turn its attention to this section of town. Its numerous abandoned buildings, dark streets, and sporadic ramshackle housing were magnets for criminals and vagrants.

With a tip from a lucid street dweller, Sanchez and her partner apprehended one of the suspects, but the other was still loose when the first 911 call came in for a bank robbery on the other side of the city.

Kate shot Potter a look of disbelief. "You've got to be kidding me."

He pulled a U-turn and sped in the direction of the bank.

"I think," he said, "it's going to be one of those days."

Chapter Thirty-four

"I didn't believe it," Grant said. He stood in the doorway of Nate's office. "They told me you came into work today, and I said, 'No, that's insane,' and yet, here you are. You've got serious problems, man, and I'm not talking about the work that Mexican punk did on your face."

"No rest for the wicked."

"Well, I wouldn't number you among the wicked, so why don't you go back home, where you should be resting."

Nate leaned back in his chair with a slight grimace. His hand went to his ribs. He fixed his eyes on Grant. "Wouldn't you say that all of us are wicked, to some degree?"

Grant leaned against the doorframe. "What I would say is, that's a pretty bleak view of humanity. I like to think some of us are a little more evolved than that, but I'm sure there are kernels of…darkness in us all. But I wouldn't call that wickedness." He realized he was studying the pattern of the carpeting and forced himself to meet Nate's gaze. "Why do you say that?"

"If I weren't at least a little wicked, would this have happened to me?" Nate asked motioning toward the injuries on his face. His eye had darkened to a purple black, nearly matching the tiny black stitches on his cheekbone and forehead. "Isn't this my comeuppance for my part in stirring up strife in people's lives? Isn't that what karma is?"

"If it comes down to karma, you'll be okay. You and *Truth Will Out* do more good than harm. You know that. Remember the little speech you gave me when I came on board? People deserve the truth, and when we give them the truth, we help them protect themselves. We've helped expose corruption in the government, in the business sector. We've warned people about manufacturing dangers." Grant held up his hands in concession. "All right, maybe the magazine slides into tabloid mode occasionally, but I believe, under your leadership and hopefully mine, that it's meant a lot more than that. And you're just as responsible for all that good as whatever harm may have come from it."

Nate seemed to study the papers on his desk. "Maybe it's not always best for the truth to come out. Some secrets bear no profit when revealed, right?"

Grant cocked his head. "Do you have secrets, Nate?"

Nate met his gaze. "Do you?"

Grant chuckled. "I guess we all do, and you're right…some are best left secret. We're all entitled to privacy, which is a way of saying no one's entitled to all the truth."

"I hate to put an end to our contemplative discussion, but I should get back to this manuscript." Nate picked up a sharpened blue pencil and tapped the eraser against the desk. "Thanks for your concern, but I won't overdo it."

Grant shook his head and shrugged. "I had to try, didn't I?"

Nate smiled at him. "That's what friends are for."

As Grant walked back to his office, his mind replayed the conversation. Upon reflection, he wasn't sure that everyone had secrets. He believed that some people's lives were simple enough, that some *people* were simple enough, transparent, that they didn't warrant keeping secrets. He was not among that group, and while he would never have called Nate simple, he had never thought of him as a man of secrets, at least not until he had seen Nate with that blonde detective…Kate. He hadn't known that Nate had gone to the police about the threats. That was one secret. The letters had been a secret in and of themselves, although not from him. Grant wondered how many more.

At his office, he closed the door to discourage anyone from intruding upon his thoughts. His mind played between Nathanael Carver's secrets and his own. He reflected on how much he knew about Nate's and began to wonder how much Nate might know about his. He ran his hand through his hair, brushing the long bangs away from his face. He let his hand rest upon his neck, and in the stillness he heard the soft ticking of his watch's second hand. Its incessant movement marked in near-perfect increments—*tick, tick, tick.* The sound brought to mind the crocodile, the one pursuing Captain Hook in *Peter Pan.* It had swallowed a clock and thus a dread ticking always preceded its entrance. With his thumb and pinkie, Grant rotated the ring on his right hand until he could see the crocodile. *Tick, tick, tick.*

There was more than one crocodile in his life, though; he had to lay out some assignments for another issue. The newest one would hit mailboxes and newsstands at the end of the week, and while the next after had already been planned, there were still gaps to fill. But his efforts were impeded. Once his hearing had become attuned to the constant ticking, soft though it was, his mind could not shut it out. The more he tried to ignore it, the more prominent it became.

Refusing to cave to the mental distraction, Grant angrily punched at his keyboard, bringing up an Internet radio station. Music he could easily block out. He drowned out the ticking with "the best of the '80s, '90s, and today," and although he could no longer hear it over Madonna's "Secret," it was still there, counting down the time.

Chapter Thirty-five

"This is ridiculous." Kate peered around the corner of a side alley behind the bank. She'd been there for over two hours, waiting with a small contingent of officers to make sure the robbers didn't try to escape through the back. She'd had no breakfast and no lunch, and around noon the gray skies had finally relinquished a steady drizzle that showed no sign of picking up or dying off. To make matters worse, the building to their right was an Italian restaurant, and the tantalizing aroma of oregano and garlic continually wafted out. Kate's stomach made the sound of tires rolling over gravel.

"If these idiots ever come out, I'm gonna kill 'em," she told Potter, who crouched a few feet away, positioned against the wall opposite her. The official report had been that two men and one woman were left inside. All the hostages, save the woman, had been evacuated.

"You're just upset because you're hungry, tired, and wet."

Kate shot her partner an incredulous look. "Yes, Potter, I think that would go without saying, but that does pretty much sum things up. Although you forgot *cold*." With the rain had come a contemptible autumn chill, causing their words to hang visible in the air. She turned her attention back toward the bank's exit. "What kind of morons are these anyway? I mean, who robs a bank anymore?"

"There was that rash of bank robberies in Olivet and Porcine a few years ago," Potter answered.

"How successful were they?"

"Not terribly."

"Exactly my point. Nobody gets away with it, and I'm a little bewildered at the geniuses who think, Oh, I'll be the one." Kate turned back to Potter. "Pig Town?" she asked, using Porcine's more common, less flattering moniker. "Do they even have a bank?"

Potter nodded. "A tiny branch office. It got hit *twice*."

Kate shook her head and refocused on the exit. Her irritation stemmed not only from the physical environs of the robbery but also from the delay the robbery had caused in their investigation. She told herself she was just being paranoid, but still, she believed that every moment they wasted here made it more likely that somehow word would seep out to Julio's sister or one of his *hombres* and any evidence that might have been at the apartment would be gone. She took a deep breath and exhaled, battering a raindrop that fell from her nose.

The moments dripped on, and the sky darkened further. Finally, someone's radio squawked that one of the men and the female hostage were coming out the front. He wasn't letting her go, just using her as a shield to get to a car parked on the street. The officers at the back left of the building swung around to the side to help box him in out front. Everyone else in the back steeled themselves, aware that the change out front could mean action was coming their way too. Sure enough, less than a minute later, a muscular man in a hooded jacket and dark glasses burst through the door, carrying canvas bags in both hands. After a quick glance, he sprinted away from the remaining police. Almost immediately a second man came out, dressed like the first and clutching a bag, but in his other hand, he held a gun. He fired a shot down the alley, causing a rookie to throw himself behind a dumpster. Kate ducked back around the corner. They'd been told only two men were left in the bank, counting the one who'd gone out front. So much for reliable information.

The robber took off after his partner.

"Police. Stop!"

The men, of course, did not stop—did they ever?— but the bags they carried slowed them down significantly, and had it not been raining, they would have probably been easily apprehended. The police that had been farthest back in the alley took off around the restaurant to head them off. Kate and Potter, who had been at the mouth of the side alley, swung in behind the officers that remained.

Kate could hear curses erupt as one and then another of the men running near her slipped on loose refuse and crashed to the pavement. Was it her imagination or had the rain suddenly picked up?

The officers in front of her tackled the slower, smaller suspect and wrested away his gun. Kate dashed by, pulling ahead of the few behind her. As she neared the remaining robber, she realized exactly what a moose he was. She slammed into the towering figure from behind. The impact was negligible. He did skid for a moment but never lost his footing completely, and when he swung around to face her, he used the momentum to send one of the money bags flying into her. The force sent Kate's gun skittering down the alley and knocked her backward into the brick wall. The air rushed from her lungs, but she nevertheless rebounded instantly. She saw the flash of a navy blue uniform to one side, but her eyes were fixed on the hand that had let loose of the bag, the hand that was reaching into the back waistband of the man's jeans.

She attacked the man's arm before he could raise the gun, but his grip was like iron. She spun to the inside, putting herself behind the gun and pinning his arm beneath her own, and tried wrenching the gun away, digging at the wrist where there should have been a pressure point but seemed to be only taut bands of muscle. She could hear grunting and crashing coming from the man's other side. Before she could even register what that might mean, the arm lifted and she found herself dangling in the air.

Now, *this* was ridiculous. Refusing to let go she kicked back with her feet, but with the awkward angle, her heels merely bounced off the man's pillar-like legs. His gun went off, and chips of brick flew away from the wall. For a moment, Kate could hear nothing but the death of countless audial nerve cells.

"Somebody help us here!" Kate yelled, her voice muffled in her own ears. Surely the others had subdued the smaller robber by now.

Her man lurched, smashing her arm and shoulder against the wall. Kate cried out between gritted teeth, but with both of them pressed against the wall, she used her free hand to punch her wrestling partner's hand repeatedly against it. The gun finally dropped, but the man yanked back his arm, crushing Kate to him. Out of the corner of her eye, she saw a baton slam into the man's meaty neck. He wobbled and his grip loosened. She fought free and delivered a spin kick to the back of his knee. The giant toppled.

Kate and the other officer wrestled the brute onto his stomach as several police rushed forward to help. It's true, Kate thought, they're never there when you need them. Even when you're one of them. For the first time, Kate realized her companion in the fight had been Nash. He was panting almost as hard as she was as he held an arm in place so the thug could be cuffed.

As much as it galled her, she knew she had to do it. As other less-winded officers led the man away, she approached Nash.

"Thanks," she said, surprised at how breathless she still sounded.

"Don't mention it, Baxter. I've got your back." Kate waited for the salacious other shoe to drop, but it didn't.

"Appreciate it," she said.

Potter called them over to the bank's exit.

"You okay?" he asked Kate.

"Yeah," she said, ducking in from the rain.

Nash walked on, leaving the partners alone. After he was out of earshot, Kate muttered, "Did you see that?"

"Well, not all of it."

"I was hanging off that guy's arm like an ornament on a Christmas tree. How humiliating."

"Don't sweat it. I'm sure everyone was a little too preoccupied to notice."

"Thanks, but that doesn't make me feel any less stupid."

She spotted Parkman, another cop who'd been in the alley with them, heading back to the exit. She told Potter she needed a minute. She followed Parkman to find him standing in the doorway with a cigarette.

"Exciting, huh?" he asked when she caught up with him.

"You could say that I suppose."

He held the pack out to her without her even having to ask. She hoped he didn't notice how her hand trembled as she reached for the cigarette and held it up for a light. She breathed in the warmth and waited for the soothing sensation she knew would follow. Her mind replayed the altercation, sure that she could have handled it better, without looking like a dork. It wasn't until afterward that she remembered to thank God that she or anyone else hadn't been shot.

When she'd gathered herself, Kate found Potter in the bank's waiting area, talking to Spence and his mini-recorder.

"Katherine, are you all right?" Spence asked. "Potter was just giving me a run down, and he said things got a little rough out back."

Potter handed her a steaming cup of coffee. Kate looked at him to ascertain how much he'd divulged. His gaze held neither guilt nor chagrin. She should have known she could depend on Potter's healthy respect for privacy.

"Yeah, it was a little rough out there, but we got both the bad guys. Been better—."

"Been worse," Spence finished. "Well, I'm glad you're okay. Take it easy on the heroics."

Kate laughed. "Don't worry about that. I always push Potter into the oncoming danger first."

Spence chuckled and Potter gave a tight-lipped smile. The look in his eyes, though, accused Kate of performing.

"I don't think we're needed here anymore," he reported.

"Good. We need to get over to Ambris's place."

"I'll get out of your way," Spence said. "With the fire on the other side of town, it's been a crazy news day."

"Tell us about it," said Kate.

Spence left, and Kate grimaced as she eased herself down onto the arm of a padded chair.

"Perhaps you should take the rest of the day off," Potter suggested. "I can handle Ambris's apartment."

Kate didn't respond. She was taking stock of the magazines spread out on the coffee table in front of her, specifically an issue of *Truth Will Out*. She recognized the cover, a photo of a little girl holding a rose at a funeral. She picked up the magazine. It was the August issue. She held it up to Potter.

"Do you suppose they have the September issue?" she asked.

"I suppose we could ask," he answered patiently, although his face bore an impatiently quizzical expression.

"Let's," said Kate as she surveyed the table again, looking for the issue in question.

Potter shook his head and walked away. In his absence Kate checked out the magazines on the other tables. She found several older issues, most of which were familiar from her research, but she couldn't find a September issue. When he returned, Potter had some helpful news.

"I got the answer to your question, though the woman looked at me as if I'd lost my mind, asking her about their magazines after they'd just been robbed. Refresh my memory, but weren't you champing at the bit to get over to Ambris's place?"

"What did she say?"

"She said it hasn't come yet. It always comes toward the end of the month, instead of the beginning. She didn't know why."

Kate held up the August issue in her hand again. "The message was, *It won't be much longer now.* Chronology."

Potter blinked twice, and between blinks, Kate sensed that almost audible *click* as he realized her point.

"I'll check out Ambris's place, and you follow up on this," he said.

Kate nodded. "If our poison pen kept to his pattern, we might actually have a break."

Chapter Thirty-six

Nathanael Carver rarely left the office early, but he figured that being battered the day before was excuse enough. Workaholic or not, a dip in stamina had to be expected. He made sure to tell Cynthia he was going home for the day. He got to the downstairs lobby before remembering that the cover designer for the Boudreau book was supposed to submit mockups to him today. Could he afford to blow it off? Boudreau had already been yapping about seeing the cover for weeks. With a groan, Nate forced himself back up to the design department. He ran into Ricky at the door.

"Hey there, big guy." The design supervisor laid a hand on his shoulder. "How are you holding up? That was so bizarro you getting attacked like that!"

"I'm hanging in there. I think my pain medication is wearing off, though, so I'm heading home. I just need to see Mason about the Boudreau book before I leave. He's supposed to have something to show me."

"Ahh, he's not here. I told him he could telecommute today. I didn't know he was trying to ditch a meeting with you." Ricky shook his head. "Mmm!"

"It wasn't an official meeting," Nate explained. "He probably planned to bring them in later this afternoon."

"You give him too much credit," Ricky said. "He's got a lousy work ethic in addition to a lousy social disposition."

Nate chuckled. "Then why don't you let him go?"

Ricky shrugged with an exaggerated groan. "Because he's also very talented. I give him menial tasks occasionally to keep him humble, but he's very gifted."

"I can only guess what he thinks of you," Nate teased.

"I can assure you it isn't flattering. I'll give him a talking-to tomorrow. He did email me some preliminary files. You want me to forward those to you?"

"Yes, please."

"They'll be in your inbox when you get home. Now, you go get some R&R. Tell Amelie I said hello."

"Will do. We'll have to have you and Theresa over for dinner; it's been a while."

"Just give us enough notice to find a sitter."

"Sure thing."

Nate convinced himself that one day wouldn't really make a difference on the designs. After all, the delay on the artwork was nothing compared to the constant delays the author had caused with the text. On the drive home, his thoughts turned to the evening. Amelie had pushed back her book club from Tuesday because of the Chapboy launch party. Even with her out of the house, he predicted the night would not be particularly restful.

A strange car sat in front of his side of the garage. Nate didn't recognize the junky little Volvo as being anything that Amelie's friends, or his, would drive.

"This week just keeps getting better and better," he muttered.

His injuries required him to move gingerly, so dashing through the rain to the front door was out of the question. He used an already damp newspaper for what shelter it could provide and kicked himself for not leaving an umbrella in the car. Once inside the door, he shook the excess water from the newspaper and his coat, sprinkling the foyer.

Amelie came from the kitchen. "I thought I heard the door. You're home early!" She gave him a quick, gentle peck, careful to avoid his tender bruises.

"I figured I could use the rest. I'm probably blocking you in. Whose car—" Nate stopped short at the sight of Mason Lenkov walking down his hallway. "What are you doing here?"

"Manners." Amelie reproved with a finger, as if he were a child. "Mason said he was supposed to show you some designs for that book you're always talking about."

Mason nodded toward the kitchen. "We spread 'em out on the table in there."

Nate could read nothing in the younger man's dark and vacant eyes. That bothered him. "How did you know where I lived?" He tried to control his tone, to not reveal how the intrusion disturbed him.

"Nathanael, honestly. Mason lives in the house right behind ours. You work in the same company and never noticed that?"

"No." Nate forced a laugh. "I guess I'm not as observant as I thought. What a coincidence."

Mason's head bobbed a few times, as if in time to some internal rhythm.

"Well, let's look at these designs, then."

Ricky had been right. Mason was good. He presented three different concepts, all of them eye-catching and in vogue with where the market was going (rather than where it currently resided), but each took a distinctive tact. They weren't just reworked versions of each other. Nate admitted, at least to himself, that Mason had exceeded his expectations, but he still wanted him out of the house. He concluded the business quickly and ushered Mason to the door.

"Are you all right?" Amelie asked when Nate returned to the kitchen.

"What possessed you to let him inside?"

He could tell Amelie didn't care for his tone by the way she crossed her arms. "He works with you. He talked about the project you've been going on about forever."

"Just because we work together doesn't make him safe."

Amelie snorted. "Since when have you been concerned about our safety?" She retreated to the living room.

Nate pursued. "Did you even look at him? With that thing stuck in his eyebrow, and one in his tongue and God knows where else?"

"Oh, please, Nate. Everyone his age has some kind of tattoo or piercing. You can't step out the door without seeing them. What decade are you living in? Besides, he's our neighbor. I know him."

"Really? How well do you know him? Did you even know his name before tonight?"

She hesitated ever so briefly before replying, "Yes, I did. I've talked to him several times."

She was lying. He could always tell when she lied. Maybe not all of her statement, but at least part of it was untrue. He debated whether to play the card he held in his hand. He hated to but did.

"What if he were the one sending the letters?"

Amelie stood stock still, and he knew he'd hit upon the possibility she'd been trying to evade. After a moment, she turned and faced him.

"What possible reason would *he* have for threatening you?" she challenged.

"I wouldn't know, but I think it's safe to say that whoever's sending the letters isn't the most balanced individual, so maybe there is no comprehensible reason."

Amelie threw her hands up. "So I guess I can't trust anyone, can I?"

Nate embraced her, mindful of his injured ribs. "You can trust me."

Amelie was brittle in his embrace, but eventually she melted into him. He took that as a good sign but wondered what she was thinking. He knew her so well after this many years of marriage, and yet certain aspects of her remained a mystery.

"When are you leaving for book club?" he asked when she pulled away.

"Oh, Nate! Surely you don't think I'd go after what happened last night? I'll stay home with you."

"There's no need to do that. I don't think I'll be good company tonight...as you've probably ascertained already. You should go. I'll just be resting anyway. I can look after myself."

Amelie furrowed her brow at him. "You were just trying to convince me that our neighbor is a psychopath, and now you want me to leave you home alone, in your condition?"

Nate had to laugh. She had a point.

"I'm sorry. I'm probably not making a lot of sense—"

"I knew you shouldn't have gone to the office today."

He took her by the arms. "I know I've put you through a lot lately." She started to protest, but he stopped her. "It's my fault one way or another, but I'm sure it'll be over soon. The police will find whoever's doing this and make it stop, and everything will go back to normal. You deserve a night out." She hesitated, patting her hand against his chest. "Go, I mean it! Maybe after club you can persuade some of the girls to go out for drinks. Make a late night of it."

"Well, we did move it back from Tuesday just for me, and the girls would be upset if I canceled on them this late."

"Oh, you hadn't canceled already?" He couldn't hide the note of disappointment in his voice.

She winced. "I kept putting it off. It's awful of me, I know, but if you really want me to go, it turned out to be a good thing, right?"

He smiled. "Definitely."

"You're sure you'll be okay?"

"Absolutely. I'll keep the gun handy." They'd been keeping the handgun loaded since their first visit to the police. Uncertainty still played on Amelie's face. He kissed her forehead. "Don't worry. I'll be perfectly safe. Nothing is going to happen to me."

Chapter Thirty-seven

This time Kate tried a more familiar tact with the behemoth administrative assistant. "Hello, Cynthia! I was just checking to see if Mr. Carver happened to be in?"

The look was less suspicious than last time but more disdainful.

"And you are?"

Kate knew full well that Cynthia remembered her, but she forced a smile and flashed her badge. "Detective Baxter. I'm one of the people who's trying to make sure your boss is okay." She tried to stop there, honestly she did. But it had been such a rotten day. "So you might want to curb the attitude and try being helpful. Unless you've got something against Mr. Carver, in which case I'd *love* to hear about it." The smile never left her face.

Cynthia's face puckered, but she answered nonetheless. "Mr. Carver did come in today, but he left a few hours ago. He said he was going home."

"Thank you," said Kate, perhaps a bit too cheerfully. "I need some information about the current issue of *Truth Will Out*. Whom should I see about that?"

"That office is down one floor. You may speak to Joyce Wickenseimer. She is Mr. Innerst's assistant."

Kate decided, however, to forego administrative interference this time. Besides, judging from her previous encounters with Grant Innerst, she expected a friendly reception from the magazine editor. At his office, however, closed blinds covered the windows, so she knocked on the door. There was no answer. Kate glanced at her watch. It was a quarter till five. She knocked again and simultaneously turned the knob. The door opened a crack.

"May I help you?"

Kate turned to find a little silver-haired woman in glasses a few feet behind her. The woman clutched a stack of heavily loaded manila envelopes to her satiny blouse. Her pink smile was friendly, her eyes wary.

"Yes." Kate flashed her badge again. "Kate Baxter with the Fulton Springs Police Department. I'm looking for Grant Innerst."

The suspicion changed instantly to wonder. "Oh! Is this about the attack on Mr. Carver yesterday?"

"Yes, in a way."

"Wasn't that just awful? I could not believe it. Something like that happening right here. My husband told me to have someone walk me to the car from now on."

Kate interrupted. "That sounds like a good idea. Is Mr. Innerst in?"

"No, he left a few minutes ago. Is there anything I can do for you? I'm Joyce Wickenseimer, his assistant."

"Yes, there is. I know this is going to sound strange, but I need to see a copy of your September issue."

Joyce laughed. "You're right; that is a little strange. I have one at my desk." From her immaculate desk, Joyce pulled the current issue from a filing cabinet, but she hesitated before handing it to Kate. "You said this was to help Mr. Carver, right?"

"Yes, it's actually pretty important."

Joyce nodded and then handed the magazine to Kate.

"Would you mind if I used your desk for just a minute?" Kate inquired. "I need to check something in this real quick."

"Oh, that's fine," said Joyce. "I'll just go back to delivering these." She hefted her manila envelopes up. "Before I go, though, can I ask you a question—if it's all right—about the man they arrested? The one who attacked Mr. Carver."

"I guess it depends on what the question is," said Kate, caught between curiosity and impatience.

"It wasn't a young Hispanic man, was it? Shaved head, wearing a black jacket and nice shoes?"

"As a matter of fact, it was. How did you hit on that exact description?"

Joyce sighed. "Cynthia and I saw him out front on our way back from lunch. He was acting kind of strange, just standing there looking at the building. I thought maybe he needed help. He was dressed so nicely; it didn't occur to me that he would be a criminal, although Cynthia was afraid he was a mugger." She whispered, "But between you and me, I think she was just being a bit racist."

Kate fought hard not to smile. "You're very astute, Joyce, and it's good to know that you saw the man beforehand. You've been very helpful."

"Oh, I'm so glad." Joyce beamed. "I'll be back in a jiff."

Kate shook her head as the secretary walked away, amazed at the disparity between this woman and her professional counterpart upstairs.

On her phone, Kate brought up a photo of the latest threat. She compared the red cursive *r*, the one constant among all the letters, in the threat to the one on the cover of the magazine. Their backgrounds matched; however, it was nondescript gray with the barest gradient in color. Unsatisfied, Kate flipped through pages looking for headline text that matched the fonts and letters used in the message: *I'm coming for you.* After five positive IDs, she was certain—the writer had used this issue. At their first meeting, Carver had said the letters had come briefly, stopped, and then started again. The later letters were the only ones he had kept. One had come every month, composed from a new issue of *Truth Will Out.* Except the last one—it was composed from a new issue, but it had come in the same month as the previous letter.

Kate stuffed the phone back into her pocket as Joyce approached.

"Excuse me, Joyce, but can you tell me when this issue came out?"

"It hasn't. It comes out tomorrow. That's why I wasn't sure whether I should show it to you," Joyce explained. "We have very strict procedures about our release and mailings. We don't let anyone outside the company see it before it's delivered to the stores and subscribers, but I figured, since you're with the police department, it would be okay."

"How long have you had this issue here in the office?"

"Since last Wednesday."

Kate didn't wait to get back to the car before she called Potter.

"Nothing's turned up has it?" she asked.

"You know this how?"

"The September issue was just mailed out this week. Whoever wrote the last letter had to have access to it beforehand. It's gotta be somebody at Roving House."

Chapter Thirty-eight

Mason watched as the lights at the Carver house blinked out. A moment later, the silver Saab pulled away and drove down the street. Mason watched it disappear and then redirected his binoculars back to the darkened house. Well, it was now or never.

He pulled on a pair of shoes and ran downstairs. He slipped into his jacket and opened the back door. A blast of rain hit him in the face. He pulled the door closed again. It was raining harder than before, and it was colder. He grabbed a black stocking cap. Maybe an umbrella? No, it might draw attention. He hurried to the kitchen and rummaged through the drawers until he found a large plastic bag with a zip top. He folded it and put it in his inside jacket pocket.

He sprinted across the yard to the back fence, the rain pounding away at him. He had trouble gripping the weather-treated wood in the rain but still managed to hoist himself over with no serious trouble. He landed awkwardly, though, slipping on the wet grass and catching himself with his hands. The return trip would be harder. He stopped, scanned the house for light or movement, saw nothing, and moved on to the kitchen door.

There was little mud on his shoes, but they were plastered with grass as were his hands. The yard must have been recently cut. Despite the cold rain, he kicked the shoes off and gritted his teeth against the cold cement biting into his now-bare feet. He wiped his hands off as best he could on the sodden denim. Then he turned the door handle. It was unlocked, just as he had left it.

SITTING AT a red light, Grant frowned. He could have sworn that Nate's car had gone through the intersection just as he had pulled up, but the rain made it impossible to say for sure. He drummed his fingertips on the steering wheel as the pop chanteuse on the radio breathily exclaimed her desire. There were lots of silver Saabs. He would go on to Nate's house as planned.

When he pulled up, there were no signs of life about the place. It wasn't terribly dark out yet, but it would be inside. He frowned again. Had it been Nate back at the intersection? This had better not be a colossal waste of time. He backed into the drive so that he could make a quicker exit and also be on the side of the car closest to the front door. He zipped his jacket up to the neck, then dashed through the rain to the overhang. He'd forgotten his car lights again. Well, this would take only a minute.

The knob, cold to the touch, resisted his effort to turn it. Grant was beginning to get annoyed. The door was supposed to have been unlocked. His body hummed with impatient energy. He dug his keys out of his pants pocket, found the correct key, and opened the door.

TRANSCRIPT FROM the Fulton Springs Emergency Response Center.

DISPATCHER: Nine-one-one. Please state the nature of your emergency.

MALE CALLER: Somebody's breaking into my house.

DISPATCHER: Where are you, sir?

MALE CALLER: I'm upstairs. I'm by myself. My wife is gone—

DISPATCHER: Sir, I need to confirm your address.

MALE CALLER: 199 Adams Road, Fulton Springs.

DISPATCHER: What's your name, sir?

MALE CALLER: Nathanael Carver. I've been getting death threats. I think it must be him.

DISPATCHER: All right, sir. We have officers in the area. We're dispatching them now. They should be there soon. Do you think you can get out of the house safely?

MALE CALLER: [*unintelligible*]

DISPATCHER: Sir, I can't understand you. Please speak directly into the phone.

Silence.

DISPATCHER: Sir, are you there?

MALE CALLER: [*whispering*] He's inside. Please hurry.

DISPATCHER: Can you get out of the house?

MALE CALLER: [*whispering*] He's downstairs. There's no other way out.

DISPATCHER: Can you defend yourself? Do you have something—anything—you can defend yourself with?

MALE CALLER: [*whispering*] I have my gun. I have it ready.

DISPATCHER: Okay, don't confront him unless you have to. Sit tight. Help will be there in a minute. Is there a place that you can hide until the police get there?

Silence.

DISPATCHER: Sir, are you still with me? Sir?

MALE CALLER: [*whispering*] I think he's moved away from the door. I'm going to try to get out.

DISPATCHER: Are you sure there's no other—

MALE IN THE BACKGROUND: Hey!

MALE CALLER: STOP OR I'LL SHOOT!

Clattering noise. Gunfire.

DISPATCHER: Sir? Sir, are you okay?

No response. Sirens.

Chapter Thirty-nine

Kate arrived at the Carver house well after Potter. Several patrol cars and an ambulance sat in the street blocking off the drive. The red and blue lights flashed as beacons in the early evening gloom and steady rain. It seemed her break had come too late. Kate parked as close as possible and sat in the car for a few minutes. She didn't want to go inside. A report over the police radio had already told her what she would find inside. It hadn't taken much imagination to piece together what hadn't been said. A huge sense of failure loomed overhead, and when she walked in that door, it would crash down on top of her.

Kate sighed and got out. She had never dried out from the afternoon standoff, so it seemed pointless to bother with an umbrella, even though the rain had picked up significantly. As she stalked up the drive to the door, she quickly surveyed the front of the house. The downstairs was ablaze with light. Two patrolmen in slickers stood outside the front door. An old Chevy was parked in front of the garage. The neighboring house on the left was dark. A realtor's sign stood in the yard. Security lights illumined the front of the house on the right. A small dog yipped incessantly, demanding attention over the rush of rain. Kate shielded her eyes from the watery onslaught to see a pouffy white head bob in and out of view through the porch window. She grimaced. That's why she had cats.

The warmth of the house welcomed her initially, a respite from the wet chill that had composed most of her day, but it quickly became stifling. A light hum of cop communication ran through the downstairs as radios intermittently buzzed, wet footsteps squeaked on hardwood floors, conversations murmured, and pictures snapped. Where the hall opened into the high-ceilinged entry, next to the stairs, in a pool of blood, lay the body of Grant Innerst.

The expression about dying young and leaving a good-looking corpse came to mind. Kate shook her head. She usually didn't meet victims until after they were corpses. She'd only met Grant twice, but both times he had exuded vitality, a distinct contrast to the lifeless form in front of her. His lips were slightly parted as if about to speak, but the open eyes were hollow.

A camera flash interrupted her thoughts as Benny from the crime lab continued photographing the body.

"Looks like two shots to the chest," he said. Kate could see the dark punctures in the white shirt for herself. "Both close range. The homeowner said he was standing here, and that matches up." Benny walked a few feet away to where Carver had been. "Of course, you'll have to wait for Andreeson for the official take. He's back at the morgue waiting for the body."

"Don't load him up just yet. I want a chance to look around before the scene's obliterated."

"Okay, but I'd really prefer not to be here all night." Benny nodded toward the den. "They're in there."

Potter stood, with a minirecorder in hand, next to Carver, who sat hunched over on a sofa, a hand covering his face.

"Are you okay, Mr. Carver?" Kate asked.

He looked up and nodded shakily. His clothing and hair were damp, although not soaked as hers were.

"We've been going over what happened," Potter said. He turned back to Carver. "Would you mind telling Detective Baxter what you told me?"

"I, uh…" Carver stopped, took a breath, and then continued. "I was upstairs. Amelie had just left for her book club, and I was going to rest for a while. I heard a noise at the front door. I thought somebody was trying to break in, so I called 911. Then I got my gun." He paused for a moment. "I could hear him walking around downstairs. He was going toward the kitchen, so I thought maybe I could get out. I knew he was going to kill me. I got down the stairs, but he must have heard me. He came back. I yelled for him to stop, but he came at me. So I fired." His head sank. "It was dark. I didn't even realize it was Grant till afterward. I can't believe it—I just can't."

Kate shot a look at Potter. "It didn't look like the front door had been broken in."

"Grant has a key," Carver said. "When we'd go on vacation, he'd check on the house for us. He was my friend. I thought he was my friend."

Benny whistled for their attention and nodded them over. Kate and Potter excused themselves. Benny held up a hoop of fishing line.

"He was holding this in his hand. I don't see any other weapon, so I suppose he was planning on garroting him," he concluded.

"A pleasant, nonviolent way to kill a friend," Kate said.

"Why didn't he have it uncurled, though?" Potter asked.

"Maybe he was nervous. Thought he could talk Carver down if they came face to face," Kate replied.

"Then why rush him?"

"You got me. I still have a big blank for motive. Anything else out of the ordinary, Benny?"

Benny shook his head.

"Hey, Benny!" an officer called from the kitchen. "When you're done in there, somebody made a mess in here."

"Be there in a sec." Benny looked from Kate to Potter. "That's the direction your intended victim said his attacker was coming from. Anyone want to come?"

"In a minute," Potter said.

After Benny left, Kate exhaled a burst of regret. "I wouldn't have picked Grant Innerst for this in the first place."

"You're not subscribing to the professional jealousy motive?"

Kate shook her head. "Not unless he totally snowed me. It wouldn't be the first time I've gotten taken, but...I don't know." She shrugged. She looked back into the den at Carver. "Why's he all wet? When did he go outside?"

"First responders said he ran out of the house as they pulled up."

"Why?"

"Creeped out by killing his friend in his own house? I don't know."

Potter went to see if Benny would turn up anything in the back of the house, and Kate returned to the den.

"Mr. Carver, Potter told me that you ran outside when the police got here. Why?"

"I was just so relieved they were finally here," he answered. "It was very disturbing, being in here with him." He nodded in Grant's direction.

"I can understand that," Kate conceded. She'd seen enough corpses to remain dispassionate, but she remembered what it was like to be responsible for one.

"Have you ever shot someone?" Carver asked before Kate could move the interview on.

She nodded.

"Do you ever get over it?" She couldn't read the intensity in his eyes as any particular emotion.

"Where did Grant live?" she asked, evading his question. She didn't want to give false hope or to dispel the humanist myth. She didn't want to answer yes.

"Olivet," Carver answered, then groaned. "I keep thinking, should I have seen this coming?"

"No idea why he would want to hurt you?"

"Not unless it were about the job, but that doesn't really make sense. He never seemed that interested in it. He'd tell me how good I had it, not just the job, but life, but he never seemed jealous."

This time, yelling from outside saved Kate from having to fabricate a conciliatory reply.

"Nate! Grant!" A frantic Amelie Carver burst through the front door, followed by an officer. She stopped short at the sight of Grant Innerst's dead body. A hand flew to her mouth, but it did not quell the scream. Her leather bag slipped from her shoulder, spilling its contents, as she collapsed to her knees.

Carver hurried over to her. "I'm here! I'm here!" he repeated as he took his wife in his arms. He murmured consolation as the two clung to each other, Amelie gasping and choking through her shock. When he had finally calmed her, they retreated to the den.

Kate, who had remained a respectful distance, picked up the bag. A brush, a container of shea butter, a small makeup bag, and a crisp copy of *Madame Bovary* had fallen out. *Look inside the bag*, an interior voice said, but Kate resisted. She put everything back in except the book. The cardboard bookmark, now bent, marked a place about halfway through the book. She rejoined the Carvers.

"That can't be true. Grant wouldn't do that. He wouldn't. I know he wouldn't," Amelie babbled to her husband.

"I know it doesn't seem possible, but he did. He attacked me."

"It doesn't make sense!"

"You don't have any idea why Grant would do this?" Kate asked.

Amelie shook her head, her eyes unfocused and a little wild. "No, he's—" Her voice caught. "He's our *friend*." And she was crying again.

This was going to take forever. Kate took off her coat, which did little to alleviate her discomfort in the house's sultry atmosphere, and sat down on a chair with a squish. She would have killed for a pair of dry underwear. She looked over at Amelie Carver, blubbering on her husband's shoulder. How did she manage to still look perfect? She was a pretty crier, which was a rarity in itself, but was she impervious to rain too?

"You called both your husband's and Grant's name when you came in." Kate didn't make it a question, just an observation.

"I saw Grant's car outside," Amelie retorted. She had inferred an accusation. "I didn't—" She broke off into huffing sobs.

Kate nodded to herself. That made sense. Potter's quiet approach drew the group's attention.

"Excuse me, Mr. Carver," he asked. "One of the officers found a substantial amount of water and grass in front of the kitchen door. Did you track that in?"

Carver froze. Kate could see gears turn behind his eyes. "No," he said. "That doesn't make sense. That door's locked."

"No, it's not, sir," Potter corrected.

"It must have been Grant," Carver concluded, though puzzlement still clouded his features. "He must have stepped out the back door while I was still upstairs. I can't think why, though."

"We'll check with the neighbors," Kate said, "to see if they saw anything."

"We're kind of neighborless at the moment," Carver said. "The house next door has been on the market for a while, and the Thompsons, on the other side, just left for vacation."

"I thought I heard a dog next door," Kate said.

"That's Beau, Edith's toy poodle," Amelie answered. "They go to Florida every year for a few weeks, but they don't always take him."

Kate asked if they knew who was taking care of the dog, but neither did.

"Here's your things, Mrs. Carver." Kate handed Amelie her book and bag. "Is *Madame Bovary* for your book club?"

Amelie nodded, dabbing at her nose with a tissue.

"Kind of funny that the protagonist's sister has the same name as you, but I guess it's not that uncommon in French. What did you think of the section where she comes to visit?"

Amelie sniffed and shrugged. "It wasn't my favorite."

"Yeah, that part is a little dry," Kate conceded and stood. "Why don't you two pack a bag? I don't think you'll want to stay here tonight. We can finish up without you."

"I don't want to go back out there," Amelie said.

"I'll take care of it, dear."

"Just let us know where you're staying, how to get in touch with you," Potter said.

Carver nodded. The two detectives walked him to the entryway and watched as he climbed the stairs without looking at the dead body sprawled beside it.

"So why the sudden literary interest?" Potter asked quietly.

"I'll tell you later."

"I think I can guess."

"You're smart like that."

"I don't think it was Grant," Potter said, switching tracks.

"What?"

"The water and grass in the kitchen. It's pooled like somebody just stood there for a while inside the door. Then it goes off in the direction opposite of the hallway. It might make sense if he had come through the back and circled through the dining room, but he came through the front. Benny says the trails don't meet up."

Carver appeared overhead, a small suitcase in either hand.

"That was fast," Kate said to Potter.

From where she stood, Kate had a clear line of sight through the kitchen windows. The windows of the house behind the Carvers' were illuminated. She pointed.

"Somebody's home over there. Maybe they saw something. I'll be right back."

On her way out to the car, Kate detoured by the Thompsons' house. She knocked on the door, just in case, and got only Beau's yipping in response. Kate turned and walked down the sidewalk. Flowerbeds with precisely spaced plants flanked the cement walkway. The plants would soon succumb to the cold weather. She stopped. A narrow rut in the soil of one of the beds had flooded with water. She followed the angle to a similar rut in the bed on the other side. Something had cut across the yard and beds heading toward the front door. Kate wondered how Edith Thompson would feel about her dogsitter riding a bike through her flowerbeds.

Kate drove around to the house on the neighboring street and parked in the drive next to a gold Volvo. Thankfully, the house had a small porch, which provided relief from the rain, if not from the chill, as she pounded on the door. When no one came, she pounded with a little more intensity.

Finally, the door yanked open with an expletive. The unshaven guy with an eyebrow stud who opened it wore an ugly expression. Heat rushed over Kate to escape the house, but despite the interior warmth, the guy was already shivering. Perhaps because he was soaking wet and half-dressed. He wore no shoes and no shirt, revealing tattoos of a dragon on his forearm and a skull on one side of his nearly hairless chest. The wide swath of gray striped boxers that showed above his jeans was plastered to his skin, disturbingly translucent. Water dripped from his trailing, grass-laced cuffs and pooled on the floor.

"I'm sorry to bother you," Kate said tersely. She flashed her badge at him. Caution displaced the anger on his face, and he shifted his weight back—details she did not miss. "I'm Detective Baxter with the Fulton Springs PD. There's been an incident at the house behind yours. Did you happen to see or hear anything out of the ordinary tonight?"

He shook his head.

"We just wondered because we saw a light on upstairs." Kate knew she had no prayer of being invited inside, but perhaps if she drew this out, he'd be politer to the next person who knocked on his door. "You probably have a clear view from there of the back of the house."

"I just got home, like a minute ago." Kate narrowed her eyes at him. "I leave the light on upstairs sometimes," he added. He crossed his arms to conserve heat. A long, ugly, red welt ran along his right forearm.

"Okay. If you think of anything, please give me a call." She brought her card case out but fumbled it into the puddle at his feet. "Oh, stupid me."

He bent over to pick up the case, and she saw the tattoo on the back of his neck, Asian characters. She'd seen them before. Where? He handed the case back to her, and she picked a piece of grass off it and handed him one of her cards.

"Did you just mow your yard?"

"Yeah, well, it looked like rain." The insolence was resurging.

"Have we met before? You seem familiar."

He shook his head again.

After he shut the door, it came to her—Roving House. She'd stood behind him in the design department. He worked the same place as Nathanael Carver. And he'd obviously been spooked by her. But would those things be connected? Was his aversion to cops personal, or did he know something about what happened next door?

Well, she couldn't stand there all night. She should check with the houses on either side of this one. She left the porch but then shot a glance back at the closed door.

Weird.

Chapter Forty

Kate sat in the dark, Louis curled up on her lap, watching some late show she cared nothing about when her phone buzzed. The illuminated screen showed a text from Spence, asking if she was awake. She reached over and grabbed the cordless from its cradle and called him.

"I was afraid I might wake you."

Kate snorted. "Not hardly." She'd been home only long enough to take a hot shower and change into dry clothes. Too much weighed on her to sleep.

"I heard there was some action at Nathanael Carver's house tonight." His voice was faint. She punched up the volume on her phone and muted the TV.

"You calling for a lead?"

"No," he said slowly. "I'm calling to see if you're all right."

"I'm sorry. I had a bad day." Boy, did that seem like the understatement of the year. "The guy I'm supposed to be helping almost gets killed. Instead somebody else does. Either way, it's not really a job well done. Then when I got back to the station—I mean right as I walk in with Potter—there's this slugfest going on. Some rednecks brought in on a domestic, and they were burly trucker types. It was a free-for-all." The words poured out of her, but she couldn't stop the torrent. "And for icing, I had two messages from my ever-lovin' parents when I finally got home, one from each—and I quote my mother—to make sure that I'm not dead in a parking lot somewhere, since I work such a dangerous job. I swear, they live in the same house but have zero communication."

Spence waited to see if she was truly done before offering his condolences. He then told her that he was leaving the paper for the night.

"Just now?"

"You, better than most, should know that it was hardly a slow news day."

"Point taken."

"Anyway, do you want to meet for coffee, my treat?" he offered.

"What I could really use is a cigarette." The words shot out like a bullet. Stupid, stupid.

An awkward pause ensued before Spence said, "You started smoking again?"

"Not really—yes, but I've already quit again. A couple times actually. Don't tell Heidi. I am so sorry; my mouth is going much faster than my brain right now."

"I won't say anything to Heidi. I'm guessing Danny already knows?"

"Yeah, he gave me the once over."

"What about a nicotine patch?" he suggested. "Have you ever tried one of those?"

"Can we please not talk about this right now?"

"Yes, of course. We can talk about whatever you want to talk about."

"Over coffee," Kate decided.

"There are only a few places still open. Where do you want to meet?"

"Not Waffle House. If we stayed too long, I'd end up having to arrest someone. I'll meet you at Steak 'n' Shake in a half hour."

Two cups of decaf, a shared brownie sundae, and a great deal of conversation (off the record) later, Kate's sense of duty began to feel a reprieve. Spence sat in a rather rumpled suit in the corner of the booth opposite her, his long legs stretched out on the seat, black shoes dangling in the aisle.

"It doesn't sound as if there's much you could have done differently," he said.

"If I'd just been faster, like smarter-faster."

"Don't make me quote Shel Silverstein's 'Whatif' to you. I don't think I can remember it all."

"You're right." Kate smiled and flicked her finger against cup of coffee number three. "The weird loose ends still bother me though."

"What's your partner think?"

"By the time we'd finished processing everything and the hubbub from the redneck smackdown had died down, it was so stinking late that we said we'd sleep on it and discuss it tomorrow. He admits the loose ends are weird, but I can tell he's leaning toward thinking they're irrelevant. There's always stuff at the crime scene that's not actually related to the crime. It's not like TV. It's as if you're putting together a puzzle with no reference picture and extra pieces. He thinks they're extra pieces. His only concession is the wife, who is up to her eyeballs in something. Once again, though, is that *something* an extra piece or a missing piece?"

"You've got good instincts. Follow them. Are you thinking she and Innerst were in it together?"

Kate thought for a minute. "No. I mean, anything's possible, but from what dismally little I know, it doesn't seem probable. You've been wading pretty deep into the publishing pool lately; is there anything more you can tell me about these people? Any insights, please?"

Spence's handsome face split in a rueful grin, and he leaned his head back against the booth divider. "I'm sorry, but at this point, it sounds as if you know a lot more about them than I do."

"Then I guess I'll keep looking. We still haven't looked at Grant's apartment or office. Maybe some answers will turn up there. And if the missus is involved, maybe her lies will come back to bite her in the behind."

Spence laughed. "That's the spirit…I think."

"Oh, crap. I just realized I have to notify Grant's family tomorrow. I hate doing that."

"You haven't already?"

Kate shook her head. "No wife or kids; both parents deceased. We have to call his emergency contact, but nobody wants to get that phone call in the middle of the night."

Spence grimaced. "That's true."

Kate lifted her coffee cup in a toast. "Well, here's to tomorrow—" She checked her watch. "Make that today—a new day with no mistakes in it, unless you count staying up till the wee hours of the morning of your own volition on a work night."

Spence lifted his cup with a smile. "And to friends."

For the first time that day, Kate felt truly warm. "Who stick closer than a brother," she added.

They clinked cups and drank deeply.

ABOUT THE same hour in a private suite at the Peacock Hotel, Amelie Carver shuddered awake. Even in sleep was there no rest from the horror of what had happened. The fear that Nate might be dead had abated only by the ugly, ugly realization that Grant was. Blood on her floor, in her house. She still couldn't understand it. She was surprised to find she had fallen asleep at all. She had spent most of the evening in shock clinging to Nate.

She looked at the other side of the bed. Even in the dark, she could see he wasn't there. She snapped on the light, casting frantic eyes around the room as if he might be hiding in a corner. She ran to the suite's sitting room. A single lamp had been left on, and its dim orange light created an ambiance more eerie than warm.

They could have stayed with relatives, but Nate had insisted they would have greater privacy here. He knew the manager, whose discretion, he said, they could count on. But now standing alone in the middle of the elegant sitting room, Amelie was not so sure anyone could be trusted.

The beep of the key-card lock froze her where she stood. The door swung open and she screamed.

Nate fell back against the doorjamb, clutching at his chest. "Amelie! You almost gave me a coronary."

Furious and relieved, she threw herself at him. "Oh, I was so scared! Where were you? How could you leave me?"

"I just—" He had not recovered his breath yet. "I couldn't sleep so I went for a walk. You were asleep. I thought you'd be fine till I got back."

"How could you say that after what happened tonight!" She was crying again. She tried to stop, but her emotions outweighed her resolve. Nate pulled her close.

"Is everything all right in here, sir? Ma'am?" A tall, muscular man had nudged the door open further and regarded them suspiciously. His dark blue-green vest and black bow tie marked him as hotel personnel. Nate eyed the walkie-talkie in his hand.

"Yes, we're fine," he said.

"Someone reported screaming from this suite."

"Just one scream," Nate corrected. "I startled my wife when I came in the door. We've had a rough night."

The man did not seem convinced. "Ma'am, is everything okay? Can I get you anything?"

Amelie shook her head. She felt rather foolish now. "My husband's right. I'm just a little overwrought right now." She delicately wiped at her eyes with a finger. "Our apologies for the disruption. It won't happen again."

After the guard left, she sank down on a sofa. "How mortifying."

Nate knelt before her, albeit somewhat stiffly, and took her by the shoulders. "At least we know that the hotel's security is fast." His remark brought a sniffley chuckle. "I told you that nothing would happen to you."

"You weren't here," she objected.

"Trust me. I would never let anything happen to you." She collapsed into him and let his reassurances comfort her.

"There's nothing to be afraid of," he said. "It's all over now."

Chapter Forty-one

Kate regretted the lost sleep as she knocked on the door of a posh downtown apartment early the next morning, or rather later that morning. Her eyes were inclined to drift shut if she didn't concentrate specifically on keeping them open. Potter had been atypically cranky that morning and had refused to take on the unpleasant task at hand, insisting he had paperwork that had to be done.

Kate knocked again. She heard the latch turn, and a brawny guy with damp curly hair opened the door. His crisp white shirt stayed partially closed by virtue of two buttons, and a striped tie lay draped around his neck.

"Can I help you?" he asked politely.

"Kipp Wilson?"

He nodded. She identified herself and asked if she could step inside for a moment. At the sight of her badge, his eyes enlarged.

"Uh, yeah—sure," he stammered, letting her inside. "I don't have a lot of time. I'm getting ready for work. I'm not in trouble for anything, am I?" He recommenced buttoning his shirt.

"No, nothing like that." Kate waited for some magic words to come. They didn't. "You're listed as the emergency contact for Grant Innerst."

"Yeah, he's my—" Kipp stopped two buttons shy of the top. "Was he in an accident?"

"Not exactly. He died last night."

Kipp stared at her, long enough that it became uncomfortable. Then he blinked and said, "What?"

"He was shot last night. He died before EMS or the police arrived."

Kipp let out a hushed expletive as he sank onto a sofa arm. Kate offered a standard line of condolence used by the FSPD and asked if he knew of any next of kin they should notify. Kipp said there was a sister living in Connecticut. He gave Kate as much information on her as he could.

"He and his sister weren't really that close. Grant's not really very open. The closest thing he has to family here would be the Carvers. He works with Nathanael Carver at Roving House."

Kate wasn't one to ignore an open door, and since Kipp had opened this one, she walked on through.

"Ironically enough, it was Nathanael Carver who shot Grant. It appears Grant attacked him, and Mr. Carver shot him in self-defense before he even realized who it was. Mr. Carver's been getting death threats over the last year."

"That's insane. That makes no sense."

"Grant never expressed any problems with Mr. Carver? Any animosity?"

Kipp shook his head in bewilderment. "Nothing he ever mentioned. He always talked about him in a positive light…but Grant was a pretty private person. He didn't always share a lot. But he would have said *something* surely, if they started having problems…I would think."

Kate frowned. "You're one of his best friends, but he doesn't share much with you? What do you talk about?"

Kipp shrugged. "Books, movies, politics. Mostly, we play racquetball, go clubbing or out to dinner. You know, on the town."

"Is there someone else that he might have confided in more? He seeing anyone?"

"I don't think so. I thought maybe he was getting back together with Isobel, but—"

"Isobel?"

"Isobel Barringer, his ex-almost-fiancée. They broke up about a year ago, but he'd mentioned her once or twice recently, just casually. I thought maybe they were getting back together, but he said they weren't. He always clammed up, more than usual, when he was hooking up with someone. I think he liked to keep that type of thing to himself."

"Yeah," Kate said. "Some people do."

Chapter Forty-two

Grant Innerst's apartment reminded Kate of Spence's duplex: black-and-white photography on the walls, candles, and pottery but nothing that hinted at femininity and a hearty dose of masculine dusty clutter and a bathroom in want of cleaning. The refrigerator was well-stocked for a bachelor, most of it a waste now.

In the living room, Potter rooted through coats and sporting equipment in a closet while Kate sifted through the contents of the desk. She flipped through the pages of a small blue pad, the contents of which turned out to be several drafts of a poem. It started with the line *A crafty crocodile weeping in the sacred Nile*. Kate read through the entirety of the last version. She didn't consider herself a poetry person, but she liked it. It intrigued her that Grant wrote poetry, what seemed to her good poetry. The desk, however, failed to yield any other surprises.

Potter had moved on to survey the rest of the room, checking the entertainment center, the drawers of the end tables, and the space behind the books in the built-in bookcases. Kate asked if he had found anything in the closet.

"There are racquets and balls, a hockey stick, but no fishing equipment. There wasn't any in his car either. Makes it seem more likely that he bought the fishing wire solely with the intention of using it as a weapon. You?"

"He writes poetry," she answered as she tried unsuccessfully to access his laptop. "He has a password on this thing. Maybe one of the guys at the lab can get into it."

"Is there really a point?"

His back was to her, so Kate rolled her eyes. Potter's mood had not improved.

"Just looking for a why," she said.

"Wow," Potter said with about as much enthusiasm as one might muster for bran muffins. "He doesn't just write poetry." Potter drew a couple of thin volumes off a bottom shelf. *"The Daylight Ends: A Collection of Poems* by Grant Innerst and *A Monk's Indulgence and Other Poems* by Grant Innerst." Potter held them up for Kate to see.

"The last one sounds dirty," she said.

"Could be." Potter replaced the books and pulled out a few books next to them. He flipped through the tables of contents. "These are anthologies; it looks like he's published in a couple of them as well. This is all pretty impressive for someone his age."

"Our age. Well, my age at any rate," Kate said, taking a potshot at Potter, who was only a few years older. He didn't reply.

They proceeded to the bedroom, which proffered a revelation of its own.

"I have a sneaky suspicion he was expecting company last night," Kate said. The bedroom, unlike the rest of the apartment, was immaculate. Pink and red rose petals were strewn over the burgundy comforter. Two empty goblets and a bottle of unopened red wine waited patiently on a linen runner on the cherry dresser. "So how do you figure that? Knock off your mentor early in the evening and still have time for a romantic romp at home?"

"Maybe it was supposed to be his alibi, the one he obviously never got to use."

"I don't know how credible it would be as an alibi when your own best friend doesn't know you have a girlfriend."

"Maybe it's a boyfriend, hence the secret."

Kate made an incredulous face. "He sure flirts up a heterosexual storm for a gay man."

"It happens, so I hear." Potter pulled open the bedside table closest to the door. He let out a whistle. "He's got a regular treasure trove in here. Everything for contraception and more, including your classic texts on technique."

"Okay, thank you," said Kate, circling the bed to a matching table on the other side. She opened the drawer. "I think I can cast significant doubt on your gay theory." She pulled out a red teddy. "Unless his significant other is a very petit cross-dresser. It's a size 4."

Their examination of the bedroom turned up no clues as to the identity of Grant's mystery partner or to Grant's motive in the attempted murder, so Kate and Potter packed it in and headed to Roving House to check Grant's office. And what they found there, while not enlightening, did prove rather damning for the late Grant Innerst. In the bottom side drawer of his desk, in a plastic grocery bag, were a pair of scissors, a package of white construction paper, rubber cement, and the butchered remains of several issues of *Truth Will Out*.

Potter looked up at Kate from where he crouched above the drawer. "Truth will out, huh?"

"Yeah," Kate said grimly. "I just wish a motive would."

Chapter Forty-three

"What have you got there?"

Kate looked up from the legal pad she was sketching on, bemused at Potter's show of curiosity. In Kate's estimation, Potter, rather strangely for a detective, had been born without the snooping gene. He more than made up for it with a sharp mind, but still. She suddenly realized he was subtly making amends now that he was less grumpy. Lunch did that for some people. She turned the pad around so that he could see it from his desk.

"Chinese?" he guessed, looking at the characters she'd drawn.

"Or Japanese. Or Korean for all I know. It was tattooed on the neighbor's neck."

"The one that worked at Roving House?"

"Yeah."

"His name's Mason Lenkov," Potter said. Kate had resumed coloring in the characters with her pencil but paused at the information. She raised an eyebrow at Potter. "He's got two priors: drug possession for marijuana and committing a lewd act with a minor when he was nineteen."

"Upstanding citizen. Been doing some research, huh?"

He shrugged. "Things were slow while you were out at lunch. I ran backgrounds on all the neighbors. Your man, Lenkov, was the only one with a record."

"Which might explain why he flinched at me. He do any time?"

"Not to speak of. A slap on the wrist, probation. The kind of guy who's probably most dangerous to himself."

"I don't know. He looked on the scary side to me, but I go for the clean-cut boys."

"What would his connection be to the case, other than working for the same company as both Carver and Innerst?"

"I don't know," Kate admitted. She tossed the pad onto her desk. "Probably nothing. Just curious, you know. He just seems fishy."

"As much as I believe that everything is connected in a global cosmic sense," Potter said, "when it comes to casework, not everything is."

"Yes, I know," Kate said through a tight jaw. She had to curtail this conversation before Potter sank into full-scale condescension.

"I told Sergeant Polanksi we'd take over one of Kotono's cases. He and Kirkley have a lot heavier load than we do right now."

She knew what he meant—time to move on. Kate stopped the fuming process before it got under way. "You're right. Let's love our neighbors." She grabbed her coat and started toward the door. "But first I want to talk to Isobel Barringer. Maybe she knows who Grant was seeing."

Kate knew it was a slim possibility. They had checked Grant's phone records, and most of the calls had been to either the Carvers or Kipp Wilson. But Isobel Barringer was still listed in his contacts, and he had called her three times in the last month. If nothing else, she had known Grant in a capacity that no one else they had talked to had. Perhaps she could shine a little light.

Chapter Forty-four

The Barringer name, like Weston and Fulton, held significant sway around Fulton Springs—politically, socially, and of course monetarily. People in-the-know considered such families to be the movers and shakers, the pillars of the community, or the wanton Midwestern plutocracy—it all depended on one's perspective.

Regardless, they were not the type of people Kate dealt with on a regular basis, and when a case called for such interaction, it usually called for kid gloves. And with assistants, lawyers, publicists, and servants running interference, the whole process was a headache. The younger, trust-fund generation often proved more accessible. Kate hadn't decided whether that was due to their cavalier, privilege-born attitude or simply because they had not yet accumulated as many closeted skeletons as their progenitors. Probably six of one, half dozen of the other.

Thankfully, Isobel Barringer, a willowy brunette with startling cheekbones, proved neither inaccessible nor standoffish. She graciously invited Kate into her penthouse apartment atop the Empyrean, the newest and tallest building in the recently renovated section of downtown. In comparison to the Peacock Hotel, its "historic" counterpart, the Empyrean was sleek and modern. In addition to being the city's most expensive hotel, it housed several shops, a restaurant, and a spa on the ground floor and luxury apartments in its top floors, the price tag of which was staggering to someone like Kate. As she entered Isobel's home, she reflected that the only way she'd ever set foot in one of these suites was due to a case.

The open living room and kitchen were done all in white and creams. Huge windows flooded the beautiful, if not quite comfortable, space with light. It seemed as if nothing in the apartment was darker than beige. Kate surreptitiously checked to make sure she hadn't tracked anything onto the carpet. As she and Isobel settled onto matching off-white divans separated by a glass coffee table, Kate's insecurity rose, this time targeting her dress and appearance. Isobel's graceful movement and simple yet elegant fashion pointed up the mannishness of Kate's plaid button-up and khakis. She felt like a clod until she reprimanded herself that this was stupid and that she was getting distracted. Why should she care what Isobel Barringer thought of her? She would, however, paint her toenails later that night in an effort at beautification.

"Now, what can I do for you, Detective Baxter? You said this has something to do with Grant. I find it hard to believe that he's gotten mixed up in anything illegal." Isobel smoothly tucked a lock of light brown hair behind an ear that dangled a diamond earring. "He always struck me as too cautious for that."

"People can surprise you sometimes." Kate wanted to avoid dropping the death bomb for the moment.

"Yes, they certainly can," Isobel conceded wryly.

"You and Grant broke up a year ago?"

"About then."

"Someone thought the two of you might have been reconciling. Is there any truth to that?"

A laugh burst from Isobel, but before it had died, it was overtaken by a fresh wave of genuine amusement. "No," she assured Kate. "That's not the case. At least not that I'm aware of." She fixed a sharp pair of brown eyes on Kate. "Detective, I do have to ask what this is all about. You don't have to tell me everything, obviously, but you're going to have to give me a reason to open my personal life, or Grant's for that matter, to your inspection."

Kate delivered the news of Grant's death with equal candor and few details. Isobel absorbed the news in composed silence, though disbelief played upon her face.

"The night he died, it appears Grant was going to have a romantic meeting with someone. We're trying to find that person to see if she can help us understand what happened."

"Well, it certainly wasn't me." A thickening in Isobel's voice betrayed emotion.

"Do you know who it was?"

The laugh was a bit muffled this time. "No, I do not. Grant and I had started speaking again. We were even what I would call friendly, mainly because I thought I wanted him back, but we weren't so intimate that he would've shared any details on his romantic life."

"He liked to keep secrets, didn't he?" Kate's question served more as a prompt than an inquiry.

"Oh, yes." A slight bitterness edged into Isobel's tone. "He did at that." Her legs were tucked up under her on the sofa, and she ran a hand down her linen pant leg, smoothing out an invisible wrinkle. She seemed willing to share more but unsure of what to say. Kate waited.

"When we broke up a year ago," Isobel said at length, "I thought it would only be temporary. When a few weeks went by and he didn't try to make things up to me, I decided to let him off the hook and start the reconciliation. He was surprised when I showed up at his apartment. I had always told him it was unsuitable, and beyond that, I'm not a person who gives in to other people easily. We smoothed things over more or less. He did not volunteer that he had been with someone else while we were apart. And when we reconciled, it didn't stop. When I confronted him about it, he didn't deny it. He said it was nothing serious, but then he wouldn't give it up either. And I'm not the kind of woman who will share.

"I overestimated my hold on Grant. I thought because of my wealth and status and looks that he needed me. I didn't take into consideration that he could quite easily find all those things with someone else, or perhaps they weren't as important to him as I thought they were. I think the idea of a clandestine affair appealed to him. He had a very romantic nature, something I do not possess on my own, and I guess that won out over his ambition, something else he had a lot of." She gave a tight smile. "Confession is good for the soul, eh? I don't know if the woman you're looking for is the same one or not. A year can be a long time, and I never knew who she was. If I had, I would have done something about her."

I bet you would have, Kate thought. She turned her line of questioning toward Nathanael Carver to see if Isobel knew of any undisclosed tensions.

"They got along famously as far as I know," Isobel said. "Grant looked up to him, which is saying something. Grant wasn't one to idolize, probably because he was truly exceptional himself. We may not have ended well, but I would never say differently. And Grant only gave his admiration to superior things or people. I don't really know Nathanael Carver, but I know that he must be an exceptional man."

Kate thanked Isobel for her time. As they stood at the door saying goodbye, Isobel posed a question. "Who told you they thought Grant and I were getting back together?"

"Kipp."

Not a blip of recognition read on Isobel's face. "Kipp who?"

"Grant's best friend, Kipp Wilson," Kate elaborated.

"The name sounds slightly familiar, but I don't think I ever met him." Isobel gave a humorless chuckle and then sighed.

"How unsurprising."

Chapter Forty-five

That evening Kate was still pondering her interview with Isobel Barringer as she walked into the Kent Theatre at Landers University. If Grant's life were so compartmentalized that his ex didn't even know his best buddy, then who in the world could give her a cohesive picture of the guy? Had anyone really known Grant Innerst?

Such thoughts vacated as she took in the set on the main stage. A flight of shining steps covered the entire forestage and culminated in a platform, on which a soaring transparent wall, divided into thirds vertically, stretched toward the fly loft. The first and final thirds contained alcoves of transparent triangular columns flanking bubbled glass panels that distorted the view behind them. A large, open doorway was cut out of the central section of the wall. Most breathtaking was an enormous Greek bust upstage of the glass wall on the right, tilted so that it seemed to be staring down at center stage. The head had to be at least twenty feet across. Kate stood in the center aisle taking in the grandeur before moving to the front of the auditorium.

She was not there to see a play, however. She was there to collect Alexandra Hamel, one of the two women wrestling with a headless, draped mannequin in the left alcove. Once she got Alex's attention, she asked what play the set was intended for.

"*Blind*," her friend answered. "It's my adaptation of *Oedipus Rex*. We start tech rehearsals next week."

Kate's exposure to the theater world was limited, but she always thought that Alex looked as if she belonged there or at least in New York. Most of Alex's wardrobe was black, as evidenced by the shoes, pants, long turtleneck sweater, and even the frames of the glasses she currently had on. Of course, black was supposed to be slimming, and Alex did carry some extra weight, but Kate didn't think that theory was what dictated Alex's fashion taste. Alex wore her hair—a little longer, a little blonder, and whole lot thicker than Kate's—down and straight.

"*Oedipus Rex*," said Kate. "I believe I've actually read that one, at least the original."

"The struggle of fate and free will, or as you would probably put it, the paradox of predestination and free will."

Kate held up her hands. "That sounds like a debate for Heidi and Spence. And maybe Danny. I try to steer clear of controversies, religious or otherwise."

Alex shook her head. "One can never steer clear of controversy."

"Tell me about it."

"Nor should one try."

"Sounds like you're coming down on the fate side of things. Anyway, the set is beautiful."

"You can thank Lola for that. I do." Alex gestured to the black-haired young woman who had been helping set up the mannequin and was now adjusting its tunic. "She's my designer. And what she's messing with will eventually be a life-size statue of Artemis."

Lola smiled and waved at Kate. In spite of her paint-spattered clothes, haphazardly pulled-back hair, and glasses, Kate could tell that the pink-complexioned girl was more attractive than either she or Alex.

"You'd like Lola," Alex teased, deadpan. "She's like you, a Protestant."

Kate scoffed, "Oh, yes, because one Protestant is just like any other."

"Well, they're all deviations from the true Church."

"And here I thought the Catholic Church was supposed to be all inclusive-friendly nowadays. Ah, but new pope, new rules, right?"

A semi-good-natured growl rose in Alex's throat as she shook her head. "Touché," she said. "And I think that's enough religious controversy for the evening."

"Agreed. I was looking forward to a stress-free dinner tonight, not a rehash of the Reformation." Kate looked back at Lola as the designer pinned a crease in place. "Is she really a nice girl?"

"Quite."

"Maybe we could set her up with Danny." The thought had just popped into her head.

Alex paused in putting on a black pea coat. "What do you mean *we*? And Danny? You know your friends better than I, but I would think she'd be more Spence's type. When did you turn to matchmaking?"

"Oh, I just think Danny could use some encouragement—or perhaps distraction—right now. And don't underestimate him." Kate would never mention that of her tribe it was Danny who best…accepted Alex. She felt that Alex, though unknowing, should somehow reciprocate.

"I'm not saying anything against him," Alex defended herself, albeit with a touch of blasé condescension, as they left the auditorium. "Lola's a very talented visual artist, even beyond the theater; that just doesn't seem like Danny's *thing*." She sighed dramatically, her cloud of breath illuminated by a street lamp. "But there's no accounting for choice of partner anyway. I've never been able to rationalize why my father married my stepmother."

Kate deemed it wisest to say nothing.

Alex smirked. "Your silence is deafening. Anyway, I never involve myself in matchmaking or even match speculation, for that matter. As Shakespeare said, 'O hell! to choose love by another's eye.'"

"Sorry I mentioned it," Kate said dryly.

"I suppose you could bring Danny to opening night," Alex suggested as they settled into the front seat of Kate's car. "He might meet her if he came backstage with you after the show. To talk to me of course."

"Why am I friends with you? Remind me again."

"Darling, every devil needs an advocate."

KATE DREADED the arrival of the check. Alex had suggested the restaurant, which had turned out to be the kind that didn't price the menu. The shrimp and asparagus risotto had been fabulous, but Kate wondered how much damage it would deal her pocketbook. Alex wore her affluence so nonchalantly that Kate often forgot it, except in situations such as this, in which Alex took money for granted. These times brought into sharp focus that they were from different worlds and unlikely friends indeed. They had met when Kate taught a self-defense course at the university, though it still surprised her sometimes that they had maintained the connection.

That evening, the conversation had meandered around Kate's work and Alex's academic pursuits, a two-pronged MFA in playwriting and stage direction with a possible PhD in the future. Alex dutifully inquired after Kate's friends, and Kate cautiously asked about Alex's family.

"Do you know Isobel Barringer?" Kate asked. She thought that the Hamels were probably part of "that circle."

"Oh, yes. Izzy and I knew each other growing up." Kate suppressed a laugh at Isobel Barringer's being referred to as Izzy. "We went to tennis camp, that kind of thing, but we weren't best friends or any such nonsense. Why do you ask?"

"It just occurred to me that you might. I met her today. I kind of had to give her some bad news."

"Was she unkind to you?"

The question took Kate off guard. "No, why would she be?"

"Because you're not rich," Alex said without condemnation or apology. "Daddy always says, 'The greater their riches—" Alex stopped short. "Excuse me. I almost forgot your distaste for profanity. We'll just bypass Daddy's epigram, and suffice it to say that I'm glad Izzy's grown up some. And I'm sorry you had to give her bad news."

"Me too." Kate polished off her water. "Did you ever meet her ex, Grant Innerst?"

"A few times."

"What did you think of him?"

Alex knit her brow in remembrance. "Very charismatic as I recall. I remember he engaged me in this discussion on Shakespeare's sonnets, and even though I knew he couldn't plausibly be interested in me, something about him said differently." She thought a moment more. "He reminded me of a description I read in *Midnight in the Garden of Good and Evil*: 'a walking streak of sex.' Only with more class and charm than that sounds. I didn't think Izzy would hang on to him for too long. She's a lot of good things but not really exciting. I didn't think she would stand up to his vitality. He's a butterfly, someone that you're drawn to but should know better than to depend on. Why, have you met Grant as well?"

Kate admitted that she had and that by and large she agreed with Alex's distillation. "Maybe you should ditch the theater and go into profiling."

Alex permitted herself a half smile. "So all this about Isobel and Grant, am I going to be reading about it in the paper shortly?"

"Well, at least about one of them."

"Then I shall have to start reading the paper," Alex said as the waiter handed her the check. Before Kate could open her mouth, her friend said, "I've got this one. Consider it a thank-you for dinner at your place last month."

"I wish I cooked as well as the chef here does."

"Sometimes the company is more important than the cooking."

On the way back to the car, Kate pulled the tattoo sketch out of her coat pocket.

"Does the university offer any courses in Japanese?"

"You're just full of random questions tonight. Yes, it does. I know the TA who teaches the beginning course. She's from Tokyo."

Kate handed the sketch to Alex. "Could you see if she could translate that for me? One of our detectives is of Japanese descent. He was pretty sure it was kanji, but he doesn't read it. I saw it somewhere, and I'm curious as to what it means."

"Most gladly."

When Kate got home, the message light on her phone blinked a warning. She ignored it—the warning, not the light—

and listened to the messages. Her mother wanted to know if she was okay and why hadn't she returned her email? Was she coming home for Thanksgiving this year? The questions went on and on. She could hear her father in the background yelling for a hammer. Who knew what home repair project he was inflicting on the house now? Kate checked her watch. After ten, it was too late to call them back now.

Instead, she snuggled on the couch with Louis and watched an old Carey Grant movie. She had the weekend off, and Potter would be checking out their new case, a home invasion that sounded drug related. For the rest of the evening, she did not think about her parents, nor did she think about how Nathanael Carver had almost died or how Grant Innerst had. She did not think of kanji-tattooed neighbors or secret romances. Instead, she ran her fingers through Louis's long striped coat and lost herself in *Arsenic and Old Lace*. She laughed at the handsome, frantic man on the screen and those funny aunts of his who thought it a charity to dispatch lonely old men. And she prayed she wasn't as clueless as the beat cops in Brooklyn.

Chapter Forty-six

Kate tied yet another double ribbon of brown and orange around the neck of yet another cellophane baggie containing candy corn, mellocreme pumpkins, Tootsie Rolls, and peanut butter kisses. Piano music played in the background, melodious ear candy of which every track sounded virtually the same. She tugged at the mouth of the clear bag marked with orange and yellow confetti so that the neck and mouth of the bag vaguely resembled a sheaf of wheat. Very harvesty.

She looked down the kitchen table, over the little packages and the materials from whence they had come, at Heidi, who was loading up another bag with candy. With her dark red hair pulled back in barrettes and no makeup, Heidi could have passed for one of her students.

"I'm sorry," Kate said. "What were you saying?"

Heidi snorted. "I haven't said anything for about twenty minutes. I gave up when you wouldn't respond to your own name." As sore as Kate was from her altercation in the alley, teaching two sessions of kickboxing to chubby women at the Y earlier that morning had nearly wiped her out, but she had already volunteered to help Heidi make treat bags for her classes. Obviously, though, she was failing to provide substantial fellowship. "If there's something you need to do, I can handle this on my own," Heidi said.

"Sorry. I'm suffering from case preoccupation. I put it out of my mind last night, but it seeped back in this morning apparently."

"Apparently," Heidi agreed. She threw a piece of candy corn, which hit Kate in the head.

"Nice," Kate said as Heidi laughed. "You've been hanging around Danny too much."

"Only because you and Spence are too busy, and I can only do so much with the women from work before the catty backbiting drives me insane. I've actually been thinking of applying at the Christian academy in Fulton Springs. I heard they have some openings for next year. It'd mean a pay cut, but it might be worth it to work in a Christian environment."

"Be careful," Kate cautioned as she curled ribbon with a pair of scissors. "It might not be as utopian as you think. Besides, you have such good opportunities for testimony at your school."

"I know," admitted Heidi. She had even started a before-school Bible study with some of her students. "It's not just my coworkers though; public education is a sinking ship. It's bad enough that it's sinking in humanism; that can be combated. But it's also being dragged to a watery grave by politics and bureaucracy, and I have yet to find a viable method for fighting that. We were doing so much better before we became a grant school. I just need to switch to a school that will actually let me teach, public or private."

Heidi's discouragement showed in the frown lines around her mouth. She had told Kate before how the strings tied to the grant money disrupted the classroom, dictating teaching methods and continually pulling teachers out for indoctrination in the latest educational fads. The result was less productive class time with their students. Ironically, Heidi was wearing a long-sleeved girls' track-and-field T-shirt for Olivet High. Kate thought that if her friend left the school, she'd miss interacting with her current students, whether in teaching or in coaching; but maybe the frustrations were starting to outweigh the positives, and there were other schools.

Kate cinched another cellophane bag closed with ribbon. "Remind me why we're making Halloween treat bags for your students when it's not even October yet."

"They're *not* Halloween bags," Heidi corrected. "Don't make me say it again. I always pass them out the week after the leaves change color."

"I didn't think you celebrated Halloween."

"I don't—it's the high feast day of the satanic church—but I do like to do little special things for the kids. Besides, it means more when you do it at times separate from when everyone else does. It also gives me an in-road to talk about my faith if the kids ask questions. Why celebrate the leaves changing color? Because it's a demonstration of God's creativity in nature. In the words of Gerard Manley Hopkins, 'The world is charged with the grandeur of God.' We cover that poem in eighth-grade lit. And you are so not listening to me again."

Kate stopped fumbling with the ribbon she was curling. "I'm sorry," she apologized. "I just keep thinking of this guy, the one who got shot. He's so enigmatic. It's like nobody really knew him."

"Some people say that you can't ever really know another person."

"Do you believe that?"

Heidi wrinkled her forehead in faux concentration. "What is it Spence always says to you?" She dropped the pretense and held up the back of her hand and tapped it. Kate laughed.

"I think the idea that you can never know someone is baloney. Of course, a lot depends on how open we're willing to be and, on the flip side, how closely we pay attention." Heidi picked up a partially filled bag of candy and held it up. "What's in this bag?"

"Candy," Kate said, speaking to her friend as if she were mentally deficient.

"More specific, please."

"Candy corn and pumpkins," Kate amended.

Heidi cocked her head to one side. "What you just said is true. You know that this bag contains candy corn and pumpkins; however, I know this bag also contains peanut butter kisses." She turned the bag around so that Kate could see the candies wrapped in black and orange wax paper buried beneath the corn but pressed against the back of the bag. "People are not just like this, but the metaphor carries. We were looking at the bag from different sides, so we saw different things. One could argue that I saw more than you did. Some people are this transparent, and some, including the guy you're talking about, tend toward opaqueness. And everyone but the most boring people have stuff buried underneath; sometimes it's even good stuff."

"Everybody's got secrets?"

Heidi arched an eyebrow. "Don't you?"

"Only fairly benign ones."

"But—" Heidi paused for dramatic effect as she ripped open a fresh bag of Tootsie Rolls. "You still have them. Sometimes, it's not about secrets, though. Sometimes, it's the things we just don't think to share or show or whatever."

"Whatever? You run out of articulation?"

Kate got pelted with another piece of candy corn. She picked it up from where it had bounced onto the table and popped it into her mouth.

"So how do you get to know someone after they're dead?"

"You talk to the people who knew them," Heidi said. Kate rolled her eyes. "I guess that hasn't been working."

"Not so much. I've been through his apartment and office, and that's broadened the picture, but he's still a mystery, especially the *why*. That's what's plaguing me. We assume we know *what* he was there to do but not *why* he was doing it. Maybe by Monday the tech guys will have found something on his computer."

"Isn't he on social media?" Heidi asked mockingly. She disdained such things. "Surely that would tell you exactly who he really was."

Kate smiled and shook her head. "Not likely. By all accounts, he was way too private a person to participate in…what do you always call it?"

"Emotional exhibitionism. I'm guessing he didn't leave a journal or any such helpful personal record behind."

"No, at least not that we've found." Kate's mind flashed back to Grant's apartment. She saw Potter drawing books off a shelf. "Or maybe he did, of sorts."

"Okay," Heidi prompted.

"Every author is known by his works."

"That's cryptic," said Heidi.

Kate grabbed her jacket.

"I'll see you at lunch tomorrow. I need to do some reading."

Chapter Forty-seven

The story of the attack on Nate had hit all the local media the day after, and by that evening, it had spread in a minor capacity to the national news. After all, how often did editors from the same company engage in mortal combat? Eirik Boudreau was already garnering free publicity, as many articles identified Roving House as the publisher of his forthcoming book. Nate told Amelie that it was only a matter of time before the man pushed his way onto television himself to comment on the situation, of which he would know absolutely nothing.

Close friends and relatives had been in contact, and Nate and Amelie's location had been disclosed to a trusted few, some of whom had visited at the hotel suite when the Carvers quickly became unable to sift through the flood of telecommunications. From that point, their attorney ran interference for them. Nate said that as soon as another story hit, they would be forgotten, but Amelie doubted that the furor of interview requests and solicitations for "a comment" would cease anytime soon. They had been told that a couple television crews were parked on the street outside their house, awaiting their return. Nate hadn't the foresight to pack some belongings that Amelie wanted, and rather than brave that gauntlet, they had the concierge purchase the items and deliver them to their suite.

Standing at a window in the sitting room, Amelie reflected on the media circus with disgust. They'd spent less than forty-eight hours there, but it seemed to be rapidly becoming home. Staring down at the busy street through barely parted curtains, she wondered if she could brave it. She couldn't understand how

Nate had dared to venture out, even in the dark. But now she had to, because Nate had been wrong. It was not all over.

The urgency had not struck her until last evening, probably because she had spent most of Friday in a daze, having not slept at all after Nate's return from his midnight jaunt. But now ramifications of what had passed drove her to action.

Amelie moved to the open doorway to check on Nate. He slept, sprawled face-up on the bed. He'd been sleeping for about fifteen minutes. She had made sure to place her handbag in the sitting room before he lay down. He had started sleeping more during the day than at night. Out of the bag, she pulled a silk scarf and a stylish pair of overlarge sunglasses, both of which Talitha had brought her the night before in a bag full of things to ease their stay away from home. She hadn't told Talitha why she wanted them, and Talitha hadn't asked. Pictures of both Carvers from various fundraisers and gala events had been on the news. Now more than ever, she feared attracting notice.

Looking in the large, gold-framed mirror above the fireplace, she tied the scarf around her head, trying to affect a sense of style rather than the essence of a babushka. She pulled on the warm jacket she had been wearing the night of the attack, and with dark glasses in hand and leather bag over her shoulder, she stole out of the suite. She didn't breathe until she pulled the door closed behind her.

She took a set of stairs that led directly outside, avoiding the lobby. Not only did she not want someone outside the hotel to spot her as "the wife of that man that was attacked," but she also did not want anyone inside to know that she had left. Nate had slept as little as she the night before, so he would be out for a good while. She could be back before he awoke. The drive to Olivet would not take long, even in weekend traffic.

Stepping outside, she slipped on the dark glasses, thankful for the afternoon sun that shone intermittently through the clouds. Otherwise, her modest attempt at a disguise would have been ludicrous. Despite the sunny rays, the world still seemed damp and chilled from the soaking it had received. Leaves that had fallen from the plantered trees adhered slimily to the pavement, devoid of the brilliant hues they had boasted just days ago.

Amelie sped all the way to Olivet, distrustful of how secure her plan actually was. In truth, she did not have the nerves to deal with all this. How she had let things progress to this point was beyond her, but then again, could she really be blamed for what had happened? Somewhere along the line she had lost control. She would not own the events of that week.

Outside the apartment building, Amelie parked between a dark blue Crown Victoria and a white compact car a few spaces down from the entrance. She reasoned the Saab would draw less attention there than if it were parked directly in front of the entrance by itself. She had a key for both the outside entrance and Grant's apartment. Mercifully, the halls were empty. Only once had she ever had the misfortune of running into one of his neighbors.

She slipped inside. It was colder inside the apartment than outside. She realized that Grant would never come back here. Odd that the thought should wash over her at this moment, but being here without him and with that knowledge somehow distracted her. She took a breath, focused, and hurried to the bedroom. She quickly cleared out what little she had in the bedside table, stuffing the contents in her bag. Then she began the search for the most damning piece of evidence.

She did not find it in the other bedside table. She thought perhaps he had tucked it into one of the books he kept there. She searched next through the drawers underneath the clothes,
careful not to leave them disheveled. She still did not find it. Perhaps his desk? Surely he wouldn't have been reckless enough to keep it in his desk at work. Grant could be absent-minded, but never stupid.

She rushed to the living room only to stop short. Seated in an armchair at the end of the room, with the curtains pulled just enough to let in a modest swath of light, sat Detective Kate Baxter, an open book on her lap and a few more on the table next to her. She looked thoroughly amused.

"Well now, this is rather dramatic, isn't it? Although I think the Jackie Onassis outfit may be a bit too much. I'd say I'm as surprised as you, but I have the feeling that isn't quite true." The policewoman paused, but Amelie could think of nothing to say as her heart threatened to pound her insides to a pulp. "After all, I did see you zip through on your way to the bedroom, and the pieces for me had already begun to fall into place."

Amelie found her voice. "What are you doing here?" She forced some authority into the question.

"Reading." Kate held up the book. It was one of Grant's collections. "You?"

Amelie looked down to see a scrap of red satin hanging over the edge of her bag. It was obvious what she was doing there, and she unfortunately could not manufacture a plausible excuse on the spot. Fate had not gifted her thus. So she said nothing.

Book still in hand, the detective rose and took a few steps toward her. Amelie could not resist the urge to retreat a step.

"Emma Bovary didn't have a sister."

"What are you talking about?"

"The night of the attack on your husband, I asked you about the protagonist's sister, from the book you were reading for your book club. But the character of Emma Bovary didn't have a sister. I know that because I've actually read it, and you obviously haven't. And I'm guessing there is no book club, unless that's what they're calling it nowadays."

"I don't have to listen to this!" Amelie tried to sound indignant, but even to herself, she sounded scared. She turned and headed for the door.

"Is this what you were looking for?" Kate called out, stopping her in midstride.

Amelie turned her head, refusing to look eager, but what she saw made her stomach churn. Pinched between the detective's index finger and thumb was a five-by-seven of a nude young woman, whose resemblance to Amelie Carver was unmistakable.

"I found it in this copy of *A Monk's Indulgence*, which, by the way, is the racier of Grant's volumes of poetry, but I guess that would explain why he kept the photo there."

Amelie could feel her face flush. She averted her eyes to a corner of the ceiling. "May I have that back? It belongs to me."

"I'm afraid not."

"What!" Panic surged at the thought of what the detective might do with the photo.

"I have to log it, and the contents of your bag there, as evidence." Kate placed the photo back in the book and closed it. "They speak to motive, which is what I've been wondering all along—why Grant Innerst would want to kill your husband. How long had you two been planning this?"

Amelie felt the air evaporate out of her lungs. "I didn't—we never did," she choked out.

A corner of Kate's mouth crooked up in bored incredulity.

"It's some kind of mistake." Amelie's voice grew firmer. "I would never do anything to hurt Nate—"

"Like sleep with his coworker?"

"Nate didn't get hurt because Nate doesn't know," Amelie asserted, her jaw tightening. "I don't know what happened at the house, but it had to be a misunderstanding because I know Grant never would have hurt Nate either."

"Mrs. Carver, we found the magazines used to make the threats in Grant's desk at Roving House."

"That's a lie. It's impossible."

The detective's eyebrows arched. "Why is that?"

"Because he didn't write them. He promised me that he didn't."

"So you thought he did?"

"When the letters first started coming, I thought maybe he was trying to be cute."

"And after you found out they were being mailed from Olivet?"

"I asked him again. He swore he didn't send them."

"And he's essentially an honest person."

Amelie groaned. "Oh, please. One indiscretion does not make someone an evil person."

"One indiscretion," Kate snorted. "You just implied that your affair's been going on for over a year, before your husband started receiving the threats."

Amelie hadn't realized how much she'd been giving away. Her legs trembled, and she moved to an armchair to sit. Everything was unraveling.

"It was a mistake," she reiterated. "Grant must have gone to talk to Nate about something. It was dark, Nate was on edge—it was an accident."

"But wasn't Grant supposed to be meeting you here?" Kate asked. "Maybe he just wanted to get you out of the house so that he could off your husband. Or maybe you planned it together, and he was supposed to meet you here afterward to celebrate."

"That is vile and not true! I had nothing to do with any of this, and I know Grant probably better than anyone else. We shared things with each other. Like that." She indicated the photo enclosed in the book. "He's the only one who knows about that part of my life. We knew that what we had would never be…more than what it was. He would not do this."

The detective's eyes remained hard.

"Mrs. Carver, may I point one thing out?"

"What?"

"You're a liar. I've known that since the day I met you. You've lied to your husband; you've lied to me and my partner. Why should I believe anything you say?"

"SO SHE not only denied any involvement, but she tried to convince you that Grant was innocent?" Kate's account of her interview with Amelie intrigued Potter, who had met Kate back at the station that evening.

"Oh yeah," said Kate, perched on the corner of his desk. "I knew there had to be more going on here, some kind of concrete motive, and it's starting to fit together. You should have seen her reaction when I told her we'd found some of her photos on the Web."

"Not good?"

"I thought I was going to have to call EMS."

"Do you really think she was in on it?"

"I can tell you one thing: if she was, we're going to prove it." Kate set her jaw. "I want her phone records, house and cell. I want her e-mail records. I want everything. There's got to be something somewhere."

"I imagine this is going to be touchy." Potter reminded her, "She is a Weston after all, and you mentioned that she and her husband were friends with the chief. Discretion will probably be called for."

Kate stood up. "Her lover tried to kill her husband. I don't care if she's friends with the governor. We're getting to the bottom of this."

Chapter Forty-eight

Sunday proved restful. After morning service, Kate's tribe convened at Heidi's for a home-cooked dinner. Heidi's propensity toward caretaking had earned her the nickname Mama Schafer from Danny, who seemed to benefit most frequently from Heidi's maternal drive. His use of the nickname, however, usually earned him a smack on the back of the head and/or a threat to suspend such generous action. The group had concluded long ago that such threats were pure bluster. Kate had mentioned to Heidi a few months ago that if she didn't give such a big reaction to the nickname, Danny would likely stop using it. Heidi said nothing for a moment before confessing that she didn't really mind it.

"What?"

Heidi sighed. "I spend my days taking care of other people's kids. A lot of them don't get what they need at home, but there's really only so much you can do at the middle-school level and still maintain the proper teacher-student relationship. They're my kids, but they'll never be my children. They'll never be my family. You guys are my family."

Kate pointed out that Heidi had a family—her parents and two sisters lived in the area.

"Yes, but they have their own families. You guys are *my* family, see? Besides," she added wryly, "Danny may be the only child I ever have."

Kate did see, being the unmarried, childless one in her family. She didn't press the issue, but she sensed that Heidi had given up on waiting for a family of her own. Kate couldn't understand that; Heidi was younger than she was.

Thankfully, the conversation around the Sunday dinner

table was more jocular. Afterward, Kate helped Heidi with the dishes and returned home for an extended nap before the evening church service. After the service, some people from her Sunday school class invited her to join them for dessert. Such occasions were rare, so Kate felt compelled to do some bridge building.

Sunday, however, did not prove restful enough to equip Kate for dealing with Monday, which proved to be very Mondayish indeed. She woke to the gray spit of rain rat-a-tatting on her bedroom window an unhealthy forty minutes before her alarm would sound. First thing at the station, she faced an interminable staff meeting explaining the new timekeeping system. The rest of the morning she gave to the case she and Potter had inherited from Kotono. The robbery didn't merit much detective work. They arrested two young men from the victim's neighborhood before lunchtime. Kate was tempted to feel insulted that Kotono had handed them a puff case, but wrapping it up quickly allowed her to get back to studying the Carver case that much sooner.

She stood at her desk, trying to stretch out her back, which seemed to be bothering her more since Saturday. Most of the stiffness and soreness had seemed to pass, but the kickboxing had set her back a few days and now she was contemplating a visit to the chiropractor. She had had no luck implicating Amelie in the attack on her husband. The lovers seemed to have been incredibly discrete in their communications. No lurid emails, letters, or chat postings had come to light. Potter had returned to Grant's house to search there. Everything they had at the moment was purely circumstantial.

Kate eyed the papers and photos covering the surface of her desk. She'd been reviewing them for the last hour or so, committing details to memory, waiting for one to jump out as more salient than the others.

She picked up a stack of Benny's crime scene photos and reviewed them again. Benny had taken shots of the mess tracked into the kitchen. No explanation for that had surfaced yet. She looked at pictures of the body—positional shots, close-ups. She paused at a picture of the hand that Benny had taken the fishing wire from. There was a shot of the closed grasp and one in which the fingers had been pulled apart enough to see the fishing wire held inside. What Kate noticed, however, was a silver ring oddly positioned on the middle finger. It sat just above the middle knuckle. It bore some kind of carving or engraving, but she couldn't really make out what. She looked through the other photos to see if there was a clearer shot of it. There wasn't.

She was toying with the idea of checking the evidence locker—she was curious to see what the ring looked like but doubted that knowing would actually be beneficial—when Amelie Carver arrived to speak with her.

"Is there somewhere we could speak privately?" the older woman asked, looking around at the people circulating through the open office.

When they were both seated in an interview room, Amelie took a few moments more to orient her thoughts. She struck Kate as a conscientious grade-schooler preparing to take a test, tidying her scarf and purse in place of straightening her pencils. Naïveté underscored her mature beauty. Kate wondered if that almost childlike air was what in part attracted men to this woman. She also wondered if it was practiced or came naturally; perhaps it stemmed from a life of pampering. Amelie clasped her hands in front of her and gazed at them. Finally, she met Kate's eyes.

"How much are you going to tell my husband?"

Kate groaned internally. She'd been hoping for something a little less boring from the surprise visit, but people were so egocentric.

"As much as I have to, Mrs. Carver," Kate said tiredly. "I don't really understand how you expect to keep this hushed up. Your lover tries to kill your husband—"

"No, no, no," Amelie insisted calmly. "I told you there was some kind of mistake."

"Right. Do you have anything *new* to tell me, or are we just going to have the same conversation over and over?"

The look in Amelie's eyes said she knew she was being patronized, but she sloughed it off.

"I spoke with Alain Guerre on the phone this morning.

After all these years, it was lovely to speak with him. He's as charming as ever. He promised to have the photographs of me removed from that online gallery. He didn't realize I would object; in fact, he doesn't really understand why I do. He's such an artist. I never told Nate about my relationship with Alain or the modeling. It's something my family wouldn't have understood—the pictures, not necessarily the relationship—but I wasn't sure how Nate would respond. So I just never told him."

Amelie looked at Kate expectantly, and Kate wondered if this woman was as dense as she was beginning to suspect. "I'm sorry," she said, "I meant something new that was helpful. Something that would perhaps shed light on what happened on Thursday or prove that you didn't help plan to murder your husband."

Amelie's eyes iced up and her jaw jutted forth.

"Mrs. Carver, I don't mean to be rude," Kate continued. "But you can't honestly expect me to be interested in your efforts to salvage your reputation. For one, that ship has sailed. For another, I'm trying to get at the truth, and it seems to me that you have a vested interest in keeping the truth hidden. We seem to be on opposite sides, and I don't have time for chitchat."

"That's not true! I want the truth too." Amelie's words poured out in a frantic cascade as Kate rose to leave. "I just think you're not looking in the right direction. There must be some explanation for why Grant stopped by the house, maybe something to do with the office. Did you think of that?"

Kate paused at the door. "If you were interested in the truth, you would be at your hotel room telling your husband this whole sordid business and asking him to forgive you. That you came here to beg me not to tell him doesn't do a lot to convince me of your dedication to the truth, or your innocence for that matter."

Amelie followed Kate into the hall. "Have you found anything that would imply I had anything to do with the attack?" she demanded.

Kate turned to face her. "It's early yet."

"That's because I had nothing to do with it!" Amelie insisted.

"Well, my partner's at your house right now with a couple other guys going over the place with a fine-toothed comb, so we haven't given up looking."

That unsettled Amelie, but she held firm. "They won't find anything."

"Well then, I would say you don't have anything to worry about, but to be frankly honest, I don't think either of us believes that." Kate wished Potter were here to deal with this woman. "Does your husband know you're here, or did you lie to him again about where you were going?"

"He knows. I told him I was coming to see if you'd found out anything more. I convinced him that he needed to stay at the hotel and rest."

Since Amelie Carver was being so accommodating, Kate decided to ply her with a few more questions.

"Why didn't you call Grant when he didn't show up for your little rendezvous?" The last call on Grant's cell phone had been shortly after five. "Were you expecting him to run late?"

"No. I didn't call because I didn't know where he was. I thought perhaps he'd been delayed at the office." The next words she practically whispered. "We never talked on the phone in front of other people, and we were very careful about making calls period."

"I've gathered. So you just left? After you'd gone to all that work decking out the bedroom for a passionate evening?"

Amelie crossed her arms. She found this admission harder to make. "The longer I was there—without Grant—the more I started thinking that I shouldn't have left Nate. It being so soon after the attack. I called to check on him, but he didn't answer, and that's when I came back."

As Amelie spoke, Kate's own phone started vibrating. She checked to see her parents' number and with a press of a button sent the call to voicemail.

"When I got to the house and saw the police and ambulance, I knew something awful had happened to Nate. Then I saw Grant's car. I know what you think of Grant—and of me—but he would never have hurt Nate. He just saved his life earlier this week when—"

"Baxter!" Sanchez called from the end of the hall. "Phone for you."

"Take a message," Kate called back.

"She says it's important."

Kate excused herself and went to her desk to take the call.

"This is Detective Baxter."

"Why won't you take my calls?" demanded a shrill female voice.

"Mom?"

"I've been worried sick about you. I thought you might be dead in some parking lot."

Kate wanted very much to scream at the top of her lungs. Instead, with a fair amount of calm, she asked just what her mother was doing calling the station. "You know you're not supposed to call me here unless it's an emergency."

"I thought that maybe it was an emergency! I called you on Friday, and then I had your father call because I thought maybe you were mad at me. And then you never called either of us back—"

"I've been really busy, Mom. I ended up working on Saturday."

"Well, what about yesterday? Couldn't you have called yesterday?"

"Sunday's the day of rest, Mom. I was resting."

"You couldn't call your mother and rest at the same time?"

"Not by a long shot," Kate muttered through clenched teeth. Her mother didn't usually get this hopped up.

"There's no need to be sarcastic! I was worried about you, and when you didn't answer my call just now—"

"I'm working!" The words burst out loud enough to attract attention from people at nearby desks. Kate caught sight of Amelie Carver leaving the hall and heading her direction. "I'm interviewing someone for a case. Now I've really got to go. I'll call you later this week, and we can talk about how awful and negligent I am."

Kate managed to disentangle herself from the call before Amelie reached the desk. Kate swung between being internally furious and mortified. She was pretty sure the manual on being an effective cop did not recommend arguing with your mommy in front of a suspect.

"I should be getting back to Nate," said Amelie, worrying the end of her cashmere scarf with her delicate hands. "I realize that you're right, that Nate will surely find out eventually, but I can't tell him. I just can't do it. Not yet."

"Mrs. Carver, I can't imagine that it will be better or easier for him coming from someone else." Kate's eye caught the photos spread on her desk. "Before you go, perhaps you could explain something to me since you knew Grant so well." She handed a close-up of Grant's hand to Amelie. "Can you tell me what's on that ring and why Grant was wearing it there, on the end of his finger?"

Amelie took the photo as if it might bite her.

"He left his lights on," she said rather enigmatically.

"Excuse me?"

"The ring is carved in the shape of an alligator and a man. They chase each other around the finger. Grant picked it up in some little side street shop in Chicago when he was still in college. He said that depending on how you looked at it, it could be either the man chasing the alligator or the alligator chasing the man. He said the ambiguity fascinated him. He wore it all the time." Kate recalled the poem she had found on Grant's desk. Amelie gently tapped a finger against Grant's ring finger in the photo. "On that finger," she continued. "But he would switch it to his middle finger as a reminder to turn his car lights off. He was always leaving them on otherwise. When he stopped at the house, he must have left his car lights on."

Amelie handed the photo back. "You see, I really did know him," she said in a low voice. "I didn't love him like my husband, but I did love him. It wasn't just about sex."

Kate's annoyance with Amelie Carver began to give way to wonder—wonder at how ardently this woman desired to justify what in Kate's eyes would always be unjustifiable.

"I told you he didn't go there to kill Nate." Amelie's features smacked of self-assurance or, in Kate's opinion, self-delusion. "It doesn't make sense to leave your car lights on when you're sneaking into someone's house to murder them. Grant wasn't stupid."

Kate almost didn't have the heart to tell her. "You're wrong, Mrs. Carver. His car lights weren't on."

The assurance on Amelie's face squinted into skepticism. "That doesn't make sense." She pointed at the picture now back on Kate's desk. "Your photograph says otherwise."

After Amelie Carver left, Kate stared at the photo and considered how much weight Amelie's testimony deserved. She should at least check with Potter, perhaps Benny, about the car lights since they'd arrived on the scene before her. She couldn't see how it would be important, but maybe they could shine some light on the situation. She grunted a mirthless chuckle at her poor pun.

As close as she could tell, the section of the ring visible in the photo showed the mouth of the alligator—or crocodile, in the poem it had been a crocodile—and the feet and legs of the man. Whatever Grant's crocodile had been an incarnation of—lust or ambition or something yet untapped—it had gotten the better of him. It had wept its tears in the Nile until Grant had ventured out just far enough, and then it had eaten him whole.

Chapter Forty-nine

"It really is getting too cold to do this," Danny puffed as he and Kate came to the end of their Tuesday morning run in the park.

"You've said that like five times already," Kate pointed out. She restretched in the sharp, chilled air.

"Repetition aids learning." Danny mirrored her actions. "Has the point gotten through yet?"

"I don't like running on a treadmill."

Danny had been pushing for a move to either the Y or a health club. Now he groaned and flung himself backward onto the ground, only to stand up immediately and begin jogging in place. "It's too cold to stand still."

"You are such a weenie."

"Sorry. I didn't realize I'd picked Helga the Viking Warrior Maiden for my running partner."

"Just wait till the snow starts."

"You've got to be kidding me." Danny started in on his speech about how running in the cold was bad for your lungs but stopped when he saw Kate was too busy checking her phone to listen. "You're not listening to me."

"I know. I've gotten bad about that. Hold on a minute."

"What's so important?"

"Alex was supposed to text me something." And she had. The succinct message gave the answer to Kate's kanji question: *it means blood song.*

"You're making a face," Danny observed.

"Does the phrase *blood song* mean anything to you?"

Danny stopped revolving in a circle but kept jogging in place. He cocked his head way over to one side. "Yes," he said slowly. "Why do you ask?"

"Just tell. Pretty please."

"It's a kick-butt graphic novel. I have a copy. The sequel was better though."

This literary turn bemused Kate since Danny wasn't a big reader. "So is a graphic novel one that's filled with sex and violence? And if so, why are you reading it?"

Danny stopped moving. "No," he said derisively. "You are so unhip."

"I'm pretty sure using the word *unhip* is unhip."

"Regardless." Danny waved her point away. "A graphic novel tells its story *graphically*, with pictures. They have words too, of course, but the emphasis is on the art."

"So it's a comic book," Kate deduced.

"No," Danny objected, "they're not! Some of them are *like* comic book anthologies or miniseries, but some of them have no root in the superhero vein. Some aren't even fantasy."

"And what kind do you have?"

"The superhero, fantasy kind," Danny stated without defense.

"That's what I thought. So *Blood Song* is one of these graphic novels?"

"Yeah, it's kind of a vampire-opera thing."

"Like a vampire soap opera? Is it a *Twilight* thing?"

"No! It's nothing like *Twilight*. It's not a copycat. Think more like vampires meets *Phantom of the Opera*. I know it sounds stupid, but really it's not. If you wanna come back to my place, I can show you."

Danny had set a brisker pace than usual, due to the cold, so Kate figured she had the time.

"It's the first book in the *Immortal Arts* series," Danny explained as he pulled a shallow box from underneath his bed. "The second book is called *Blood Portrait*, and the third is due out this spring."

"Let me guess, *Blood on Stage*?"

"Cute. No." He removed the lid from the box, revealing his stash of graphic novels. "It's supposed to be called *Blood Chronicle*." He sifted through his modest collection, which, as he intimated, comprised mostly Justice League and Superman books, until he found *Blood Song*. He thumbed through the novel, which was substantially thicker than a regular comic book, showing it to her. "See, it's only three colors: black and white and red, but because they use varying shades and because the art's so awesome, it doesn't make it boring or anything."

As with poetry, when it came to illustration, Kate didn't consider herself an expert, but the book seemed expertly done to her. She took it from Danny and flipped through a few more pages. Danny was right about the color: the minimal variance accented the bold, sharp style of the art, and the deepest and brightest red was mostly reserved, of course, for blood. She turned another page to find a frenzied bloodbath.

"A little gruesome, isn't it?"

"Yeah, I suppose, but I mean it's vampires, so you kind of expect that."

Kate arched an eyebrow at him.

"Do not tell Heidi about this," he said solemnly. "She already gives me enough grief for being an oversized kid."

Kate held back a laugh. "Don't worry. Your glorified-comic-book-collection secret is safe with me. And don't let Heidi fool you," she added. "She likes you just the way you are."

She closed the book and stopped short when she saw the authors' names on the cover: Travis Buchanan and Mason Lenkov.

"Helloo?" Danny drew her out of staring at the cover.

"Sorry. I'm just a little surprised. I met one of the authors recently."

"Cool!"

"That's where I saw *Blood Song*; he has it tattooed on the back of his neck in Japanese. When you said it was a graphic novel, I figured he must have been a fan. I never would have guessed he was the author. I'm not sure which thought disturbs me more."

"Which author?"

"Mason Lenkov. He lives over near Inoca Park."

"I didn't even know they were local. Can you get me an autograph?"

Kate laughed. "I don't think so. He wasn't very polite, and I don't think he'd favor seeing me again."

"Oh, c'mon," Danny egged. "Do you realize what an autograph would do to the market value of this puppy?" He tapped the issue Kate still held in her hand. "Plus, it would be totally cool. What artist doesn't enjoy meeting a fan?"

"They exist. Not a good idea, Danny, trust me. Can I see the sequel?" Maybe she could distract him from his request.

Danny dug *Blood Portrait* out of the box and handed it over. "I'm telling you, it's a great idea. You have an in already. Nobody'll care if you got off on the wrong foot. I'll do all the talking, and you know I can talk. I'm a likable guy."

Kate thumbed through the sequel while Danny pushed his plea. It didn't take long for her to tune him out. Rather than centering on an opera singer as the first book did, this one dealt with a portrait artist, but some of the vampire characters Kate recognized from her cursory review of the first book. She flipped to the back looking for author blurbs, but the last page of art arrested her attention.

"Who's this?" she interrupted Danny.

"Ameretat. She's kind of like the queen of the vampires. They just introduced her in the end of this book, kind of a minor character, the type of thing where they talk about her throughout the book but she doesn't show up until the end. Why do you ask?"

"She's very well drawn."

"Well, yeah, the whole thing is. The storylines are pretty decent too, for vampire stories. So whaddya say? Are you gonna take me to meet him?"

"If you let me borrow these, I'll see what I can do."

Danny looked at her warily. "Are you serious? You'd have to be really careful with them. They aren't cheap."

Kate promised to take good care of Danny's books and that she'd give serious consideration to taking him to get them autographed. She would indeed. It would be a convenient excuse to pay the artist another call. Something was going on with Mason Lenkov. The art on the last page led Kate to believe that her initial twinges of suspicion about him were correct, and she wouldn't be surprised at all when his secrets led back to the Carver household, for the artfully drawn Ameretat bore a remarkable resemblance to Nathanael Carver's wayward wife.

Chapter Fifty

Stuck in a car with little to do other than eat an incredibly late lunch and watch the front of an empty house, Kate thought this might be an opportune moment for some partner bonding.

"You know," she said around a bite of a tepid hamburger, "When you came to the station, for the first several weeks—I don't know, maybe even months—I thought Potter was your last name." Kate sat on the passenger side, her feet up on the dash so that her knees almost touched her chest.

Potter swallowed a bite of his own sandwich before responding. "Yeah, I get that a lot."

"I'm sure I must have heard your last name when you first came, but it just went out of mind."

Potter bit off half a french fry.

"So is Potter like a family name?" Kate tried again.

"It's my mother's maiden name."

"I've heard of that being done."

Then extraordinarily, Potter volunteered personal information. "When my parents got married, my mother wanted to keep her maiden name, but my father was totally opposed to the idea. They fought about it a good deal, but eventually she yielded. She said that marrying him was more important than getting her own way."

"Well, that sounds loving."

Potter shot her a look. "Story's not over. When I was born, they had picked out a name together, something common—Jacob or Jeremy, I forget what. Anyway, my father was out of town on a short business trip when my mom went into labor early. She took advantage of his absence and gave me her maiden name to…get a bit of her own back."

"Wow." The two partners lapped into silence. "We're not really bonding here, are we?"

"Nope."

Well, she had tried.

"This is a ridiculous stakeout," Potter said.

"I couldn't come up with any better options, and you weren't volunteering any either."

"I didn't say the idea was ridiculous, just the stakeout. Seriously, wouldn't you agree?"

Kate looked out her window. "Yeah, if you put it like that. Perhaps it wouldn't seem so stupid if you didn't think of it as a stakeout. Just think of it as waiting."

They were parked in the Carvers' driveway, watching the Thompsons' house, waiting for the dogsitter. Even though Potter was helping her to continue the investigation, Kate knew his patience was straining.

"You're partially to blame, you know," Kate said.

Potter checked his watch and replied, "This is your idea. The kid better have something good." He stretched back and closed his eyes.

Both were right: the "stakeout" was Kate's idea, but it was inspired by what Potter had told her that morning. Rather than asking him point-blank about the lights on Grant's car, she had asked him to describe the street and the front of the house at the time of his arrival. Most of his description had meshed with what Kate herself remembered, including the lights to Grant's car being off, but one little detail had excited her. Potter remembered a red bicycle propped against the steps of the Thompsons' house, a bicycle that had not been there when Kate arrived.

Unfortunately, the Carvers had not known the identity of the dogsitter, nor had they known where the Thompsons were staying in Florida or how to contact them. If their possible witness was a teenager, as Kate suspected, he would be getting out of school anytime now, and Kate was guessing this would be his first stop. Little Beau would be more than ready to be let out.

They'd been waiting for a half-hour when Potter's phone rang. The conversation was brief, and for Kate's hearing, consisted mostly of nebulous expressions such as "how very interesting" and "no, that's very helpful." Potter's report afterward compensated by being far more enlightening.

"That was the crime lab. I took Benjamin with me when I went back to Carver's house. Thought maybe we should have a more thorough look at the mess by the back door."

"What did they find?"

Potter's face squinted and grinned in an odd contortion of amusement and consternation. Kate could hear a telepathic drum roll. "Mason Lenkov's fingerprints on the inside of the kitchen door, specifically on the doorknob."

"That *is* very interesting! See, I told you there's more going on here."

"It would seem you are right," he conceded.

But before they could discuss the new information further, a shaggy-haired kid, about fourteen, rode a red ten-speed through the front yard to the Thompsons' door.

"Same red bike?" asked Kate.

"It was dark, but I think so."

The kid dismounted and threw a wary glance in their direction as he hitched up his jeans so that his drawers no longer showed beneath the hem of his windbreaker and then ran up the steps.

Good, thought Kate, he's somewhat observant. She and Potter nonchalantly vacated the car.

"Hey there!" she called out, stopping the kid before he got through the door. "Are you taking care of Beau?"

"Yeah," the kid called back. He stayed at the door and left his hand on the doorknob. Beau yipped up a frenzy on the other side.

Kate introduced herself and Potter, letting the boy examine their badges, and then asked his name, which was Colin Wigley. Throughout the exchange, Beau's racket did not abate.

"Colin, why don't you get Beau, and you and I can take him for his walk?" she suggested. "I just have a few questions to ask you. No big deal."

Colin agreed but not without hesitation. His caution struck Kate as smart. Potter rolled his eyes and got back in the car. On their walk, she started with some background small talk, asking what grade Colin was in, how he knew the Thompsons, whether he had watched Beau for them before. They paused as Beau investigated and then relieved himself on a corner stop sign.

"You usually let Beau out right after school?"

"Yeah," said Colin, a bit more relaxed with Kate now. "Right before and right after."

"I ask because my partner thought he saw your bike last Thursday parked out front later, like around five-forty."

"That was the night all the police cars came, right?"

Kate nodded encouragingly.

"Yeah, I got detention that day, so I had to stay after school. I forgot about Beau when I got home. When I remembered, my mom wouldn't drive me over because she was mad I got detention *and* because I forgot the dog, so I had to ride my bike in the rain. But we live on Crescent Street, so it's not that far. The stupid dog had pooped all over the living room."

Colin jerked on Beau's leash to get him moving again as they walked back toward the house.

"Did you hear the gunshots?"

"Yeah, but I didn't know that's what they were. Friday, I saw on the news that that guy was shot. My mom totally freaked about it. I told the kids at school I was next door when it happened, but most of them don't believe me. Just my friends."

"It's good to have friends. Why didn't you stay and talk to the police that night?"

Colin shrugged. "Well, I really didn't see anything. I didn't even know what happened. Besides, I was cleaning up dog poop when it did. Trust me, my mom kept asking me over and over if I saw anything. She wanted me to come talk to you guys, but Dad said if I didn't see anything, it was pointless."

"Did you look outside when you heard the shots?"

"Yeah, just for a second. Beau, get away from there!" Beau had started rooting in someone's rosebushes. Colin shortened his leash.

"What did you see?" Kate asked. She didn't want the interchange to get derailed.

"Nothing, just a car in the driveway."

"Can you describe the car to me?"

"It was small. I don't know what kind. It wasn't a sports car. I think it was black, but it was kind of dark. There wasn't anybody inside, but the lights were on."

Chapter Fifty-one

*D*oesn't make sense. Kate had a long list of things related to her case under that heading. Foremost was why Grant's car lights were *on* during the attack and *off* afterward. Amelie Carver had a point: leaving the car lights on while executing the murder didn't make a lot of sense. Was Grant that slipshod? Or perhaps just that arrogant? And why had Grant saved Carver earlier in the week when he'd been attacked by Julio Ambris? Why not let Julio do the work for him?

Of course, Kate also wondered what Mason Lenkov's prints were doing on the inside of the Carvers' back door. How long ago had he been there? Had he made the mess found in front of that door? Who had left the door unlocked? And how could any of this even relate to the case? She could hardly see Lenkov as a conspirator with Amelie or Grant. Could she?

She knew this much: he had lied to her about just getting home. His house had been lit up and well heated, and he had been half stripped. So why had he lied, and more importantly, was it relevant?

Kate was mired in her own personal game of twenty questions and felt like she was losing. One last question still bothered her, one concerning Grant, and it had led her back to Roving House, where the night watchman, who patrolled not only this building but several others on the block, was letting her in.

She thanked him and, as they rode the elevator up together, asked if people at the company usually worked this late.

"Oh, no—not unless they're all here for a deadline. It's kind of an all-or-nothing thing for the most part. Only the higher-ups have keys to get in after hours. If somebody forgets their purse or something, they have to call me to let 'em in."

"I just wondered because outside I could see lights on upstairs."

"That's the cleaning crew. They come in at night, empty the trash, clean the bathrooms and stuff while everybody's gone."

Kate wanted to go through Grant's office again. Potter had been back over the Carvers' house and Grant's apartment but not the office. That one last question on Kate's mind was, Why would Grant Innerst compose the threats to Nathanael Carver at his office when he could have more easily done it at home? He lived alone and would have virtually no chance of being discovered there. Yet this was where they had found the materials. Even taking into account what the guard had said about the limited number of employees with after-hours access, it didn't make sense to Kate, especially given that they'd been mailed from his neighborhood. Unless it was the risk. Could it have been the thrill of writing the threats right under Nathanael Carver's nose, or at least the floor below? That might fit the picture of Grant that Kate had been able to assemble; however, to her, it still seemed the stupid option.

While the security guard watched with great interest and a myriad of questions, Kate snapped on her latex gloves and researched Grant's desk. She was even able to search through his computer files and email this time, having obtained his passwords from the Roving House IT guy, although she didn't find anything connected to the attack on Carver. She didn't even find much from or about the affair, just a few vague messages. Amelie had been right; they had been circumspect in their communication, if not in anything else.

After she had finished up and assured the watchman that passing the police academy wasn't as easy as he thought, she flagged down one of the custodians who were still bustling about. It turned out that the cleaning service didn't necessarily use the same people for the same buildings from night to night. The crew supervisors, however, did not rotate, and once Kate tracked down the one for Roving House, she asked again whether many or any of the employees of the publisher worked this late. She asked specifically about Grant Innerst, whom the custodial supervisor didn't even know. She pointed out the office.

"Not usually. But the banged-up guy's been here late at night for about a week."

"The banged-up guy?"

He pointed up. "The one on the third floor, bandages and bruises on his face."

Kate went upstairs, and sure enough, Nathanael Carver sat typing away in his office, a little lit cube in the otherwise dark third floor. Kate approached and stood in the doorway.

"You—" She broke off as Carver jerked violently back, so much that it startled her as well. "Sorry, I didn't mean to scare you," she said, simultaneously trying to suppress her laughter.

Carver sighed and laughed a little himself. "That's all right. It even happens when people are here working. I tell all my employees to approach with a certain amount of noise."

"What I was trying to say was that you were the last person I expected to find here."

Carver waved his hand over some papers on his desk. "I had a book to finish editing. I can't afford to fall behind schedule. Then the compositor and proofreaders would either be rushed or fall behind as well, and we'd miss our slot at the printers and have to delay the release of the book, which is already being publicized. Or we'd have to pay for a rush printing, which would be almost as bad." Carver leaned back in his chair with a small stretch. "But it's finished now."

"Is this Eirik Boudreau's book?"

"Yes, order your advanced copy today."

Kate smiled. "I'll think about that, but having met the author recently, I'm not sure I could say I'm a fan. Why not come in during the day?"

"It's easier to avoid attention at night. The publicity has died down a little bit, but it's still there. Plus, I'm really not looking forward to dealing with everybody here after what happened with Grant, especially not all at once. It was next to impossible getting any work done after I got attacked by that

Mexican guy. I can't imagine what my return after this will be like. Everybody wants to see you, talk to you."

Kate nodded.

"Why are you here? If I may be so inquisitive."

"I was going through Grant's office again to see if I could turn up anything new."

Carver frowned. "Why?"

"We're just going over all the sites again," Kate said non-committally.

"I'd heard you'd been back to the house. Amelie still balks at the idea of going back home, but I'm hoping it won't be much longer. The Peacock's room service is excellent, but I get cabin fever. Another reason to come here at night."

"Speaking of your house, do you know Mason Lenkov from the art department here?"

"Not terribly well, but yes, I know him. He's the cover designer for this book." Carver tapped the manuscript pages on his desk. "But what does he have to do with our house?"

"Has he ever been over to your house?"

"Actually, he was just there the afternoon before the attack. He brought by some designs to show me."

"Did you look at them in the kitchen?"

Carver laughed in amazement. "How did you know that?"

"We found his prints on the inside of the back door, but he must have just touched it when he was in the kitchen with you."

"Yes." Carver elongated the word ever so slightly, his eyes thoughtful. "You must be right. He was talking in the kitchen with Amelie when I got home."

"Well, that's at least one question we have an answer to."

Kate bid the editor good night and, even though it was late and she was tired, opted for the stairs rather than the elevator. She desired physical movement and was in no rush to get back to an empty house, her mood in the midst of souring. She cogitated over her doesn't-make-sense list, unwilling to scratch Mason Lenkov completely off yet. Carver had seemed a little...unsettled? disturbed? at her revelation. Why if the explanation was logical?

She exited onto the street. The late-night air chilled her face. She moseyed back to her car in the parking garage and then on impulse climbed up to the third level where Julio had attacked Carver. Good ol' Julio had finally made bail and was awaiting his day in court. Kate slowly walked to the site of the attack. Of course, no blood remained now, no sign of struggle—well, that was not quite true. This patch of concrete had been scrubbed down so it was actually cleaner than the surrounding area. Kate stood there trying to divine some answers to her questions, as if the spirit of Grant Innerst had chosen to hover over the spot that marked his heroism. Then she realized she was wasting precious time that could be spent sleeping.

As she pulled out of the garage, a tiny orange glow in the attendant's booth caught her eye. She looked over to see him exhale through the screened window. He smiled and waved. Her eyes followed the cigarette in his hand as she absentmindedly returned the greeting. She deserved a smoke, to compensate for her current frustrations. Suddenly she remembered that she still owed her mother a phone call and that it would be an ugly one. Boy, did she ever deserve a smoke.

On the way home, she made the mistake of stopping at a gas station. Stopping wasn't really a mistake because, after all, she did need gas. She wasn't so non-self-aware as to not recognize her own rationalization, even in process. But looking at the cigarettes—there wasn't really a way to sugarcoat that mistake. If she bought them, she would have to tell Danny. He'd been true to his word about checking up on her, and she wouldn't lie.

"Did you need something else, honey?" asked the amorphous, unkempt woman behind the counter. A lit cigarette jutted out from between the woman's first two stained stubby fingers. She raised her other hand to her haggard face to receive a sticky, wracking cough.

Kate could almost hear Danny's voice: "Now why don't you ever see someone like that on a cigarette ad?"

Kate smiled politely. "No, just the gas. Thank you."

AMELIE WOKE when Nathanael entered the room.

"I wish you wouldn't go out late like this."

"Well, there's nothing to worry about anymore, is there?" he reminded her, although since speaking with the detective earlier, he was less convinced of that. He sat on his side of the bed but didn't move to undress. "When that designer came by the house, did he come in the front door or the back door?"

Amelie clicked on a lamp but shielded her eyes from its light with a hand. "The front door. Why?"

"I was just thinking about that mess the detectives found by the back door."

"Wasn't it just grass and water? Who knows how it got there. Maybe one of the police people tracked it in."

"Did he go over by the door?"

Amelie pushed herself into a sitting position. "Mason? I don't think so. Why are you thinking about this now?"

"No reason. I keep thinking about everything that happened that night. Don't worry about it. I'm sorry I woke you."

Amelie turned out the light, leaving Nathanael in the dark with the ripening suspicion that they weren't so safe after all.

Chapter Fifty-two

Even though the editor hadn't been around Roving House since the shooting, the thought of going up to Nathanael Carver's floor disquieted Mason. But when he'd suggested to Ricky that Bob, or whatever-his-name-was, could come down to the art department just as easily, Ricky had told him to get off his lazy keister and get up there. He had actually used the word *keister*.

When Mason walked into the third-floor open office, his stomach knotted up. Nathanael Carver was working in his office. He hadn't been there for days; why was he here now? Mason turned around to go back downstairs. He would just email the other designer to come talk to him, and Ricky could just go—

"Mason!"

Mason didn't move.

"Over here!" the tenor voice called again. Mason turned to see a chubby guy with an all-but-gone hairline waving at him as if he couldn't clearly see where the guy was. Mason started toward the cubicle, hoping the dork would shut up before he drew attention to him. As he walked, Mason glanced toward the office to see if Carver had heard. He had. He was looking at him. Mason swore to himself and ducked into the compositor's cubicle, whose short walls offered insufficient visual defense.

The guy, whose name *was* Bob, chattered about how great Mason's cover design was while he brought up the files. It was totally uncool to have someone so lame tell you how cool your work was. Once the files were up, Mason showed Bob which elements could easily be pulled into an interior design for the book. Bob turned out not to be quite as big of a moron as he'd anticipated, so he didn't have to tell him how to put them together. The body font had already been set, but they discussed what typestyles to use for the headers, title page, and so forth. There was so little to it that Mason decided book designers must want to shoot themselves from boredom. All the fun was in doing the cover.

Mason found it difficult to focus on their conversation though, because he would occasionally take a peek at Carver's office and the editor watched them constantly. Mason left the third floor unnerved. Back at his desk, Kassie tried to comfort him.

"Is everything okay? You've been kinda jumpy lately." Her head lolled to one side, accentuating the slenderness and length of her neck. Her skin was so pale. She said tanning beds caused cancer and that spray tans were for posers. He decided she might make a good model for the vampire books. He could picture someone leaning in for a bite of that neck. He wouldn't mind doing it himself. He shook his head clear.

"Got a lot on my mind." He wasn't good with too much to think about. It addled him. He couldn't focus, just fret. One thing at a time, he could do that. That's what his mom always used to say, *One thing at a time*.

"I did something stupid," he blurted. "And now I don't know what to do."

Her eyes got all big and compassionate. "Aw, I'm sorry. Can I help?"

He shook his head, then changed his mind. If Carver was back at work, he might be back in their house too. For the moment, he wanted as much space between him and Carver as possible.

"Can I stay at your place tonight?"

"Sure thing."

She wrapped an arm around his shoulder, and even though they were at the office, Mason didn't mind.

Chapter Fifty-three

"The grass is long," Kate observed as she and Danny walked up to Mason Lenkov's front door.

"Fascinating," said Danny.

"More than you realize."

As she knocked on the door, Danny stood behind her, jiggling about, holding both of his volumes of *Immortal Arts*.

"Would you hold still? Do you want him to think you're an idiot?"

"I'm nervous, and I've had entirely too much coffee today."

The young man who opened the door was not Mason Lenkov. His stylishly haphazard hair and scruff of beard were light brown. He wore dark-framed glasses, flip-flops, cargo pants, and a tweed sports coat over a T-shirt that declared "Models Wanted" in fuchsia letters. Kate also noticed a distinct lack of facial jewelry.

"Is Mason home?" she asked.

The guy smiled. "No, I'm sorry, he's not, but he's definitely popular today. You're the second person to come looking for him."

"I met Mason last week and wanted to introduce my friend to him. Do you know when we might catch him?"

The guy shook his head. "I'm his roommate, but I just got back into town on Friday and I haven't really seen much of him since then. He's kind of hooked up with some girl from work, so I think he's spending a lot of time at her place. How'd you guys meet?"

Kate introduced herself and explained that she'd been investigating an "incident" in the neighborhood.

"The shooting? I read about that. It was the house right

behind ours. Crazy!"

"Do you know the couple who lives there?"

"No clue. My name's Travis, by the way."

He held out his hand. As Kate reached to shake it, she received a sharp nudge from Danny, who'd been silent up till now.

"Travis Buchanan?" she asked.

He nodded, somewhat surprised, and Danny took over, holding up his books. "I'm kind of a fan." He spoke rapidly, "I was hoping Mason would autograph these for me. I didn't know you guys were roommates or local even. Would *you* sign them?"

Travis laughed. "Sure. Come on in, and I'll find a marker."

"Is it just the two of you? Kind of a big place for just two guys," Kate commented as she looked around the living room. It smelled quite stale.

"We use the extra rooms for a studio and an office," Travis explained, coming back from the kitchen with a Sharpie. "Sorry about the mess. I haven't had a chance to clean up since I got back. I've been out a lot too."

"Could I see your studio?" Danny asked as Travis autographed his books.

"Well, it's not mine technically; it's Mason's. The office is mine. He does all the artwork, and I do the writing. Then we hire a couple guys to do the inking and the lettering. But I don't think he'd mind. We've shown it to the two or three other fans who've managed to find us." Travis evidently was enjoying the attention. He clapped Danny on the back. "I'll even show you some drawings we have for the next book. Mason did them while I was gone."

"Awesome."

"Your jacket's torn," Kate interjected from where she stood by a row of pegs in entryway. A black, lightweight jacket had a serious gash below the elbow.

"Oh, that's not mine. It's Mason's."

"I have a friend who sews, if he can't find someone else to patch it up," she said.

Danny caught her eye with an incredulous look behind Travis's back and mouthed the word "random." But what Kate had actually been thinking about was the fresh scrape on Mason's arm when he had come to the door that night. She looked across the room and through the glass sliding doors that led to the backyard. She could see the second story of the Carvers' house over the privacy fence.

She followed Travis and Danny upstairs, only half-listening to their conversation. Travis showed Danny into the small studio as Kate surveyed the other doors. The one directly in front of the stairs was probably a bathroom or closet. Another was open, and inside she could see, amidst clothes scattered on the floor, some open luggage: Travis's room. And he was the one who was going to clean up? She turned her attention to the two remaining doors. One was barely ajar; the other, closed completely.

She went for the closed door, asking loudly in her most innocuous voice, "Is this your office?"

Travis's head poked into the hall. "Oh—wait—no, that's Mason's room. He doesn't like people…in there." Travis's words died out as he, with Danny behind him, now stood in the doorway and could see what Kate saw.

One wall of the chaotic room was papered in Amelie Carver. Drawings showed her in various states of dress or undress. The nude images showed a certain amount of imagination as they did not correspond entirely with Alain Guerre's photographs. But Mason had photos of his own—albeit of a more amateur and candid nature—posted on the wall between drawings. Binoculars and a large camera perched guiltily on the corner of the nightstand next to the window.

"Wow," Travis said. "This is not good."

"No," Kate agreed, "not good."

BACK IN the car, Danny asked, "I'm not going to get Mason Lenkov's autograph, am I?"

"It's not looking likely," Kate said.

"That's okay. I really don't think I want it now." He held up his *Immortal Arts* books. "In fact, these may go on eBay tonight. I'm kinda creeped out."

"That's understandable."

Kate pulled around the block.

"Where are we going?"

"I need to check something while it's still light out."

"Well, you're going to have to hurry."

She pulled into the Carvers' driveway. She grabbed some gloves and an evidence kit and, with Danny in tow, went around to the backyard.

"Are we detecting? What are we looking for?" he asked as she looked around the door leading into the kitchen.

"Don't touch anything!" she commanded.

She crossed to the fence. Peering through the narrow slats, she lined herself up with the sliding doors of Mason's house, and with the help of a lawn chair, she examined the top of the fence until she found what she was looking for, a shred of black fabric wedged between two boards.

"I WENT detecting with Kate today," Danny boasted at dinner.

"Really?" asked Spence as he plucked a breadstick out of the basket on their table. He raised his eyebrows at her. "She never takes me detecting."

She smacked him playfully on the arm. "Come off it."

"Whatever," said Danny. "You go to crime scenes all the time. She told me you were at the bank robbery last week."

Danny went on telling about his adventure with as much detail as Kate would permit while the group waited for Heidi to arrive from her volleyball match. The dinner became celebratory when she arrived and announced that both the JV and varsity teams had won.

As dinner wound down, Danny asked if anyone wanted dessert. Everyone passed on the grounds of either being too full or the hour being too late.

"It's not too late," he objected.

"Danny, I have school tomorrow," Heidi reminded him. "I have to be up earlier than you."

"Okay," he relented. "I've been staying up too late anyway. I'm becoming addicted to late-night TV."

"Why?" Kate asked.

"I don't know." Danny shrugged. "It started with not being able to sleep, so I'd watch TV till I got tired, and now it's like I'm used to watching TV at those times; it's habitual."

"What are you watching?" Spence asked.

"Well, there's a *Law & Order* on at eleven, and they rerun *Buffy* at one."

Kate shook her head. "You and your vampires."

"So what do you watch at twelve?" Spence asked.

"I usually channel surf. The problem is there's absolutely nothing on at twelve. It's all infomercials and really bad reality programming, like *Cheaters*."

Spence and Kate groaned, but Heidi didn't know what the program was.

"It's this reality show," Danny explained, "where they interview people who think their partner is cheating on them, and then they investigate the cheater and show the confrontation." He turned to Kate. "Hey! You could go work for them."

"Funny."

"I thought you didn't watch it?" Spence challenged.

"Sometimes I watch the showdowns."

"How humiliating!" said Heidi. "Why would anyone do that on television? Really, don't they already know? If they're willing to go to these *Cheaters* people, they must already know."

"Knowing something and having evidence are not the same thing," said Kate. "I speak in a professional capacity."

"Heidi's right, though," Danny said. "They already know; otherwise, they wouldn't be there, yet they still get so angry—and frequently violent—in the showdown. My question is, why fight over someone who doesn't really care about you? I say cut 'em loose."

"Some people don't view their adultery that way," Kate said, thinking of her conversations with Amelie Carver.

"I imagine it has more to do with pride than anything else," said Spence. He was looking for something on his phone. "We've been studying the book of Proverbs at church, and this reminds me of something, if I can find it."

"One of those news shows, *Dateline* or *20/20*, aired a program on adultery a while back," Heidi interjected. "They talked about how rampant cheating was. They had this woman on—I can't remember how many times she'd been married, but she'd cheated in her last few marriages. Her attitude was that it was normal. She said, basically, that people should just accept it. I found it highly hypocritical, though, since during the entire interview they had her face shadowed. If it's the status quo, if there's nothing wrong with it, why not show your face?"

"The term *cheating* implies I'm taking something that's not lawful for me," Spence said. "It isn't a self-contained sin. If I commit adultery, it doesn't damage just me and the person I cheat with. It hurts my spouse and her spouse. Not to mention the entire family when kids are involved. It's betrayal. Most people don't take their vows seriously anymore, but it still hurts when their partner breaks them. There's no way it can *not* be personal. So they respond out of that hurt emotionally and, as Danny said, often violently.

Here's that passage I was telling you about; it's talking about the ramifications of adultery. 'For jealousy enrages a man, and he will not spare in the day of vengeance. He will not accept any ransom, nor will he be satisfied though you give many gifts.'" Spence set his phone on the table. "People are essentially the same today as when Proverbs was penned. Cheating, enrages a man—or woman—and that rage can't be bought off or easily placated."

"And this is why it's better to be single," Danny stated, only half-seriously. "Who needs that risk and aggravation?"

Heidi and Spence proceeded to debunk Danny's statement, but Kate tuned them out. She felt as if she had been providentially handed a piece of her mystery, perhaps not the last piece, but the most important. Something she should have realized long ago.

"He knew." Kate muttered these words to herself but loudly enough to halt the conversation at the table.

"Excuse me?" Danny asked.

"I'm so stupid!"

"Well, I'm not one to disagree, but what are you talking about?"

"I've got to go. I'll tell you later."

Kate bolted from the table and was gone. The three friends exchanged bemused looks. Danny pointed at Kate's nearly empty plate.

"I am not paying for her meal."

Chapter Fifty-four

"See what I mean?" Kate eagerly asked Potter as the clock ticked its way toward midnight.

He held up a hand. "Let me listen to it one more time."

He and Kate had taken a laptop into an interview room for an assurance of quiet. He pressed the play button, and they both listened as the mp3 of the 911 call played back again.

"Nine-one-one. Please state the nature of your emergency."

"Somebody's breaking into my house."

"Where are you, sir?"

"I'm upstairs. I'm by myself. My wife is gone—"

"The address, sir."

"199 Adams Road, Fulton Springs."

"What's your name, sir?"

"Nathanael Carver. I've been getting death threats. I think it must be him."

"All right, sir. We have officers in the area. We're dispatching them now. They should be there soon. Do you think you can get out of the house safely?"

[Unintelligible.]

"Sir, I can't understand you. Please speak directly into the phone."

[Silence.]

"Sir, are you there?"

[Whispering] "He's inside. Please hurry."

"Can you get out of the house?"

[Whispering] "He's downstairs. There's no other way out."

"Can you defend yourself? Do you have something—anything—you can defend yourself with?"

[Whispering] "I have my gun. I have it ready."

"Okay, don't confront him unless you have to. Sit tight. Help will be there in a minute. Is there a place that you can hide until the police get there?"

[Silence.]

"Sir, are you still with me? Sir?"

[Whispering] "I think he's moved away from the door. I'm going to try to get out."

"Are you sure there's no other—"

"Hey!"

"STOP OR I'LL SHOOT!"

[Clattering noise. Gunfire.]

"Sir? Sir, are you okay?"

[No response. Sirens.]

After the call ended, Kate held her tongue and let Potter absorb it. They were not so much listening to what they could hear as to what they couldn't—the silent gaps in the call. When he looked at her, she leaned forward on the table, emanating a restrained excitement, and said, "No static, no rain—nothin'."

"It does give one pause. Did you talk to the operator?"

"Yep. She remembered it because every time the line went silent, she thought she'd lost the call, but then it would pick back up."

Potter thought for a moment. "It was a cell call," he realized. Kate nodded. "He was muting it."

Kate reached over and played a section of the call.

"Do you think you can get out of the house safely?"

[Unintelligible.]

"Sir, I can't understand you. Please speak directly into the phone."

[Silence.]

"Sir, are you there?"

"I think the first time he just covered up the phone, and when—"

"He realized the operator could still hear, he muted it," Potter finished.

"So who was he talking to, and why did he keep muting the call?"

"It's starting to look a lot less like self-defense," Potter said dryly.

"Tell me about it."

"What led you back to the 911 call?"

"Would you believe me if I told you it was God?"

Potter tilted his head toward her. "No."

"I always knew there was something off about the call, but I couldn't put my finger on it until I had an idea of what I was looking for. Some friends and I were talking about adultery, and I thought to myself, what if he knew? He's a very sharp guy after all, and his wife, she's a bad liar. I could read it on her every time. So then I thought, he had to know. I've been running through the entire case again, looking at it from that angle, and all the question marks started clearing up. Like why he wanted us to drop the case. He called us in to make the threat look legitimate but didn't want us nosing around too close to the murder."

"It wouldn't be hard to drive out to Olivet to mail the letters to himself."

"Amelie told me that after the letters started coming, she broke things off with Grant for a while, and remember the letters stopped. He probably started them up again when he realized Grant and Amelie hadn't ended things permanently."

"And when the letters didn't curtail it this time, he decided to end the affair himself."

"And it makes sense that we found all the letter stuff in Grant's office and not the apartment." Kate gestured ecstatically. "Both times I went by his office, it was unlocked. Carver could've easily planted the stuff there, but the apartment would have been harder."

"The bags." Excitement began to creep into Potter's voice. "He went upstairs alone to pack the bags when he and Amelie left the house. It took him no time at all. He probably had already packed the magazines—"

"With some clothes on top to hide them. Or maybe he'd already moved them to Roving House." Kate leaned against the wall and crossed her arms, reining in her nervous energy. "If it hadn't been for the lights on Grant's car, he might've gotten away with it." She shook a finger in the air. "He ran out when we got there because he was already wet and he needed an excuse."

"He'd already been out in the rain to turn the lights off."

"Because what kind of killer leaves his lights on when he goes in to murder his lover's husband?"

Potter stood up. "Come with me." Potter led her back to his desk, where he rifled through some papers until he found the report he was looking for.

"The last call Innerst got was shortly after five—from Carver's cell phone," Potter said. "I didn't think anything of it before. Care to bet that call was some excuse to get Innerst to come to the house?"

"I'll take those odds. He knew Amelie would be gone, waiting for Grant, and that Grant probably wouldn't risk calling her while she's still at home with Carver."

"And Carver wagers that Innerst will come so as not to throw suspicion on himself and Amelie."

"It's almost perfect," Kate said. "He even waited for the neighbors to go on vacation."

"He's been planning this for a long time. He's one smart SOB."

"Once I stop being so excited, I'm going to start being pretty ticked that he played us for fools."

"He got us on his side and then sent us on a wild goose chase."

"An alligator chase—or crocodile," Kate corrected, thinking of Grant's ring and poem.

"What?"

"Never mind. We catch him in the end."

"How? Everything we have is circumstantial, and he can deny knowing about the affair."

"I think we may have a witness."

"Who? Colin Wigley?"

"No. Mason Lenkov."

Chapter Fifty-five

Voices at the door awakened Mason. He'd spent the better part of the night clicking the piercing in his tongue against his teeth as he puzzled out what to do, but finally he'd come up with a plan. Enough of one to let him sleep at least. He rolled over to find Kassie missing from the bed. Then he heard her at the door saying, "He's not here." That focused his attention. Were they talking about him?

A man's voice asked, "If he's not here, why is his car parked outside?"

Who would be looking for him here? Surely not Carver. It wasn't his voice. Mason slipped from between the covers and into his jeans. He crept to the bedroom door and peeked out. Kassie stood in her pajamas at the front door, holding it open enough for him to see the man on the other side. He couldn't see him very well, but well enough to know that he didn't know the guy.

Mason started looking for his shirt in the darkness. He could hear Kassie ask how the man had gotten her name, but a woman's voice answered the question. Mason stopped. He knew that voice. He went back to the door and listened. Whoever she was mentioned Travis. Suddenly he recognized the voice—the woman cop who had come to the house.

Mason backed away, unsure of what to do. Why were the police looking for him? He had a few good guesses, but it was hard to know for sure. He looked around for a means of escape, already knowing there was no viable exit in the bedroom. The windows were small, and they were on the third floor. Should he just stay put and trust Kassie to get rid of them? It sounded like she was trying.

He froze at a knock on the bedroom door. His back was to it, but he could hear the door swing open under the weight of the knock.

"Mr. Lenkov," the man said, "we need you to come with us."

THEY HAD not arrested him. Mason knew about being arrested. Arrested twice, convicted once. They had not handcuffed him; they had not read him his rights. He was not arrested. While this was very important to Mason, it did little to alleviate his tension because he knew they could still arrest him, and it would be particularly easy since they were now at the police station.

They had started off with a lot of questions about the Carvers: how well did he know them? had he ever been in their house? when was the last time he had been there? why had he been there? Mason had answered tersely and warily and up till now truthfully. They weren't fooling him. He knew they wanted to know about "that night," the same night the woman cop had come to his door. He had just finished recounting his afternoon visit to the Carvers' house.

"So what did you do in the kitchen when Mrs. Carver went to answer the door?" the man asked. He was sitting across the table from Mason. The woman lurked in the background.

That was a very specific question, a very odd question, a question that told Mason he was most definitely in trouble. "Nothing," he muttered.

"You didn't unlock the back door so that you could let yourself in later that night?"

Mason snorted. "No."

"Then why are your prints all over the door?" the man asked.

Mason didn't say anything.

"We know you were there, Mason," the woman said. She started talking about how he had torn his jacket on the fence and how she knew he had lied to her about just getting home that night, how he had grass from the Carvers' yard all over his shoes and jeans. "And we have a pretty good idea why you went back there too. I've seen the little tribute to Amelie Carver in your room."

Mason felt like his veins had just been lit on fire. He smacked a hand on the table. "That's private!" he shouted. "You had no right to be in there."

"Right now, I'm more concerned about Amelie Carver's privacy. You had no right to take those pictures. I don't need to explain to you what stalking is," the woman continued calmly. "Or that you could be in a lot of trouble. We don't want you to be in trouble, though, because we need your help." She stopped, and the man picked up speaking in her place.

"We need you to tell us what you saw and heard when you went back to the Carvers' that night. If you tell us the truth, we'll do what we can to help keep you out of trouble."

Oh, it was a deal they were trying to make. He looked them over. He didn't trust them. Leaning back in his chair, he folded his arms tight against his chest.

"I want a lawyer."

KATE HOVERED restlessly around her desk while Mason consulted with his newly acquired attorney. Potter leaned against his desk watching her with heavy eyes.

"Do you think he'll testify?" she asked the question she assumed was burning through both their minds.

Potter shrugged. The motion accentuated his weariness. "I'm wondering if it matters."

Kate sighed. She'd been trying to ignore the point that Potter had implied. Even if Lenkov did testify, his creditability was nil. Any self-respecting defense attorney would shred him on the stand…unless they had a way to back up his testimony.

"We need some way for the jury to feel like they can trust him," she said.

"Slim chance on that one. I don't trust him myself."

"Neither do I. That's why we need some way to corroborate his story."

"You mean provided he gives us his story."

"Yeah," Kate said and kicked Potter's chair.

He looked at her sharply, but then his eyebrows arched in a silent question, and she heard their minds interlock—*click*.

"Do you think he'd do it?"

Chapter Fifty-six

Mason Lenkov surprised Nathanael Carver later that morning by stepping into his office uninvited. He seemed to have lost that nervousness that Nate had perceived recently. In fact, Mason made himself quite at home. Without a word, he shut the door behind him, laid a closed paper grocery bag on a chair, and then proceeded to close the blinds to the inside windows. Nate found this sudden swing to brashness hard to bear.

"Can I help you?" he asked in a voice that intimated no such desire.

Mason said nothing, just continued closing the blinds. His smell, sweet and vaguely smoky, wafted over to Nate. Nate rolled his eyes. The guy was probably stoned out of his head. Should he call security? Instead, while Mason's back was turned, he unfastened the clasp on his briefcase, pushing the top up just enough to let his hand in.

Mason slouched down into a chair, placed the paper bag on his lap, and stared at Nate with his dark, blank eyes. Still he said nothing. He took a deep breath and let it back out.

"Listen—" Nate began, but Mason chose this moment to start speaking.

"I thought we should talk."

"About what?"

"I know."

They both sat so still that the small sounds of the office—the ticking of the clock, the hum of the CPU, the rush of air through the vents—threatened to envelop them.

"You know *what*?"

"I know," Mason repeated.

"I'm afraid I don't know what you're talking about. Are you hopped up on something? You're not going to do something stupid, are you? I've been attacked twice this month, and I don't think I can handle a round three." Nate placed his hand on the phone.

"Once," Mason corrected, holding up a finger to clarify. Nate thought he saw it tremble, but he couldn't be sure. "You've only been attacked once."

"You're mistaken, Mason."

The designer's head swiveled ever-so-slightly in a negative response. "I was there, in your house, when you killed Grant Innerst."

Now it was Nate's turn to say nothing, but Mason, who excelled at silence, matched his pause.

Finally, Nate said, "You're lying. I don't know why you're making this up."

"I don't know why you killed your friend." Mason shrugged. "I don't really care."

"You must be confused. You were in the house earlier that day." Nate picked up the receiver. "I think we need to get you some help. You're obviously on something."

"I unlocked the kitchen door so I could get back in later."

Nate stopped dialing. "Why?"

Mason carefully unrolled the top of his paper bag. "I was looking for a keepsake. When the lights went out and your car left, I thought you were both gone. My bad, huh?" Out of the paper bag he pulled a clear package, something light blue in a large zip-top bag. He leaned forward and laid the package on the desk. The bag held a sweater with pearl buttons, one that Nate recognized as Amelie's. "I'm returning it. I think she looks beautiful in it, but it's not really what I was looking for, but I didn't get very far." Nate didn't move. "If you don't believe me, you can open it. It still smells like her."

Nate's free hand instinctively curled into a fist. "You're lucky I don't come over this desk and smash your face in."

"You don't want to do that." Mason leaned back in his chair casually, but Nate thought he saw fear or something like it flicker through his eyes.

"Are you sure, absolutely sure, you want to continue this conversation?" Nate asked. He set the phone down and placed his hand next to the briefcase. "It might not go the way you think it will."

Mason swallowed. "I heard you tell Grant the files were in the kitchen. He came in there looking, but he didn't find them because there weren't any. Sure scared me. That's when I hid in the laundry room. Found the sweater. I stayed there until you went out the front. I didn't want to get shot too."

"What do you want? Money? You really think you can blackmail me?" Nate could hear the tension in his own voice, could hear the raging beat of his own heart.

Mason looked at his hands and shook his head. "I just want to be included."

"What?"

"You know, dinners, nights out, barbecues. I want to be a part of you guys' life." Nate couldn't believe what he was hearing. "And I want to paint your wife."

"There is no way that I am letting a freak like you anywhere near my wife."

Mason shrugged. "Then I tell the cops everything. How you knew it was him. How you told him to wait and then killed him. They've already come and talked to me because they found my prints in your kitchen."

"What did you tell them?"

"Nothing yet."

"And why would they believe a psychopath like you over me?"

"It's your head." Mason stood to leave.

"Sit down!"

The sharp hiss of Nate's words didn't make Mason comply, but it did stop him midmotion. Nate had already plunged his hand into the briefcase, and now he withdrew his gun.

Mason looked back at him, his dark eyes no longer blank but huge with fear. He opened his mouth but no sound came out.

"Did you think I wouldn't be ready for you? You're pretty stupid, you know. If I could kill Grant—what's to stop me from killing a nothing like you?"

Mason found his voice. "Hopefully, a whole lot of cops."

The door to the office opened. Someone yelled, "Gun!" and everything blurred until Nate found himself handcuffed, staring at Detectives Kate Baxter and Potter Davis flanked by uniformed officers. In the corner, Detective Davis assisted Mason, who was fumbling with the buttons of his shirt, the open front already revealing a wire.

Detective Baxter took Nate by the arm. "Mr. Carver, if you got cabin fever at the hotel, you're going to hate prison. You're under arrest for the murder of Grant Innerst."

She read him his rights as she led him out of the office. As he passed through the doorway, he could hear over her recitation the sound of Mason's vomiting on the floor.

Chapter Fifty-seven

Kate debated whether she should say something to Amelie Carver. The older woman sat on a bench in the lobby of the police station, looking vaguely comatose. Kate sighed and joined her.

"You were right," she said. "Grant was innocent."

"I thought it was an accident." Amelie's voice was small, the words defeated. She had accepted the truth already. She had known both men well: Grant, so much that she knew he wouldn't commit murder, and Nathanael, well enough to know that he could, even if that realization came desperately too late.

Rallying, Amelie turned to her. Her eyes glinted a little life, a little defiance. "You think this is all my fault, don't you?"

Well, that's somebody's guilt talking, Kate thought, but she replied with measured words. "I believe everyone is responsible for their own actions."

Amelie could not answer what was both absolution and condemnation.

"It's not really my business, so feel free to tell me so," Kate began. "But if you love your husband so much, why the affair?" Amelie looked at her wordlessly. Kate shrugged and asked again, "Why?"

Amelie looked away and closed her eyes. She breathed in. Kate could not tell whether she was searching for the answer herself or merely trying to block out the station's noise. "One night we were waiting for Nate. He was late joining us for dinner at Marcadé's, and I started telling Grant about my time in Europe, about Alain, the modeling and everything. He had been teasing me, and I think I wanted to shock him. But it felt good to share it with someone." Amelie opened her eyes. "He *was* surprised…and intrigued. I could feel the pull in him. I felt like I had those days back somehow, when life was fresh and exciting. So I kept sharing, and he shared back. Then we were sharing more and more. He was so vibrant, so full of life and energy, so young. He made me feel all those things again. I needed to feel young."

When Amelie said nothing else, Kate stood.

"I hope it was worth it."

BY THE end of the next week, fresh cases had deftly pushed the Carvers and Grant Innerst out of Kate's mind. She would have plenty of time to think about them when Nathanael Carver went to trial, but for the moment, there were more important things, such as cooking for company.

She looked into the oven to see how the lasagna—her mother's recipe—was fairing. She had just gotten off the phone with her mother, whom she'd called to refresh her memory on the baking instructions. This was their third amicable conversation since Kate had received a chastising phone call from her father. An undeclared agreement seemed in tact that stipulated no police talk from either end, and thus relative peace was being maintained.

She looked around the living room, which wasn't terribly clean, but she decided the tribe would have to take what they could get. Who had time to cook *and* clean? Someone knocked at the door.

"Hello there," greeted Heidi as she handed Kate a large bowl of salad. "I thought I'd swing by early and see if you needed help with anything."

"If you want to straighten up the living room, I won't stop you. I still have dessert to finish up."

"I have a confession to make," Heidi said as she started clearing the couch. "I came early so that I could also pick your brain on something."

"You're welcome to what's left," Kate called from the kitchen, where she was stirring Coke into chocolate cake batter.

"You know how I've been thinking about switching jobs?" Heidi waited for Kate to acknowledge her with an *uh-huh*. "I've been thinking that perhaps I should consider another field. Maybe it would be good to get out there and do something else."

"Like what?"

"There are so many publishing ventures in Fulton Springs; I figured with my language-arts background, I might be able to get a position copyediting or as an editorial assistant."

Kate stopped stirring. "Editing?"

"I've edited theses and dissertations for grad students at Landers," Heidi responded. "If I could handle those, I'm sure I could handle books and articles." She came to the kitchen door.

"So what are you wanting my input on?" Kate poured the batter into a pan.

"I was hoping you could give me some inside information on one of the companies that has open positions listed."

"How would I do that?"

"Well, I thought you might have contacts." Heidi ignored the slant-eyed glance Kate threw her. "It's Roving House."

Kate groaned.

Acknowledgements

I offer my sincere thanks to the following individuals who helped this novel along: Naomi Snow and Melissa Matos, my two loyal first readers who not only read all the early drafts but engaged in countless discussions of the plot, characters, et cetera; editor Nancy Lohr, who did everything she could to champion the project; Emma Nelson and Hannah Smith at Owl Hollow Press, who were willing to take on the book and help me put it in the hands of readers; the wonderful Gwen Holt, who introduced me to the fine folks at Owl Hollow; Sarah Hurt, Tyler Bucholtz, and Valli Rassi, the professionals who answered my questions about law enforcement and emergency services; and last but by no means least, the educators, from elementary to post-graduate school, who specifically encouraged my writing and storytelling, whose words of support I kept in my heart: Marilyn Greulach, Jennifer Rule, Connie Knoflick, Ramona Skertich, Karen Mennen, Cindy Merrill, Dr. Raymond St. John, Robert Olmstead, Marlin Barton, Leslie Pietrzyk, and Jamie Langston Turner, who guided the writing of the first few chapters.

Soli Deo Gloria

Photo credit: Craig Oesterling

ORIGINALLY FROM the Midwest, Paul Michael Garrison has spent roughly half his life in Upstate South Carolina. In addition to writing and editing, he has worked in the fields of higher education and website management. He whole-heartedly endorses the Oxford comma.

Paul Michael holds degrees in publishing, theater, and creative writing. His short fiction has appeared in *Windhover* and *Quantum Fairy Tales*, and he frequently performs with the Greenville Shakespeare Company. Whether on stage or in writing, he enjoys the art of becoming someone else. *Letters to the Editor* is his first novel.

#LetterstotheEditor